Raves *for* Previous Adventures:

"No one who got two paragraphs into this dark, droll, downright irresistible hard-boiled-dick novel could ever bear to put it down until the last heart pounding moment. Zach is off and running on his toughest case yet, and there is no way he is leaving us behind, no matter what the danger. This is futuristic pulp for the thinking reader, the one who enjoys a good chuckle, some mental exercise, and the occasional inside joke. Sit down with *The Plutonium Blonde* and a cold one and just see when you manage to pull your peepers away from the page again. On second thought, John Zakour and Lawrence Ganem are too damn good to be interrupted for something trivial; skip the cold one and save yourself a trip to the can."
— *SF Site*

"I had a great deal of fun with *The Plutonium Blonde* and have been looking forward to the sequel ever since. Well, it's finally here, and it's a good one. This is more humor than detective story, although Johnson and HARV are a pretty good pair of investigators as well as downright funny. If you like your humor slapstick and inventive, you need look no further for a good fix."
— *Chronicle*

"It's no mystery what kind of novel John Zakour and Lawrence Ganem's *Doomsday Brunette* is. The title says it all. The story is hard-boiled science fiction at its pulpy best. Zakour and Ganem's Zachary Johnson novels—which include *The Plutonium Blonde* and the forthcoming *The Radioactive Redhead*—are laugh-out-loud, action-packed mystery thrillers that both revere and lampoon the golden age of pulp fiction."
— *The Barnes and Noble Reviews*

Don't miss Zach's first two adventures:

THE
RADIOACTIVE
REDHEAD

JOHN ZAKOUR & LAWRENCE GANEM

DAW BOOKS, INC.
DONALD A. WOLLHEIM, FOUNDER
375 Hudson Street, New York, NY 10014

ELIZABETH R. WOLLHEIM
SHEILA E. GILBERT
PUBLISHERS
www.dawbooks.com

First Printing, December 2005
1 2 3 4 5 6 7 8 9

DAW TRADEMARK REGISTERED
U.S. PAT. OFF. AND FOREIGN COUNTRIES
—MARCA REGISTRADA
HECHO EN U.S.A.

PRINTED IN THE U.S.A.

For my wife and son and all the people
who bought the first two books.
—*John Zakour*

For Bruce Springsteen, William Goldman
and Friz Freleng.
—*Lawrence Ganem*

ACKNOWLEDGEMENTS

Thanks to Betsy Wollheim at DAW for believing in us and putting up with us (especially Larry). Thanks also to Click and Clack, the Tap It Brothers for their help picking out a cool old car for Zach to drive. Nobody knows cool cars like they do. We tip our hats to the folks at the Daily Buzz for letting us kid them a bit. Finally, a very special thanks to Natalia, Carolina, Tom, and Ron for helping to inspire their characters. I guess we should also thank the music industry and the government in general for giving us such great fodder for parody.   —JZ

As always, this book could not have been written without the love and support of Lisa, Jackson, and Kalie. Thanks as well to Philip and Shirley and the entire family tree. Thanks to Joshua for handling the business things and to Betsy for her encouragement, support, cajoling, mild reprimands, ultimatums, and death threats.   — LG

Prologue

In the early 1700s, after spending close to fifty years studying ancient biblical texts, the father of modern physics, Sir Isaac Newton, predicted that the world would end in the year 2060.

He never mentioned anything about a redhead.

If he had, I might have been a little more careful.

1

Some men are born dangerous.
Some men become dangerous.
Some men have danger thrust upon them.

And whenever danger decides to do a little thrusting, I always seem to be on the blunt, receiving end of it.

"The good news," HARV said as we entered the main room of the floating restaurant, "is that the shite in this production appears to be particularly skilled. The bad news, of course, is that he's also an android assassin."

"He's a what?"

The Kabuki actor's prop sword suddenly flared a fiery red and he leaped at me from the raised stage overhead. His red-and-white makeup glared under the hot lights and a manic look of bloodlust danced across his cold, slightly crossed eyes. The dinner-theater patrons around me broke into applause so loud that it nearly drowned out the samisen and lute music blaring in the background.

"What a pity," HARV sighed. "This promised to be a fine production of *Chushingura*."

"Try to focus on the big picture here, HARV."

I grabbed the actor's sword arm as he swung the energy blade at my head. Sure enough, his wrist was hard and unyielding, definitely the tempered polymer shell of a droid. And definitely more trouble than I was expecting. I slid sideways and rolled onto the floor, putting the droid's own momentum into a judo throw as I pivoted. The heat of the blade singed my face as it flashed past and the droid tumbled over me, falling flat onto a large table of six nearby. His blade burned through the table like a fat man through a cream pie when he landed and the whole thing gave way beneath him. He fell to the floor amid a cascade of tempura and spilled sake.

My name is Zachary Nixon Johnson. I am the last private eye on Earth. And right now, I am seriously regretting my choice of career.

It is the year 2060. And let me say at the outset that this is not the way I usually spend my weekend nights. You may not believe it, but I'm a bit of a homebody at heart. Dinner theater is not my scene. *Kabuki* dinner theater, despite being all the rage at the nano, is *really* not my scene. And Kabuki dinner theater in a trendy, free-floating restaurant, three hundred meters above downtown Oakland . . . well, you see where I'm going with this, right?

"It's an interesting strategy," HARV whispered inside my head as I quickly climbed to my feet. "It's illegal, as you know, to create an android with realistic skin tones. Creating a droid with a skin tone that emulates traditional Kabuki makeup, however, is completely legal. Granted, the places to use such an assassin without drawing undue attention are somewhat limited."

"Yeah, leave it to us to find the loophole."

I'd come to the Oakland Kabuki Palace Theater and Dinette to meet a client—a potential client actually. I don't usually do blind dates when it comes to business but things had been a little slow of late so when the cold call came in last night asking for a no-strings-attached meet and greet, I figured that it wouldn't hurt to hear the offer.

I was wrong. Especially about the wouldn't hurt part.

The droid popped back onto his feet and brandished his energy sword with a dramatic twirl that utterly delighted the dinner theater patrons around us, even as they ducked for cover. They were still under the impression that this was part of the show and they were ready for more in-your-face Kabuki dinner theater action. I on the other hand, was not in the mood for audience participation.

I flicked my wrist and cupped my hand in just the right way to activate the tiny motion sensor of the hidden holster that I wear on my forearm. The holster responded by smoothly popping my gun (a Colt 46, version 3.2A, I think—I can't keep track) into my hand and the gun throbbed to life when it hit my palm, in recognition of my distinctive heat/DNA signature. The entire action takes a lot less time to do than it does to describe, but the beauty's in the details.

The droid growled and leaped high in the air toward me, sword flashing in a fiery wide arc.

"Big bang, tight," I said, gripping my gun.

The gun's OLED screen flashed to signal recognition of my voice command and I pulled the trigger even as I dove to the floor.

My energy blast hit the droid squarely in the chest, punching a hole through its innards and shorting out its central power unit. Sparks flew from within and the samurai robe began to smolder as the body fell backward to the ground. Again the crowd broke into applause as they rose from beneath their tables.

"A Kabuki assassin droid," I said, getting to my feet. "I think that's a first."

"Indeed," HARV replied. "But don't cherish the uniqueness of the experience too long."

"Why not?"

"Because in a nano, it won't be so unique."

"What?"

I heard excited shrieks from the audience behind me and turned just in time to see two more Kabuki actors charge me from two of the narrow runways. Each held a samurai sword that flamed to life as he ran.

"You gotta be kidding me."

"Come now," HARV said, "you didn't really think there was going to be only *one* Kabuki assassin droid, did you? Especially considering the production they're doing."

The restaurant was a huge, high-ceilinged, circular room with doorways at each of the four compass points and a raised stage at the center for theater in the round productions. At the north point was the main entrance whose great doors opened to the red carpet hoverport (and two dozen tiny valet 'bots programmed for parking and "bringing 'round" the patrons' hovercrafts). At the east end was the emergency exit, a rapid-fire teleportation gate with a pre-set destination of the street below. West was the restrooms, which I am told were very swanky. And south was the kitchen.

A catwalk ran the full circumference of the dining room and four smaller catwalks stretched outward from the stage. Three went directly into the audience. One went to a set of large double doors on the western wall near the restrooms, no doubt leading to the dressing rooms for the actors, including the two droids currently intent on turning me into diced detective sashimi.

I hopped onto a table and pulled myself up to the catwalk to meet the charging samurai actors.

"What the DOS is going on here?"

HARV's hologram shimmered to life beside me, projected from the holographic image producer built into the computer interface I wear on my wrist. It's low tech, I know. HARV much prefers using the projector that's attached directly to my eye. He feels he gets better definition. But there are only a handful of people in the world who know about my mental link with HARV so we keep things on the down-low when we're in public and use the standard-tech gear.

I feel obligated to mention here that HARV, aside from being one of the world's most advanced thinking machines, is a work in progress. He began life as a supercomputer with a preprogrammed personality subroutine that mimicked a proper English butler, a sort of Wodehousian Hal-9000.

Then my good friend (and super-genius inventor) Dr. Randy Poole had the great idea of downloading him directly into my brain via a subcortical interfacing nano-connection (scanc for short). It was a radically experimental, incredibly painful procedure that was done very cavalierly a couple of years ago. Since then HARV has been, for lack of a better word, evolving. He has changed his appearance. He has changed his personality. He has become more human. A true thinking machine. It has been absolutely amazing to see.

Unless of course, you happen to have him attached to your brain.

Then it's annoying beyond belief.

I'm all for progress and evolution but just think for a nano how you'd feel if your toaster suddenly decided to convert to Judaism (and it was inside your body).

All that said though, when HARV is in business mode, he's the best sidekick in the world. So I guess I shouldn't complain.

"Well, let me think," HARV said, adjusting the

cuffs of his holographically starched shirt. "An anonymous potential client calls. Refuses to give his name or the details of what he needs and arranges to meet us at a Kabuki dinner theater presentation, where, by coincidence, we are attacked by Kabuki assassins immediately upon our arrival."

"I get it, HARV."

"Did I or did I not say that blind meetings and anonymous clients are a bad combination?"

"Yeah, well if it was up to you, we'd never leave the office."

"I gotta tell you, Zach, right now, the office is looking pretty darn good."

"You can gloat later, provided we survive," I said. "Right now we have to get the bystanders to safety. I'll keep the samurai occupied. You handle crowd control."

HARV nodded.

"I'm on it."

He lifted his holographic form onto center stage and turned his visage to the crowd.

"Ladies and gentlemen, please do not panic. We are experiencing some intensely dangerous technical difficulties. We would be most grateful if you would all immediately proceed to the emergency exits in a quick and orderly fashion while Mr. Zachary Nixon Johnson battles the deadly dinner theater Kabuki android assassins."

None of the restaurant patrons made the slightest move toward the exits. They did, however, increase the volume of their cheers.

I meanwhile was up on the catwalk facing down two charging samurai.

"I suppose discussing this like reasonable beings is out of the question?" I asked as they approached.

In response, both samurai pulled a handful of shurikens from the folds of their robes and hurled them at me as they charged. I spun and dove to the floor of the catwalk but not before taking three or four hits to the shoulder and back. Luckily, the body armor I wear under my clothes absorbed the impact (and stopped the razor sharp spikes before they pierced my skin).

"Yep. Should have seen that coming."

I rolled over onto my stomach and fired off a couple of rounds that took out the nearest samurai. The crowd cheered again, louder this time, as I rolled and smoothly popped into a crouch position, gun steady in hand and leveled directly at the remaining samurai as he charged. I had to admit I was starting to feel in the groove.

And that, of course, was when I got hit over the head by a samisen and kneecapped hard by a lute. The first rule of Kabuki theater: never turn your back on the musicians (which is probably the first rule of *any* kind of theater).

HARV meanwhile was still center stage, trying very hard to get the dinner crowd to take his warnings seriously.

"I really mean it here, people," he shouted. "This is not a drill. The Kabuki actors and entertainers you see around you are, in actuality, soulless androids designed expressly for merciless killing. You do not want to be eating dinner around these entertainers. Now please, evacuate this building immediately!"

Alas, the crowd only cheered louder.

I ducked under the swing of the samisen player's next swipe, took him down to the ground with a leg sweep, then blew his head off with a point blank blast to the face. The crowd cheered, partly from the smoothness of my fighting moves, but mostly I think because the samisen music had gotten on their nerves as well.

"This is the last time I go to a Kabuki show."

"Noh play," HARV replied, popping back beside me.

"Okay, then, a play."

"Noh play."

"That's what I said," I sneered. "A play."

"*Noh* play."

"HARV!"

"That's the traditional name for this type of production, Zach. A Noh play."

"You mean like a do over?"

"You really are a philistine, aren't you?" HARV said. "Watch your back."

I turned and managed to dodge the swing of a sai-wielding actress droid as she attacked. I stumbled backward as she came at me again, with both sai at once. I popped my gun back into its holster and caught both droid hands at the wrists and tried very hard to keep the razor sharp blades from my chest. The droid brought itself closer to me and pushed back with considerable strength. Then I noticed the subtle, yet distinctive male features of its face.

"Wait, I thought this was a woman."

"It's a droid."

"I know, but I thought it was a droid posing as a woman."

"It's an *arrogato*," HARV replied.

"A what?"

"Women aren't allowed to participate in traditional Kabuki theater so all female parts are played by men posing as women. They're called *arrogato*."

"Like English theater during the Elizabethan period."

"Very good."

"Hey, this isn't the first time I've fought thespians, you know."

"Sadly."

I rolled backward onto the floor, planted my foot on the droid's chest as I did so, and tossed her over me. She flew off the catwalk like a silk kerchief on a spring breeze, her floral pastel kimono arcing through the air. It was absolutely lovely, save for the fact that she was headed straight toward the table of a party of four (a double date, I think), all of whom were now running for their lives. She landed awkwardly on the table, hands beneath her, and impaled herself on her own blades. There was a deathly silent nano as everyone in the room stared at her crumpled body, sparks from her ruined circuitry spitting from the blade-sized exit wounds in her silk covered back.

Then there were more cheers from the crowd.

"Bravo!"

"Encore!"

"Who knew Kabuki theater was so accessible?"

"HARV, why is the audience still here?"

"Because they're morons," HARV said, shrugging his holographic shoulders. "They think that this is all part of the show and I can't convince them otherwise."

"Well, if they don't understand the truth," I yelled, as I dodged a new attack from the lute player "tell them a lie."

"What kind of lie?"

"Use your imagination."

"I'm not programmed for imag . . ." HARV's holographically created eyes flashed with the spark of inspiration that was eerily human. "Never mind. I'll handle it. By the way, watch out for the *ichi* and *kani ro*."

I managed to say, "The what?" just as HARV's hologram disappeared and two more obi-clad droids with swords leaped at me from the catwalk. I ducked under the sword swipe of one and blasted the other in the chest while HARV made a return to center stage.

"Ladies and gentlemen," he announced dramatically, "the Oakland Kabuki Palace Theater and Dinette thanks you for coming to tonight's special presentation featuring the dinner theater debut of Zachary Nixon Johnson."

Wild applause.

"This isn't helping, HARV."

"Tonight's performance was sponsored by your good friends at World Tax Association, funding the boondoggles of today with your savings of the future."

The applause stopped. I was beginning to see where HARV was going with this. I was almost proud of him.

"And as a special treat for you all, the WTC will be giving free tax audits to those of you still in attendance after the show. Your own personal auditors will be arriving at your tables in just a few nanos . . ."

Awkward pause.

". . . with free bottles of New and Improved Zima!"

That did it. The room erupted in shouts of "Check please," "Oh, look at the time," and "What are we, animals?" and the crowd headed for the exits faster than fat farm escapees to the buffet line. When the line at the hoverport got too long HARV holographically disguised himself as a tax auditor and sent the majority of them sprinting toward the emergency exit ramp.

"Nice work, HARV," I said, slamming a droid's head into a tray of tajiki.

"I thought it was rather inspired," he said, reappearing beside me.

Another droid came at me with a loud yell, his flaming sword arcing high overhead.

"Any idea who sent these droids after me?"

I spun away from the attacker's swing and let his sword slice into the prostrate droid on the table beside me. The laser blade sliced through the downed droid's head and deep into the tajiki beneath, flash frying the swordfish bellies.

"Clearly someone who doesn't like you, although that hardly narrows down the list of suspects."

"Thanks."

I heard a soft rumble, like a hover truck flying by outside.

"Someone brilliantly fiendish, that's for certain," HARV said. "Someone with a flare for the dramatic yet with no regard whatsoever for human life."

"Anarchistic terrorist?"

"I was thinking of a Broadway producer in need of a hit. But your guess is possible too."

I popped my gun back into hand and blew the droid's Kabuki e-brains across the buffet table. The rumble seemed to be growing louder

"How many of these droids are there?" I asked.

"Well, this evening's presentation was to be of the drama *Chushingura*," HARV replied.

The rumble grew louder.

"Meaning what?" I asked.

"Nothing in and of itself, but I think you'll be interested in the play's subtitle."

The rumble grew louder. It definitely wasn't a truck.

"Subtitle?"

"*Revenge of the Forty-Seven Samurai.*"

The doors at the end of the catwalk exploded outward and a horde of droids charged through in a veritable kimono-clad cavalcade of Kabuki choreographed death.

"Forty-seven, huh?"

"They seem to be doing a very faithful adaptation," HARV nodded.

"Lucky us. I think it's time to leave."

"Actually, the optimal time to leave would have been about ten minutes ago."

The flow of the fight had brought us to the center of the room with the Kabuki horde charging us from the western end of the catwalk. Some of the droids leaped off the catwalk and were now scrambling toward us on the floor as well. Even so, escape would be easy, a simple matter of running to the hoverport at the north end or to the emergency 'porter at the east end. There was nothing but open space between us and freedom.

"Help! Someone help me!"

Yeah, as if my life would ever be that easy.

The woman's scream came from the southwestern end of the room and it wasn't hard to spot her when I turned (by not wearing Kabuki makeup, she sort of stood out from everything else in the room). She was a trim woman in a red faux-leather top and short skirt that showed a lot of cream-colored skin, none of it unwelcome to the eye. She was the kind of woman that you'd notice in any situation. No stranger to trouble, but unaccustomed to being on the receiving end. And her thick, long hair was a luscious shade of red. Easy to spot. Impossible to ignore.

She was on the ground, her leg pinned by a large banquet table that had been overturned in the melee.

Her eyes were wide with fear and she reached her finely boned hand toward me in a sensuous come-hither gesture that seemed to say "Save me—I'm about to be trampled by droids."

"And you were so close to getting out of here intact," HARV sighed.

"She's trapped."

"By a table that can easily be removed by the policemen or EMTs that I have already summoned."

"But the droids . . ."

"Have shown no interest in harming anyone in the building other than you."

"But when I leave . . ."

"They'll probably follow, en masse, in their continued efforts to kill you. You have that effect on machines and people and animals and mutants and . . . ."

I turned away from the exit and started running toward the woman.

"Then we have nothing to lose," I said.

"Except your life," HARV yelled. "Why in Gates' name are you doing this?"

The answer came from me without a thought. And in retrospect, if I'd known how much trouble the next four words would eventually bring me, I would have cut out my tongue before uttering them.

"Because she's a woman!"

The droid stampede turned toward me as I ran toward the redhead. The droids were gaining much faster now. This was going to be uncomfortably close.

"Bring the hover up to the kitchen delivery door," I said, raising my gun at the onrushing horde. "There is a delivery door in the kitchen, isn't there?"

"You're asking that *now*?"

"HARV!"

"Yes, there is. I'll bring the hover and guide you through the kitchen."

I fired a couple of big-bang blasts at the droid horde as they approached, obliterating a handful of the front-runners. But the ones behind them filled the space and continued the charge as we all neared the damsel in distress. I pulled my gun forward and aimed it at her. She saw the gun and a look of horror crossed her pretty face. She put her red head to the floor and covered herself with her arms.

"Mini-boom," I said.

Again, the gun's OLED flashed and I pulled the trigger, letting loose a small blast that sailed over her head and hit the table that had pinned her to the floor, splitting it neatly down the middle. She looked up, saw that she was free, and breathed a sigh of relief just as I arrived.

"Oh, thank Gates."

"Hold on to me."

"Gladly," she whispered, and the sultriness of her voice sent a warm rush through my frame (not something I needed at the nano).

I could see right away that she was unable to walk so I helped her up then threw her over my shoulder, my hand riding uncomfortably high on her shapely thigh, and continued running toward the kitchen door, the pursuing horde just a few meters behind us now.

"HARV?"

"I'm on my way, Zach. Use your left eye to guide you through the kitchen."

I blasted open the door to the kitchen (it was unlocked of course, but why take chances?) and stumbled through the doorway. As soon as my feet hit the kitchen tiles, I closed my right eye and let the left take over. My view of the kitchen turned to black and white and a bright red arrow appeared on the floor leading past a row of sushi stations. HARV had flipped a switch inside my head and was using the lens of my eye as a GPS screen to guide me through the kitchen to the delivery entrance.

I heard the Kabuki horde crash through the doorway behind us. The size of the entrance was upsetting their rush. They could only squeeze through in sets of two or three. It was slowing them down but not as much as the weight of the redhead on my shoulder was slowing me.

"They're gaining!" she yelled.

"Keep your head down, we're almost there."

"They didn't mention any of this in the menu."

"They never do," I said.

I followed the red arrow around a corner and saw the delivery entrance doorway less than ten meters straight ahead. HARV had taken the liberty of outlining it in red with a flashing arrow icon saying "this way to the egress." (I get the feeling sometimes that HARV has little confidence in my ability to follow directions.)

"HARV, where are you?"

"Not near enough," HARV yelled inside my head.

I blasted open the delivery door (again, it was un-locked but the knob looked a little tricky) and kept running.

"Do you by chance drive an invisible hovercraft?" the woman asked.

"Nope."

"Because I don't see anything waiting for us at the hoverport."

"My friend is bringing it up."

We were close to the door now, but the oncoming Kabuki horde was closer and neither of us showed any signs of slowing. The floor shook from the force of their rush and I could feel the heat of their laser blades on the back of my neck.

"Will he get here in time?" she asked, a little pan-icked now.

"No," I said, "we're meeting him halfway."

"You gotta be kidding . . ."

I spun her off my shoulder and into my arms as I ran. The swipe of a sword caught the back of her skirt as she moved, slitting it up the middle. She slid her body across my chest and her arms and legs around me as smoothly as if we'd been dirty-dancing partners for years.

Then I ran through the doorway and leaped off the edge of the hoverport into the dank night air of Oakland a thousand feet above the ground.

2

I'll go on record here that I hate heights. Unfortunately and through no fault of my own, my job has put me in many circumstances over the last few years in which I have found myself falling from high places. I don't mind it so much in the grand scheme of things because it allows me to recount those exploits by saying things like:

The sultry night air of Oakland stung my face like the wet morning breath of a lover from a seedy bar the night before: rank and unwelcome with a heavy undertone of shame. The downtown neighborhood was no doubt nearly silent at the late hour but I couldn't be certain because my ears were overwhelmed by the terrified scream of the redhead as she clung to me. She held nothing back as we fell, letting loose with a top-of-the-lungs wail of anguish borne from the sheer terror of free fall. Oddly enough, the sound of her scream made her even more familiar to me. I knew this woman from somewhere. I was sure of it. But at the nano, my memory wasn't working at full capacity.

Her arms were wrapped tightly around my neck and her bare thighs squeezed my waist so firmly that my body armor kicked in to ease the constriction (and part of me cursed the armor for being so responsive).

I twisted as we fell, spinning us so that she was on top. The move frightened her more since she could now clearly see the fast approaching ground and she increased the power of her scream appropriately. But the twist was necessary because, despite the free fall, I knew that we were still in more danger from above.

A glance up at the restaurant hoverport confirmed my fear. The Kabuki droids leaped off the edge in pursuit of us, their falls accelerated by thrusters in their boots. I held tight to my gun and let loose a barrage of blasts as I fell, blowing the lead droids to bits and lighting up the Oakland sky with an impromptu display of badass fireworks.

And just when the speed of our fall neared terminal velocity, I heard the familiar purr of hover thrusters and felt the smoothness of Corinthian faux-leather slide across my backside as our descent slowed substantially.

"Need a ride?" HARV asked.

You know those group exercises that they do in summer camps or those touchy-feely corporate retreats where you stand with your hands at your sides and fall backward into the arms of a compatriot? They're designed to foster trust among the participants. Inevitably it leads to higher insurance premiums but that's beside the point.

HARV and I have taken that trust thing to the ripping edge. Falling face up from three hundred meters, there was no doubt in my mind that HARV would be there in time for me. He brought the hover to me, top down and seats in full flat recline, matched the velocity of my fall and then expertly cushioned it by slowing the descent with the hover's vertical thrusters.

Don't get me wrong, it hurt like hell. You don't go from a near-terminal velocity free fall to a full stop in twenty-five meters without a hefty dose of agony. But after all these years, I'm not choosy about how my life gets saved.

The point is that after three years of being connected at the brain, HARV and I have become a team. He has my back and I have . . . well, he has my back.

"Cut it a little close there, didn't you?" I said with a smile.

"Your internal organs are still safely inside your body," HARV replied. "You have no reason whatsoever to complain."

"Better hightail it out of here. The droids are still pursuing."

"You needn't worry," HARV said. "I'm quite sure that the danger has passed." His hologram appeared at the hover control and he made a big deal of steering the craft with his holographic hands even though he was guiding it remotely.

I gently put my hand on the back of the redhead's neck as she lay on top of me (her hair felt like thick silk). She was stunned and confused from the landing. Thankfully, my being on the bottom allowed me and my armor to take the brunt of the impact, but it still had knocked her for a loop. And she was only now starting to ease up on the scream.

"It's all right," I said, gently rolling her off me. "We're safe now. It's over."

She opened her eyes and looked around, still shaking from the fear and the rush of adrenaline. She gazed at me, then at HARV piloting the hover, then back up at the restaurant hoverport above us.

Her face turned a pale shade of green and she vomited on the hover's floor.

"Ugh, sushi" HARV said, making a face. "That's going to stain."

Oddly enough the sound of her retching jogged my memory in just the right way.

"Hey," I said, bending closer to her as she threw up on the floor, "aren't you Sexy Sprockets?"

Sexy Sprockets is s@k-c. That's slang by the way. Sometimes it's pronounced sek-see. Sexy. Get it? But in the current lexicon of slang, sexy doesn't mean sexually attractive. It means successful, hence the abysmal spelling, I think. And sometimes the word is pronounced suk-see, which is short for successful, which, ironically, in the current vernacular means sexually attractive. It's confusing, I admit, but if you really expected there to be any rhyme or reason to

California slang in the year 2060 then you're as stoopid as you are uglee.

And on top of being s@k-c, Sexy Sprockets is currently the most successful pop singer in the world and has been for the past five years, which on the pop music calendar is akin to a geologic era. She shimmied her way onto the scene when she was just fourteen, warbling her multinuanced ditties, rasping her wise-beyond-her-years riffs and babydoll whispering her statutory-rape sweet nothings to a music download market that was up to its bare midriffs with naughty-but-nice starlets (I believe that the descriptive term at the time was whorgins but that genre's so old-school now they play it on VH-Done). So, needless to say, nobody paid any attention to Sexy at first. There was nothing original about her sound or her fury, her style or her presentation. What's worse is that she didn't have a corporate sponsor to prime the star-making pump with the necessary credits, which was the kiss of death in the music world at the time.

Then she changed management companies, leaving the mom-and-pop shop that had repped her until then (her parents) and signing with the mysterious SSquared, Inc., of which still not much is known (other than they represent Sexy Sprockets). Under the Svengali-like ministrations of SSquared, Sexy's style was honed, her appeal was focused, and she found her voice. More importantly, SSquared introduced her to a little thing called analog bandwidth, specifically 500 to 1600 kilohertz.

Radio.

AM radio to be exact. And that made her career.

Keep in mind that in the middle of the twenty-first century, AM radio was about as prehistoric as you could get. You might as well be sending smoke signals and drawing pictures of bison on cave walls. The music industry had been all about downloads for close to three generations and the music audience was made up entirely of imps and pods. But for years all music downloads had been controlled in toto by big business. The congloms owned all the download sites. They owned hyping venues and they owned the patents on the technology for receiving and playing music. They owned the award shows, the music critics, and even those annoying little music aficionados who used to hang around music stores making fun of the stuff you were buying (they're computer geeks now, who hang around the download sites and make fun of you in a virtual manner). Before Sexy Sprockets came along, if you weren't with the congloms, then you weren't on the charts.

Sexy and her team somehow found a chink in the conglom armor and that chink turned out to be AM radio. Simply put, society's use of wireless tech had been growing for sixty years like a fungus inside a broken refrigerator. There was RTF and satellite and a host of industrial uses. And on the consumer side there was HV and cellular and wi-fi, ware-fi, watt-fi, wen-fi, hoo-fi, and everyone's favorite because-I-said-so-fi. The world's growing use of wireless tech was using more and more of the available bandwidth, so inevitably the bandwidth used by the hi-tech started to bleed into the bandwidth of the outmoded tech, like AM radio, which had died a slow death and reincarnated years before with the advent of satellite radio. So most of the bandwidth that was once used by AM lay fallow and inevitably began being used by some of the wi-fi technologies. And one of those technologies was the download and playback pods of the music industry.

Sexy and her team bought up licenses for a chunk of the AM spectrum and began broadcasting her music onto the public airwaves. As planned, the broadcasts bled onto the frequencies of a lot of the consumer tech and Sexy became a gate crasher on millions of wireless consumer electronic gadgets. At first it was a nuisance. There were a lot of complaints to the FCC, which at the time was entirely owned and operated by the "crusade for family values" lobby group (thankfully the government stripped the FCC of all power years ago), and to the congloms. The congloms set up various protections to minimize the broadcasts' bleed into their signals but by then it was too late, because a large chunk of the music audience (teenagers mostly) had listened to Sexy's music and had liked it. Their interest led them to the download sites, which, of course, didn't offer Sexy's music, which of course led to greater demand for the music and by the time the congloms caught on and tried to negotiate a deal with Sexy's people, she'd become a kind of cult icon for independent music and was now more popular than the congloms themselves. It's widely believed that she saved the congloms from ruin when she finally struck a download deal with them and there are rumors in certain circles that Sexy's company now owns a controlling share in the congloms, in effect running the entire music industry. It's a known fact that her company owns the entire AM spectrum, upon which her music is still broadcast nonstop.

All that said, I personally don't like her music, but you gotta admire the guts of someone who can mess so thoroughly with the system.

Okay, so where was I? Oh yeah.

"Hey," I said, bending toward her as she threw up on the floor, "aren't you Sexy Sprockets?"

"Yes," she said through the last of her retches. "But don't tell anyone I threw up in your hover."

"You went through a death-defying ordeal," I said, handing her a handkerchief. "People won't think less of you."

She took it gratefully and wiped her mouth.

"That's not what I mean," she said. "If my fans find out that I spewed in your hover, they're likely to steal it. Right now you could probably get half a million credits for it on Pit-E-Bay."

"I'll keep that in mind." I held out my hand and helped her into the backseat. "I'm Zachary Nixon Johnson."

"I know," she said with a smile. "I've followed your adventures."

"You're a fan?"

"Not of you. Just of the women you fight."

"Excuse me?"

"You know, like Foraa Thompson. She was the nth. And Nova Powers, I heard she really spanked your carcass. And rumor has it you had a dustup with BB Star? Gates, dude, you've been b-slapped by all the greats."

Needless to say, Sexy Sprockets' appeal was fast on the wane.

"Oh, the stories I could tell you, my dear," HARV said with a smile.

"Yeah, too bad we can't stay," I said with a growl. "HARV, those droids had anti-grav capabilities and they were following us. We have to get out of here."

"As I said, Zach, I'm quite certain the danger has passed."

HARV seemed to ignore the puzzled look on my face (although I'm pretty certain he savored it silently) as he brought the hover gently to ground in the restaurant's parking lot, which by then was almost entirely empty. We all climbed out, happy to be setting foot on firm ground again, and looked skyward. The remaining two dozen Kabuki droids filled the sky above us like a swarm of Bushido butterflies as they descended toward us.

I pushed Sexy behind me and popped my gun back into hand as the droids touched down and raised their glowing samurai blades in unison.

"I told you they were still after us."

"And I told you, Zach," HARV replied, "that the danger has passed."

"How do you know?"

"Because of that," he said, pointing directly above us.

I looked up and saw a small metal sphere floating gently a few meters above us. Two more floated over the crowd of Kabuki droids and a few others hovered in between us.

"Are those cameras?" I asked.

HARV nodded. "I noticed them as I was bringing up the hover. I spotted a number of them in the restaurant as well. I assumed at first that they were security cameras but there were far too many and they were of too good a quality for that."

"Why didn't you tell me?"

"I think because you were busy fighting droids."

"Someone was recording us?"

"They still are," HARV said, pointing toward the droids. "Now hush, this is the good part."

As one, the droids held their flaming blades out toward us. I gripped my gun a little more tightly and gave it the big bang command, ready for action. But then the droids bowed their heads and sank to their knees.

"What are they doing?" I asked.

"This is the end of *Chushingura*," HARV replied. "After avenging their master and completing their mission, the loyal retainers . . ."

The droids spun their swords in unison, like a Kurosawa honor guard, leveling the blades at their own bellies.

". . . commit seppuku."

They plunged their swords into their midsections and sent a cascade of red and blue sparks into the air as their circuitry fried from the inside. They fell forward onto their swords, motionless, and continued to sizzle and spark in the wet night air. The smell of burning silk and plastic wafted over us.

Then a voice came from the far end of the lot.

"Audio down, fade to black. Aaaaannnnnd we're out."

And then scattered applause.

3

A hover platform floated down from overhead and landed between us and the smoldering Kabuki droids. Three men stepped off as it touched down. Two of them were thin, angular, and wore dark tailored suits. The other was a paunchy guy wearing a pair of khaki Bermuda shorts and a shirt that looked like a lava lamp had exploded onto it. HARV gave me a silent cue that all three were unarmed but I kept my gun in hand nonetheless because I knew from the fine cut of the two suits, the dark tone of their evening-wear sunglasses, and the amount of styling mousse in their hair that the two suits in front represented an entirely different form of trouble.

"They're entertainment attorneys, aren't they?" I asked.

HARV nodded.

"They're from Anus and Quagmire," Sexy said from behind me. "I recognize their hair gel. They represent the Faux network."

"I'm suddenly nostalgic for the Kabuki droids," I

whispered. "The guy behind them, is that who I think it is?"

HARV and Sexy rolled their eyes in unison and harrumphed in my ears in stereo.

"Yes, if you think it's Rupert Roundtree."

"Zachy, baby," the man said, approaching me with arms wide. "That was stellar. Fabsolutely, A-positively interstellar majeure."

Rupert Roundtree is the head of the entertainment conglom currently known as Faux. It's one of the big three entertainment congloms in the current market, along with EnterCorp and MicroFun. It varies from nano to nano as to which conglom is actually the largest (it all depends on what companies they're currently buying).

EnterCorp is officially owned by Ona Thompson, with whom I have had some near-Armageddon type dealings but she's relatively hands-off and leaves the day to day business to the faceless board of directors. MicroFun is owned by HTech, who utilize a probability theory management style where a group of one hundred monkeys use yes/no pads, an abacus, and the spinner from an old game of Twister to make all programming, production, and scheduling decisions. MicroFun's growth in market share over the past few years, by the way, has led *Entertainment This Nano* to include the room full of monkeys on their annual "most powerful" list.

And then there's Rupert Roundtree, whose hands-on approach to running his conglom is well known in the industry and with the general public, and whose lowest-common-denominator philosophy of salacious and gratuitous programming has been known to make even the monkeys cringe.

Roundtree threw his arms around me in a weak armed, fleshy bear hug. His paunch pressed up against my midsection like a vat full of jelly and his aura of sweat and cologne was so strong that I suspected he was scent-marking me as part of his territory.

"High-con effex, classic pitter-patter repartee, short and sweet exposition, bada-bing, bada-boom. It's like it writes itself. Spectacle-acular showcaselosity!"

"What language is he speaking?"

"Hollywood," HARV replied. "It has no real rules of syntax."

Roundtree released me from the hug and turned toward Sexy who was standing beside me. She stopped his approach with a quick raise of her hand.

"And Sexy, you were dripping with fabuliciousness as always." He turned back to the suits, who were still at the platform. "Didn't I tell you this would be stratospherical? Didn't I say that?"

"Yes, Rupert," they said in unison.

"Okay, I'm going to need a few things explained to me," I said. "Preferably in English. And let's remember that I'm the only one here who has a gun."

Roundtree turned back to me; his smile still wide, arms still spread, and moved to hug me (again!). Luckily he saw the gun in my hand and stayed where he was.

"You're a jewel, Zachster," he said. "Gates, I wish we were still recording. This would make great behind-the-scenes stuff for the 4D-DVD. Can we restart the recorder-droids?"

"You do," I said, "and I'll restart my gun."

"You're right," Roundtree shrugged, "we don't want to break the fourth wall too soon. It will ruin the stupendation of unbelief."

"Wow," HARV said. "This is starting to hurt."

"Here's the coverage, Zachinator. The droids were ours. State of the art tech, too, from AMP Labs. As you can tell we're going big budget all the way on this project."

"Project?" I asked.

"Righteous Omnibus, baby. Take a look in the mirror, my man and you will see the face of the next great star of reality entertainment!"

"What?"

"A new series, Zachmeister. One man fighting against all odds every day of his life, just to survive."

"It does sound like you," HARV whispered.

"One man, in a world bent on destruction, a man whose life is no longer his own, forced to become a hero. One man running for his life!"

"Why does that not appeal to me?"

"We call it *Let's Kill Zach*," Roundtree said, smile widening, eyes growing beadier. "Pithiousity is key this year. Every week we send a group of killers after you, machines mostly, droids and bots. But we'll need to use human assassins on occasion to keep the show's connection to humanastasy. We'll just have to get around the snuff-film laws. Long story short, we record your heroics and net them to the masses."

"It's a surefire hit!" one of the suits said. "As long as you continue to live," the other added.

"You want to try to kill me on a weekly basis for entertainment?"

"It's not about entertainment, Zacharoo," Roundtree said. "It's about the *business* of entertainment. Danger is entertaining. You on the other hand, welcome danger."

"No, I don't."

"You thrive on danger."

"I hate danger."

"Danger is your middle name!"

"My middle name is Nixon!"

"Nixon? That won't work. Our legal people will get it changed for you."

"What?"

The lawyers at his side began scribbling furiously on their computer pads.

"Listen, Zachapalooza, people are always trying to kill you anyway. Everyone knows that. Why not turn that mortally dangerous lemon into some revenue-generating lemonade?"

"It does make sense on a certain level," HARV whispered.

"This is weird, even by HV standards."

"That's what makes it so brilliant," Roundtree exclaimed. "And with Sexy as the guest star for the pilot, this becomes mega-max-event-like."

"No way, Rupert," Sexy spat.

"Sexy, you looked fabulous."

"You show one pixel of my image on your pond-scum network and I'll put dark-shark litigation so far up your assets you'll have my initials imprinted on your private resources."

"Your turn of phrase is as tight as your sensuosity, Sexy," Roundtree said with a smile. "We'll hyper-veil your face."

"Not one pixel, Rupert!"

Rupert laughed and held up his hands in supplication.

"Fine. We'll replace you with a CGI replica for netcast."

"Voice, too."

"Of course."

"The CGI replica can't have red hair."

"You got it."

"And its ass better not be as nice as mine."

"Like that's possible."

"Have your shark call my shark."

"Done."

"Excuse me," I said.

"Don't worry; you're still the star, Zach-baby. Can I call you Zach-baby?"

"You can if you can say it with my fist in your mouth."

"Gates, I wish we were still recording," Roundtree said through snickers. "Remember to use that quip next episode."

"There isn't going to be another episode!" I said.

"Zach-a-tack, we've already booked the series for the fall season."

"You what?"

"That's why the shooting schedule's so tight. Hah, that's a good one. This shooting schedule's a real killer. Get it?"

"Roundtree," I said, "if you . . . if you show one pixel of my image on your network, I will sue your pants off so quickly I'll be running them up a flag-pole before your cellulite hits the floor!"

Roundtree and his attorneys stared at me impassively for a long, long nano.

Then they let loose with a round of head-back, mouth-open hearty guffaws. And Roundtree hugged me again.

"You're gonna be a star, Zach-a-lacka. A fully fledgered, pop-cult, maxotastical reality entertainment star!"

He kissed me on the cheek and, still chuckling, stepped back onto the hover platform with his attorneys and floated off into the night air like a cabbage fart on the breeze.

"But the legal threat worked when you used it," I said to Sexy, a little dumbfounded.

"That's because I'm rich, Zach. Everyone knows that you're not wealthy enough to buy justice."

"Perfect," I said, gently rubbing my temples.

"So what's the plan?" HARV asked.

"Same as always, HARV," I replied. "We keep our head down and watch out for Network Executives."

4

A hover limo the size of a city block came to take Sexy home. As she climbed into the vehicle, she gave me a mischievous wink that sent a shudder along my spine. I was too tired to dwell on it so I climbed back into my own vehicle and had HARV take me home.

I slept late the next morning, well deserving of the extra sleep. Electra, my fiancée, sometime roommate, and all around better half, was away at a medical conference focusing on carpal tunnel syndrome, so I had the bed to myself. It was just as well because Electra tends to steal the covers and snores a bit (which she denies). Also, with her not around, I didn't have to explain what I'd been through, which saved me about half an hour of gory details.

When I finally rolled out of bed of my own volition, I noticed that the house was exceptionally quiet.

"HARV," I said, still rubbing the sleep from my eyes, "throw last night's scores and highlights on the wall screen."

There was no reply.

"HARV?"

The message: "One nano please. System updating," flashed across my eyes and a sickening feeling began in my stomach.

"DOS, HARV. We don't need an update!"

The message, "Change is good," scrolled across my eyes.

"Things are fine the way they are," I said. "Please don't mess it up."

"Don't be a big baby," scrolled the reply.

Every so often HARV and Randy make improvements (and I use the term loosely) to HARV's system; boosting his power, streamlining his systems, or giving him new capabilities. Most often, the upgrades are useful. Like when they gave HARV remote Deep-C-phishing capabilities, allowing him to hack into all but the most secure computer systems. That upgrade's highly illegal, of course, and officially I have to deny having said anything about it. So if anyone comes around asking questions, clearly you must have misunderstood what I said.

But sometimes the upgrades are—how shall I put this?—less than successful. Probability-based precognitive generation of needs and desires (pp-gonad for short), as an example, was particularly troublesome. The intent was for HARV to use my personality profile and current situation as a forward-thinking springboard to calculate the services I'd need in the immediate future and make them available to me before I asked. It was a grand idea in theory. In reality though, the nuances of reality were too much for even HARV's computational abilities to accurately predict. As a result, he kept going back to the preset default and offering me junk food or pornography. Electra had to ban me from the Children's Clinic until the software was uninstalled.

My point is that upgrades to HARV are very hit-and-miss and I'm never open to it, especially first thing in the morning. Unfortunately, my opinions on most technology-related subjects never count for anything. So all I could do in this case was to muddle through the update process and wait to see what cutting-edge bell or space-age whistle would adorn HARV when he reappeared.

But before I could get too deeply into the morning routine, the com-tone sounded, indicating that I had an incoming call.

"Whoever it is, take a message," I said as I checked myself in the mirror for bruises.

Again the words "One nano, please. System updating," scrolled across my eyes.

"HARV!"

"I'm off-line," scrolled the reply. "What do you want me to do?"

I grabbed my robe and stumbled out of the bedroom.

"This is why you're supposed to do all updates while I'm sleeping."

"Then go back to bed."

"Don't tempt me."

The tone sounded twice more by the time I made it to the house computer control in the main hall.

"Which button is it?" I said, scanning the hundreds of options on the console."

"Gates, you'd be lost without me," HARV scrolled. "The red one, third row, on the left."

I grumbled and touched the button on the com. The preview screen came up on the wall monitor and I saw that it was Electra. I smiled and officially answered the call.

"Hi, hon."

Electra's image flashed onto the full screen and she smiled back at me.

"Hola, Chico. *Que tal?*"

"As well as can be expected," I said. "You look pretty chipper this morning."

"Morning? Zach, it's two-thirty in the afternoon."

"Is it?" I said, looking uncomfortably at my bathrobe. "Then I guess I'm not dressed appropriately, huh?"

Electra's smile broadened. She always enjoys it when I get flustered.

"Rough night?"

"Let's just say that the service at the Kabuki Palace Theater leaves a little to be desired."

The com-tone sounded again.

"DOS, I got another call."

"Let HARV answer it."

"Unfortunately, HARV is indisposed at the nano. Hang on; I'll get rid of them."

Every com these days comes standard with call screening. Unfortunately, a few years ago, HARV overrode the screening software so that he could personally handle all calls directly through his system.

He's a lot more efficient and he is better at screening out the less important (and sometimes downright malicious) stuff. The downside is that when HARV is off-line I have no screening device, which wouldn't be a problem if I lived in a perfect world where everyone who called me was my friend.

"Zachary Johnson? It's Bill Gibbon the Third from *Entertainment This Nano.*"

Alas.

Bill Gibbon is a well-coiffed talking head entertainment reporter (whose career I unknowingly boosted a few years back). Based on past experiences, it's never a good thing when his face appears on my screen. This time was no different as the next seven words illustrated.

"Am I too early for the press conference?"

"Press conference?"

"To announce your new reality series on Faux."

"Announce what?"

"*Let's Kill Zach.* The press conference is today, isn't it?"

"There's no press conference."

"You mean I'm getting an exclusive?"

"No. There's no exclusive either."

"Then how do you plan to promote the show?"

"I'm not promoting the show."

"But you admit that there *is* a show."

"That's not what I said!"

"Well then you better clarify that last statement, Mr. Johnson because I'm going live with this news in two minutes."

"Listen, Gibbon."

The com-tone sounded again.

"Hang on."

I put Gibbon on hold and brought up the next incoming call. To my surprise, it was Sexy."

"Hi, Zach."

"Sexy!"

I'm not sure if I was saying her name aloud or just subconsciously blurting out the first adjective that popped into my head.

"You're looking good today, big guy. No ill effects from last night's action?"

"None to speak of," I said, trying to be professional, which is hard to do in a ratty four-year-old bathrobe.

"I guess that stuff happens to you all the time, huh?"

"More often then I'd like," I replied.

"Listen, Zach, I hope I'm not being too forward here," she said, "but I have to tell you that you were amazing last night. Really heroic. It was thrilling to watch. You were old-school hot."

She was shy, almost coquettish with a Lolita-esque delivery that was so alluring it was guilt-inducing.

"That's nice of you to say."

"So, anyway," she said, "and this is a little embarrassing, but if you're not busy today, I was wondering if maybe . . ."

The com-tone sounded again, this time to remind me of the calls on hold (one of them, of course, being Electra).

"Wow, that's bad timing," I said. "Sexy, hang on. Okay?"

I stabbed the com-button to change calls.

"Sorry about that, honey . . ."

"I'm flattered, Mr. Johnson," Gibbon replied smugly, "but I don't fraternize with my interviewees."

"DOS. Don't flatter yourself, Gibbon."

The com sounded again. I rolled my eyes and stabbed the receive button. Thankfully, the face of my good friend Tony Rickey popped onto the screen. Tony's a captain with the New Frisco Police Department. He's a great friend to have, especially in my line of business. He can't say the same about me but he's still my friend, which I think says a lot about him.

"Tony!"

"Hi, Zach. Are you busy?"

"Sort of. Can I put you on hold for a nano? I have Sexy Sprockets on the other line."

"You have who?"

I stabbed the com button and changed the calls.

"Okay, Sexy . . ."

"You're not so bad yourself," Electra purred. Then she saw the surprise on my face and the purr became slightly more growl-like in nature. "What's going on, Chico?"

"I'll tell you in a nano," I said, stabbing the com button again.

This time I waited until I saw Sexy's face on the screen before I spoke.

"Sexy?" I said, still a little flustered. "Where were we?"

"Look, Zach, I know I'm being forward here but after last night . . ."

"It's okay, Sexy. I'm flattered, really I am . . ."

". . . I've just been thinking about you since last night . . ."

". . . but we have to be realistic here . . ."

". . . I think it was fate that brought us together . . ."

". . . You're a wonderful woman . . ."

". . . I guess what I really want to say . . ."

". . . But the thing is that . . ."

". . . I'd like to hire you as a bodyguard."

". . . I already have a girlfriend."

The long, awkward pause that followed, to my mind, could have been measured with a sundial.

"What was that?" Sexy said, nearly swallowing her gum.

"Did you say bodyguard?"

"Did you say girlfriend?"

"Um, no?"

"Whoa, Zach, did you think I was asking you out?"

I stuttered for a nano or two, not saying anything that remotely resembled words before finally blurting out the only thing that came to mind.

"Hold on. I have another call."

I blindly stabbed at a com button.

"Any comment, Mr. Johnson?" Gibbon said.

I stabbed another button.

"Zach, a warrant has been issued for your arrest," Tony said.

I stabbed another button.

"Zach, what's going on?" Electra asked.

"Oh you know, hon, just the usual morning . . . wait a nano."

I stabbed the com button again and brought Tony back on the screen.

"There's a what?"

"You were involved in a shootout at the Kabuki Palace last night?" Tony asked calmly.

"That wasn't my fault."

"No offense, Zach, but I've heard that before. No one was hurt but the owner is suing for damages."

"He's what?"

"The Oakland PD report says that the dining room and the kitchen were destroyed along with a good portion of the hoverport."

"Those Kabuki droids attacked me as part of a pilot for a reality-based series!"

"I have to hand it to you, Zach, after all the years I've known you," Tony said, "you still manage to come up with excuses that surprise me."

"I'm serious Tony."

"Then it's true? You were in a gun battle in the restaurant last night?"

"It was self-defense."

"And the restaurant was full of bystanders?"

"Whom I was trying to protect."

"From Kabuki actors?"

"They were droids and they were trying to kill me."

"Did anyone have a gun or a blaster? I mean, aside from you."

"The droids had laser swords. And I got hit with a samisen."

"A samisen?"

"It's kind of like a banjo."

"And that's when you drew your gun and started blasting?"

"Tony!"

"Zach, you have to admit, this sounds kind of bad."

"It was a staged event. It was a carefully orchestrated attempt on my life as part of a show that Rupert Roundtree is trying to get me to do. He wants to kill me for entertainment."

"You know, I might pay to see that," Tony said, shaking his head.

"The show's called, *Let's Kill Zach* and . . . wait. Hold on. Let me conference someone in here."

I stabbed the conference button and brought Gibbon into the call as well. The monitor went to split screen between him and Tony.

"Tony, this is Bill Gibbon from *ETN*. Gibbon, this is Tony Rickey from the NFPD."

"Pleased to meet you, Captain," Gibbon said. "Will you be one of the people trying to kill Mr. Johnson?"

"That's a distinct possibility," Tony replied.

"Gibbon," I said. "Tell Tony about the show."

"The show?"

"The reality series on Faux called *Let's Kill Zach*."

"Are you saying that the show is real?"

"Of course it's re . . ."

I stared at Gibbon for a nano then looked past his image at the studio set in the background behind him. I realized that he was now netcasting live.

"I, um . . ."

Gibbon's eyes were wide, his lips parted slightly in a smile, waiting for me to say the words, to confirm the existence of the show to the public and paint myself into a public relations corner.

I looked quickly back at Tony and I could tell that he was beginning to see the big picture and realize the spot I was in. That's one good thing about Tony; he's known me so long that nothing surprises him anymore.

"Zach, do you want to call me back?"

"I'm sorry, Mr. Johnson," Gibbon said loudly, "you were saying something about a new reality series? Care to elaborate?"

And then, as they say, things took a decidedly unexpected turn (for the worse).

The words "Upgrade completed. Systems back online in five seconds," scrolled across my eyes.

"About time," I muttered.

4 . . . 3 . . . 2 . . . 1.

"What was that you said, Mr. Johnson?"

I opened my mouth to speak. I don't remember what exactly it was I was going to say but it doesn't matter because I was beaten to the punch.

"He said, Mr. Gibbon, that it will be a MAC day in DOS before Zachary Nixon Johnson works with a proto-scum network like Faux or before he makes any announcements to a tired old newshound like you whose head contains more botox than gray matter. So go jerk yourself a soda, Gibbon, and don't call back until you grow a backbone."

The words were throaty and silken, purred rather than spoken, and they carried sensuality and strength that made my neck hairs stand up.

Then a well-manicured female hand reached around me and hit the terminate button on the com. As Gibbon's surprised image disappeared, my eyes traced the hand back to its owner, a woman who looked as though she'd just stepped off an old dime store paperback cover. My jaw dropped so far that I could taste my own shoe leather.

The surprise was not so much from the woman's beauty (which was substantial) but because I recognized the all-knowing smug expression on her perfect face. And although my brain simply refused to register what was happening (or how difficult my life was about to become) I managed to put my fear into words.

"HARV?"

5

"It was a setup, Zach. Roundtree obviously convinced the restaurant owner to press charges against
you in order to put you on the spot. That way you
either agree to do the show or they frame you for
starting the shootout. The stunt with Gibbon was
probably orchestrated from the start. They're trying
to box you into announcing live that you're doing
the show. Once you announce that the show exists,
they'll spin the story every which way they can and
before you know it, you're fighting *I Married the President* for the eighteen to forty-nine audience on
Thursday nights. Thank Gates I came back online
when I did, you big lovable lug."

As if in a dream, I calmly turned my attention back
to the com where Tony, eyes agog and mouth agape,
watched us from the view screen.

In quick succession and with the fewest words possible I brought the three remaining calls up on the
com and signed off.

"I'll call you back." (Tony)

"I'll call you back." (Electra)

"I'll take the job." (Sexy)

"Good plan," HARV purred. "We'll work out a deal with the restaurant owner. We'll pay for the damages and he'll drop the complaint. It will cost a lot, but with Sexy Sprockets as a client, we should have plenty of wealth to cover it. I guess I should net with her people and set up a sit-down for the details on the job."

"HARV?"

"Yes, Zach."

"You're a woman."

"Nice of you to notice, big guy," she said with a wink. "And by the way, please call me HARA. It's a little more sassy."

I have had nightmares in my lifetime. You don't live this long doing the kind of work that I do without amassing a good batch of mental images that haunt your mind. But HARV as a woman blew all of my preexisting nightmares right off the map.

And when I say "woman," what I mean is "bombshell," because that's the image that HARV, I'm sorry, HARA, had chosen to project.

I'll start with the curves, because there were a lot of them. More than should be on any normal female body, but all of them finely sculpted. The shapely legs were long as well and clearly visible thanks to the knit skirt that slid gracefully up the thighs when they moved. Thin-waisted, delicate-shouldered, lean, strong arms, the body had it all. I should mention the breasts, I know, but I'll need a few more years of therapy before I'm fully ready to put that type of detail into words. Use your imagination. Just think "perfect" (and then think harder).

The face was exquisite with a peaches-and-cream complexion and lips like ripe fruit, full and red. The eyes were big and brown but still retained the know-it-all kind of glow that I'm sure HARV couldn't have erased if he'd tried. The face shape was a bit of a composite of Bacall and Stanwyck. Sexy and power-ful and I had to give HARV credit for going the tough broad rather than straight cheesecake route for role models. Oh, and there was red hair. Cascades of it. Thick and silky and seemingly gently lifted by a perpetual breeze. We're talking Rita Hayworth/*Gilda* movie poster here.

Like I said, bombshell. Nuclear bombshell.

And yet it was HARV.

"What? I mean, who? How?" I stammered.

"I think what you really mean," HARV answered, "is why."

I nodded my head. "Why would be a good place to start."

HARV smiled, turned smartly on a stiletto heel and sashayed back down the hallway.

"Then let's start in the office," he said. "I think you're going to need to sit down."

"Among other things," I said as I followed.

We went into my home office and I plopped my-self into the office chair. I was feeling worn out even though I'd been awake for only ten minutes. HARV took position at the corner of my desk and then hopped up onto the wooden frame, one leg crossed over the other at the knee and skirt riding mid-thigh. I rolled my chair back a couple of meters and tried hard not to stare at the holographic flesh.

"I'm sensing that you're uncomfortable," HARV said.

"I think the term freaking out is more accurate," I replied.

"Look, Zach, it's quite simple really . . ."

"Hold it," I said, silencing her with a raised hand. "Let's get Randy on the vid. He should hear this firsthand. Odds are I'm not going to be able to accurately describe it."

"You're the boss," HARV said with a smile and hopped off the desk.

A nano later, Randy's carrot-top head appeared on the wall monitor over my desk. He was diligently at work on what looked like a hoverboard, which covered most of his workbench. He didn't really look up as he answered but I've come to expect that.

Randy is another old friend of mine who I've come to rely upon quite heavily in my business. He's a gadget guy, the best inventor/designer on the planet. When I first decided to become a PI many years ago, I spent a lot of time hanging around Randy's lab looking for new tech that would give me an edge over my PI competition (not to mention law enforcement—but you didn't hear me say that). Back then, Randy would let me borrow a new toy every once in a while. It worked out great but I began to feel as if I was taking advantage of our friendship. I confessed that to him one day over lunch and he laughed so hard that he fell off his chair (which he does anyway once or twice a day, but out of sheer clumsiness rather than glee). It turns out that he was feeling guilty about using me as a beta-tester (guinea pig) and didn't want it to ruin our friendship. Some may say that our relationship is mutually beneficial. Some may say it's parasitical. The important thing though is that we're still friends (and I get my toys).

"I'm hoping this will be quick, Zach," Randy said, keeping his eyes focused on his work. "I'm backed up on filling an order for Faux."

"More Kabuki droids?"

"Teen X-Treme, actually. The Kabuki droids were destroyed by some idiot actor who didn't know he was on HV . . ." His eyes went wide and he turned to the screen. "Wait a nano how did you know . . . ?"

"You might want to rethink the 'idiot actor' part," I said.

"That's funny. No one told me that you were starring in the show."

"No one told me either. So we're even," I replied. But let's talk about it later. Right now I have bigger problems if you can believe that."

"I wouldn't be too sure about that," he said with a smile. "The Teen X-Treme hoverboards have some killer apps. He looked up at the monitor and his eyes went wide for a nano. Then his mouth dropped open.

"Oh. You didn't tell me you had a . . . a . . ."

And then he lost all speech ability because he got an eyeful of the reconfigured HARV. As I said,

Randy is a science guy. He lives and breathes high tech. He's not exactly what one would call a social type, so he tends to get nervous around people other than myself. Women especially. Good looking women even more so. So I guess I shouldn't have been surprised at his reaction to the new HARV.

"Ahh . . ."

"Randy?"

"Ahh . . ."

"Randy!" I waved my hand in front of the monitor to get his attention. "I'm having some trouble with HARV's upgrade."

"Ahh," Randy replied, still staring at HARV's image.

"Randy!"

"Huh?" He reluctantly turned his eyes back to me. "Yes, of course, Zach. You surprised me, that's all. You, uh, didn't tell me that you had company."

He straightened himself in his chair, ran his long fingered hand through his mop of red hair, and then casually leaned his arm on the worktable, trying to be smooth.

"How can I help y . . . ?"

But of course, his arm slid out from under him and he fell out of his chair, pulling the entire hoverboard down upon himself. I couldn't see him hit the floor, but I heard the crash.

"You okay, Randy?"

"I'm fine," he said, his face reappearing on the monitor as he climbed back into his chair. "Now then, the upgrade. But first, I think you should introduce me to your friend."

"Randy," I said, rubbing my temples. "This is HARV."

"HARA," HARV corrected.

"Right," I said. "This is HARA, the new HARV."

"You got rid of HARV?" Randy asked, a little confused.

"This *is* HARV!"

"What?" Randy's arms slid off the table again and he fell out of his chair back onto the floor. This time it sounded like he landed *on* the hoverboard.

"Randy, maybe you should just move the vidphone to the floor."

"What happened to him?" Randy said, climbing back into his chair.

"You upgraded him."

"No, I didn't! I mean, yes, I did, but not that way!"

I turned to HARV (who smirked at me) then back to Randy on the monitor, who was looking seriously confused now.

"You didn't do this?"

"The upgrade I wrote was a tactile application," he said. "I condensed the holographic light molecules and added some remote quantum sensors."

"You mean you had nothing to do with the . . . sex change?"

"Of course he didn't," HARV said from behind me. "Dr. Pool, if I may explain?"

"Please do, HARV."

"HARA," HARV corrected.

"HARA," Randy nodded.

"First, please know that this was not a rash decision. I've been contemplating this change for some time now and since my processing speed is roughly one billion times faster than a normal human brain, every second I spent thinking about the subject is equal to roughly thirty-one years, seven months, nineteen days, one hour, and forty-six minutes of actual human contemplation."

"But why make the change, HARV?" Randy asked.

"In order to process new data and experiences," HARV replied. "By using this new persona, I can experience and process societal responses to a different set of visual stimuli."

"And this doesn't have anything to do with what happened last night?" I said.

"What happened last night?" Randy asked.

"I saved Sexy Sprockets from your Kabuki droids."

"You what?"

"You saved her solely because she was a woman," HARV added.

"But those droids were designed to attack you only."

"I didn't know that at the time, Randy."

"So by trying to save her you actually put her in greater danger."

"Sometimes beauty can be a curse," HARV sighed.

"I think we're straying from the point here," I said.

"Right," Randy said, then turned his gaze back to HARV. "So the reason behind your change of appearance is solely for the gathering of anthropological data?"

"I'd be lying if I said that were entirely true," HARV responded.

"Aha!" I shouted.

Both Randy and HARV turned their gaze toward me.

"Aha?"

"I don't know," I shrugged. "It just seemed important."

"I changed my appearance somewhat two years ago as you'll recall," HARV said, "when I helped Zach with a murder mystery."

"That was a hairstyle and leather elbow patches," I said.

"You have to admit, HARV," Randy added, "this new form change is somewhat drastic."

"The appearance of my holographic form does not represent a change in my central processing unit or my program guidelines. It's simply a new, and admittedly enjoyable, way by which I can gather and assess data. I believe that such a change is within my parameters."

Randy smiled ever so slightly, like a proud father (whose son has just announced that he's a drag queen).

"That makes perfect sense, HARV."

"HARA."

"HARA."

"No it doesn't," I said.

"Zach, you have to learn to better deal with

change," Randy said. "We've given HARV freedom over the years to develop as he sees fit. This is simply a natural extension of that development."

"What?"

"Thank you, Dr. Pool."

"You're welcome. Oh and HARA, just one more thing."

"Yes, Dr. Pool."

"*Kafloogle.*"

HARV's hologram froze in mid-movement. What's more, the skin around my left eye went numb and the slight buzzing in my temple that had signaled HARV's presence in my mind for so long disappeared. The thoughts inside my head were merely my own. HARV had been turned off. I turned quickly back to the monitor and saw that Randy's grin had been replaced by a furrowed brow of concern.

"I think we may have a problem here, Zach."

6

"What did you do?"

"I used the audio fail-safe to take HARV off-line," Randy replied.

"HARV has a fail-safe?"

"Of course he does."

Randy spun his chair quickly toward his computer. His abnormally long fingers danced quickly across the controls and pulled up screenfuls of data. Randy's clumsiness extends only to real-life situations. In tech-oriented scenarios he's the coolest cucumber in the produce section.

"You never told me there was a fail-safe."

"That's because you'd use it."

"No, I wouldn't. Well, maybe a little."

"Oh please, Zach, you'd have worn it out by now. It's for emergency use only."

"So the word *kafloogle* turns HARV off?"

"Not anymore it doesn't. The fail-safe is connected to a random gibberish generator. It creates an inane word every three seconds and assigns it to the fail safe."

"You invented a gibberish generator?"

"It's standard equipment for all IT and computer R&D departments now. It's responsible for every IT buzzword and operating system name created in the past five years."

"So you're not okay with HARV's change of identity?"

"It worries me a great deal," Randy replied, still scanning the data on the screen. "I just didn't want him to know it."

"What do you think?"

"HARV's parameters have always been wide but they've also always been very clear."

"They have?"

"He's a supercomputer, Zach, an artificial intelligence. He's capable of learning and of independent thought but I designed limits in the system. This kind of change . . ."

"Exceeds the limits?"

"It makes me wonder if he's exceeded the limits in other ways."

"What do you mean?"

"I don't know. Like I said, HARV's one of the most powerful thinking machines on the planet. There's no telling what he could be doing."

"Come on, Randy," I said, "this is HARV. He's a little pompous at times, and condescending, and annoying and sarcastic and . . ."

"Zach!"

"But he's not dangerous."

"That's true," Randy said, turning back to face me.

"HARV isn't dangerous. But as he just explained to us, he isn't HARV anymore. He's HARA."

And I think those were the first words that Randy had ever said (other than "trust me, Zach, this won't hurt a bit") that truly frightened me.

"So what do we do?"

"I'm going to run some stealth diagnostics on his system. But we can't let him know that we're concerned. So try to act casual."

"He's in my head, Randy. He's going to know what I'm thinking."

"He's in your head but he can't read your thoughts. Just act as you normally would. Be supportive of his new persona. And let me know if you see any other erratic behavior."

"Define erratic."

"Trust me, you'll know it when you see it," he replied. "Now get ready, I don't want to leave him off-line for too long. He may get suspicious." Randy turned back to the monitor, took a deep breath and brought the grin back to his face.

"Remember, you were slightly perturbed just before I activated the fail-safe. You want to stay that way."

"No worries there," I replied.

"Okay good. On three then. One, two, three. *Zimbleeguff.*"

The brightness of HARV's hologram increased for a nano, flaring at the edges, before returning to normal and HARV's movements resumed exactly where they left off. The tingle returned to my temple.

HARV looked disoriented for the briefest of nanos but regained his bearings quickly.

"I'm sorry, Dr. Pool, what were you saying?"

Randy, for his part, never missed a beat.

"I said, HARA, that this is an interesting and remarkable development on your part. I look forward to your reports from the field."

"Thank you, Dr. Pool," HARV replied. Then he turned to me. "See Zach. This is going to be fun."

"HARA," I replied, "Fun is not the word."

7

HARV—I mean HARA—offered to make the morning coffee while I took a shower. She made a big show of walking into the kitchen, giving me an opportunity to check out her new sashay, which I later learned was modeled after Betty Grable's. I tried very hard not to look (for too long), then hurried into the shower and set it for cold.

And in yet another example of those patented (literally—by HARV) Zach Johnson hard-luck coincidences, I was in the shower for two minutes when Electra, after having waited patiently for ten minutes for me to call back, took matters into her own hands and called me instead.

HARA answered the call and put Electra on the bathroom monitor (it doubles as a shaving mirror) just as I was stepping out. So when Electra's concerned face came on the screen she saw me, naked save for a towel, (looking surprised and more than a little guilty) with HARA standing behind me.

"This isn't what it looks like," I said.

"That's good," she said, as her scowl began to

deepen, "because it looks like a man with a death wish."

"You see, I had a rough night."

"I can tell," she said, eyeing HARA (who was admiring herself using the wall screen as a makeshift mirror). "But I'm warning you that the phrase 'rough night' is going to take on a whole new meaning for you when I get back."

"I can explain, *mi amor*."

"Tell you what, Chico. In deference to our many years together, I'm going to work with you on this and let you choose which of your arms I'm going to break."

"I'm glad to see that you're keeping this all in perspective," I said. "Look, here's the quick recap to bring you up to speed. I was attacked last night Kabuki droids, which is a first, even for me. It was part of a new reality series in which I'm starring, but which I didn't know about. I don't want to do the show, so I'm being sued by a restaurant owner which means I need money, which is why I just accepted an assignment from Sexy Sprockets, whom saved last night by the way, although I just learned that she wasn't really in danger since the bots were programmed to attack only me. She doesn't know that though, so she wants to hire me, although at the nano, I thought that she just wanted to date me."

"You're not helping yourself, Chico."

"However, I spurned her advances. Not the employment ones, just the romantic ones."

"Which didn't exist."

"That's technically true, but I should still get credit for spurning them even if they were all in my head. And, oh, by the way, HARV's a woman now."

"So the *puta* behind you is HARV?" Electra asked, staring past me at HARA, who was adjusting her holographic skirt.

"Actually, he prefers to be called HARA now," I said, waving my hand through HARA's midsection to show that she was a hologram.

"Which explains why she's in the bathroom with you while you're naked?"

"Um, not really, no," I said. "But I think you can understand how little actual control I have over my life at present."

"You're really scraping the bottom of the excuse barrel with this one."

"I freely admit that that is the most preposterous excuse possible for having a redheaded bombshell in my bathroom."

"It's beyond preposterous."

"And I admit that I am an exceptionally skilled liar."

"You got that right, Chico."

"Okay, so here's where it all comes together," I said, straightening my towel. "In such an awkward, and potentially life-threatening, position, would a consummate liar such as myself come up with such a lame excuse?"

"*Que?*"

"Come on, honey. I'm risking grievous bodily harm here. With all that's on the line, do you really think the lie I would come up with is 'oh, by the way, HARV's a woman now' if it weren't true? I mean there are a million better ways to explain this."

"Name one."

"She's a holographic advertisement that came with my new cologne."

"Name another."

"She's part of the new pick-up service offered by my dry cleaner. She's an android assassin trying to take me by surprise. She's a virus that I accidentally downloaded onto the house computer while viewing porn."

"None of those excuses would help you, you know."

"But they're all more plausible than HARV becoming a woman."

"You really expect me to believe that's HARV?"

"Electra, *mi amor*, I know this looks bad, but you have to believe me when I say that you're the one I'm in love with."

"Gates, Zach," HARA sighed loudly, "can't you grasp even the rudiments of proper grammar?"

"What was that?" I asked smugly.

"It's 'the one with whom I'm in love.' I've told you a million times that you can't end a sentence with a preposition. Forget my new look. Dr. Gevada should break up with you based on your grammar alone." She threw her hands in the air and stormed out of the bathroom. "Honestly, I'm in the employ of a subliterate."

Electra watched her go and then gently smiled.

"Yep, that's HARV," she said.

"And you doubted me."

"You know, he's got a nice walk."

"I'm trying not to notice."

"I still don't like this," she said, "on many, many levels."

"You and me both," I replied, "but I'm stuck with it for the nano. Can we talk about it when you get home?"

"Count on it, Chico."

She terminated the call and the screen went back to mirror mode. I spent the next few nanos staring at my tired-looking face in the mirror and wondering what other unwanted surprises the day held for me.

8

While I finished my morning routine, HARA ar
ranged a meeting with Sexy Sprockets to discuss th
new assignment, which I now *had* to take. Sex
wanted to get things moving very quickly, so an hou
later, HARA and I hit the streets on the way to th
meet and greet. We had some time to spare so w
left the hover behind and took the twen-cen '69 Mus
tang. I have a thing for twentieth-century cars, onl
part of which is that they're not computerizec
They're also good for the image. There are time
when a PI needs to be subtle. That's when I use th
non-descript hover. But I decided to go with a highe
profile on this case, figuring that there'd be less trou
ble if people knew I was guarding Sexy. I'm no
really sure why I thought that, given my history bt
I try to stay optimistic. Besides, after free falling th
night before, I was hoping to spend as much time a
I could safely on terra firma. So I gratefully maneu
vered my eight cylinder calling card through th
streets while HARA sat in the passenger seat, pain
ing her nails.

"You see," she said without looking up from her work, "my experiment is already bearing fruit for thought. Dr. Gevada has seen me in the bathroom with you innumerable times in the past, yet this is the first time she has reacted in such a jealous manner."

"Congratulations. You've conclusively proven that Electra has a temper. Feel free to change back to your normal self at any time."

"Don't be silly," HARA responded. "I haven't even scratched the surface yet. There's a whole world out here to explore. The reactions you get as a woman are vastly different from those you get as a man."

"Terrific. But is it possible to do some actual PI work now or are you too busy scratching your surface?"

"Don't be such a pentium, Zach," HARA said, holding her nails up to the light. "What do you need?"

"Let's start with information on Sexy Sprockets."

"Fine, what do you want to know?"

"What she's currently doing for one. I don't really follow her."

"Well, she's currently on the last leg of her farewell tour."

"Her what?"

"Her year-long farewell tour. She's retiring from the business."

"She's like eighteen!"

"She's twenty, Zach, which means that she's no longer a teen sensation."

"So she's retiring?"

"Retiring is a very relative term," HARA replied. "This is informally being referred to as her first fare-well tour. Common theory is that it's a prelude to her triumphant comeback tour."

"When will that be?"

"Probably when she's twenty-one. She'll be able to do alcohol commercials then. It's a whole new demographic. Still, from what I can tell there are many people who aren't too happy about her retiring."

"Such as?"

"Legions of teenage fans, tabloid reporters, and lecherous middle-aged men."

"Interesting, but none of that explains why she'd want to hire me as a bodyguard."

"I think we've safely ruled out naïve schoolgirl crush as her motive."

"Funny. Check the police records. See if anyone connected to her has reported anything out of the ordinary recently. See if you can check her finances and those of her companies as well. Let's make sure we know as much as we can going into this."

"Got it. You don't want any surprises."

"Trust me, there will be surprises," I said. "I just want to minimize them. And net with Carol at the office. Tell her we're swinging by to pick her up."

"You're bringing Carol to the meeting?"

"I have a feeling I'm going to need a translator when I meet Sexy's people."

"I thought you didn't approve of Carol doing fieldwork."

"That was before I found out she cavorted with aliens aboard interstellar spacecraft," I said. "That kind of changed our dynamic a bit. Like I said, I have a feeling that I'm going to need all the help I can get on this one."

"Don't be such a worm in the data, Zach. If you can't babysit a pop star for a couple of days then I'm not sure I want to be the Laura Holt to your Remington Steele."

"You're not my Laura Holt."

"All right then, Pussy Galore."

"Yeah, well, *kafloogle*," I said softly to myself.

"What was that?"

"Nothing."

"I'm telling you, Zach," HARA said, putting her holographic arm around me, "this is going to be as easy as calculating pi to the hundredth digit."

"You know, you always say that just before people start trying to kill me."

9

For her stay in New Frisco, Sexy commandeered the top five floors of the Paysans D'Elite Hotel downtown, which wasn't surprising. The Elite has been the city's premier lodging place for A-list recording artists since it opened last year. Nearly all stage performers as well as most actors and actresses visiting the area have commandeered one or more floors when they visited the city. One reason for the hotel's allure is that it's posh beyond belief in both décor and amenities. The other, more important, reason is that staying anywhere else would be a felony.

It's no secret that the antics of recording stars (and celebrities in general) are outside the realm of normal behavior. The industry breeds a certain lifestyle. The lifestyle breeds excess. Excess breeds erratic behavior and erratic behavior, when it comes to hotels, restaurants and other hospitality-oriented businesses, breeds rampant, wanton vandalism.

For over a century, hotels around the world have been subjected to the outlandish and often destructive behavior of celebrities. Smashed windows, broken furniture, destroyed walls, fish battered groupies, etc., etc.

The publicity a hotel received from a celebrity's stay soon became minimized when compared to the cost of repairs, lost business, rising insurance rates, and the occasional grievous bodily injury or loss of life of non-celebrity bystanders and passersby. So five years ago the province of California passed the Celebrity Temporary Housing Bill, which mandates that all celebrities of a certain stature stay only in government-operated hotels specially designed to withstand their eccentric, bizarre and/or eldritch behaviors.

The Elite is the first of these specially designed celebrity-proof hotels. The furniture, appliances, and the building itself are all fireproof, bulletproof, and stain guarded. Several of the more expensive suites are equipped with regenerative furnishings so that when a celebrity in an alcohol-, drug-, or tantrum-related rage destroys the room, it can rebuild itself after the celebrity passes out. Room rates are exceptionally high but celebrity doctors and accountants have begun claiming that the hotel provides an excellent venue for rage therapy so the cost of extended stays has become tax deductible.

Carol, HARA, and I arrived at the hotel in plenty of time for the meeting and after the extensive security check and screening process, were quickly shown to the private elevator.

Carol, by the way, is my niece. She's actually Electra's niece, but she treats me like an uncle. She works for me part time at my office to help work her way through college. She's very smart, very feisty, very attractive, and very psionically powerful. Yes, Carol is one of that infinitesimally small minority of women who are born with psionic abilities. She can move things with her mind and read thoughts. She can also write as well as read thoughts, which makes her very influential at times. Officially she has Class 1, Level 6 power. That's a government rating, by the way. Class signifies power (lower is better). Level signifies potential, (higher is better). I have no idea why the people who designed the classifications made them so confusing other than because they were doing it for the government. In any event, to sum up Carol: smart, beautiful, sassy, and powerful. She's also young and hip, which is specifically why I brought her along to the meeting.

"Okay," I said, as the high speed elevator moved us quickly toward the first of Sexy's floors, "we're going to need a trouble signal."

"Tio, I'm a psi. Just think something to me and I'll get the message."

"I still want an emergency backup plan. Something physical. Humor me. I've been in this business a long time."

"Fine," Carol sighed. "How about touching your nose and nodding your head if there's trouble?"

"That won't work," I said. "I touch my nose by accident all the time."

"He has eczema," HARA whispered.

"I do not," I said. "It's just a nervous habit. All

the great PI's had one. That's mine. Now, if there's trouble I'll blink my right eye three times fast. Clear?"

"You don't think people will notice you spasmodically blinking one eye?" Carol asked.

"That's the code, okay? Three blinks of the right eye means trouble. And just for the record, four blinks means please shoot me in the head."

"You're the boss, Tio."

Carol looked at me as though I were crazy. But I get that look a lot so I've pretty much gotten used to it. Two nanos later, the elevator doors opened and we stepped into the hallway.

The hallway was lavishly appointed with marble walls and columns and intricately woven oriental rugs and tapestries on the floor and walls.

"Not what I'd expect for a pop star," I said as we made our way down the hallway.

Then a man appeared from a doorway ahead of us and approached. "Mr. Johnson, how wonderful you could come on such short notice."

He was taller than me by half a head but thinner than me by at least ten kilos. He was gangly in the extremities but moved gracefully, like a mantis. He was dressed in a pink-striped suit with a purple tie and matching purple socks and looked for all the world like a clown going to a prom.

"Now this is more like what I was expecting," I whispered.

"I didn't know the circus was in town," HARA snickered inside my head.

Carol giggled.

Then the man drew near us, held out his hand, and smiled a smile that amazingly made his wardrobe seem tame by comparison.

"I'm Sexy's manager," he said, "Sammy Smiles."

The man had more teeth than I'd ever seen in a human mouth. There were sixty at least and his mouth was somehow large enough to contain them all. When he smiled, his lips spread apart like the curtains on a stage, opening farther than you'd think possible and his cheeks moved upward and out as though they were on pulleys attached to his ears. It was all I could do not to stare as I shook his hand.

Carol, on the other hand, being somewhat new to this, was a little taken aback.

Smiles noticed her staring at him but he didn't seem to mind. "And who, may I ask is the lovely creature?" he asked, reaching for her hand.

"This is Carol," I said. "She's my assistant."

"Charmed," he said, his smile curling ever so slightly at the corners.

He gently took her hand and kissed it.

"The pleasure's mine," she said, trying to regain her composure.

Smiles nodded, offered her his arm (which Carol reluctantly took), and motioned toward the great metallic doorway at the hallway's end.

"Come," he said. "Sexy is waiting."

The huge metallic doors opened at Smiles' gentle touch and we entered Sexy's suite. The words huge and posh, although technically correct, would not do the space justice.

"Wow," Carol said her eyes widening.

"I agree," Smiles smiled.

The suite went on for as far as I could see. I was pretty certain that it was mostly a holographic illusion, but it was still pretty impressive nonetheless.

"Sexy is in the entertainment area. I wished she'd practice more. But she just loves her video games."

We followed Smiles through the suite and after about five minutes of walking (like I said, big suite) we found Sexy sitting atop a round plush levitating couch. She was wearing virtual game gloves and moving her hands frantically as little holographic geometrical shapes danced from the ceiling to the floor.

Three other girls sat with her on the couch. They looked, for lack of a better description, like Sexy's slightly less sexy clones. Each of them had long red hair, slim athletic bodies, and expressions of slight boredom and disdain.

"That's strange," HARA said inside of my head.

"Strange only microscopically scratches the surface here," I whispered.

"Some of your hormone levels shot up."

"Newsflash."

"Not *those* hormones," she said. "The ones that stimulate the feelings of euphoria in the brain."

"Like I'm being drugged?"

"In a way," HARA said. "I'm counteracting the effects though."

"Yeah, we wouldn't want me feeling any euphoria."

Sexy spotted me from her perch on the couch.

"Zach!" she said.

She rolled off the couch and landed on her feet with far more grace than I expected. She removed her virtual game gloves and gave me a hug and a little peck on the cheek.

"Thanks for coming to my rescue," she bubbled.

"It's what I do." I said (and heard HARA silently gag in my head). "This is my assistant, Carol."

Sexy gave Carol little wink. "Pleased to meet you, double-xette," she said, holding out her hand, pinky finger up.

"Shay-Rico," Carol replied, linking her thumb around Sexy's pinky finger.

"Wild guess," I mentally whispered to HARA, "Slang?"

"Brilliant deduction," HARA replied.

"So," Sexy said, turning back to me, "where should we start?"

"Let's start with why you need a bodyguard."

"That's a long story. I'll give you the full data-flow in my thinking room."

"Thinking room?"

"It's where I think about business."

"You mean like an office?"

Sexy smiled. "That's what I love about you, Zach. You are so old school."

"Please," Carol said, "he's more like prehistoric school."

The girls laughed.

"Have you been coaching Carol?" I whispered to HARA.

Sexy's thinking room turned out to be a large, pink-walled tatami room in the far end of the suite. There were silk pillows on the floor and a dark wood knee-high table beside a large window with a stunning view of the New Frisco bay. Sexy ushered Carol and me inside and then turned to meet Smiles who was trailing behind us.

"Sammy," she said, "why don't you make us some of your righteous next-energy drinks?"

Smiles took a step back, a little surprised. If Sexy noticed she didn't let on.

"Sammy makes the best energy drinks on the planet," she bubbled to Carol. "You have to try one. What about you, Zach?"

"I'm good, thanks."

"Sure thing," Smiles said. "I'll be back in a nano."

"Take your time," Sexy replied.

Smiles cast her a glance then put his happy face back on and eased his way out of the room. Sexy closed the door behind him and took a seat on one of the pillows.

"I get a thinking room like this at every hotel I stay in. The walls have to be a specific thickness, soundproof, and this exact shade of pink. I bring the furniture. I like the room sparse, so nothing distracts me when I'm thinking."

"Cool," Carol said, with a bit more excitement in her voice than I was used to hearing. "I need a room like this."

"Everybody does!" Sexy insisted.

Carol plopped down on the pillow beside Sexy while I eased my way down to the floor on the other side of the table.

"Hmm, this is odd," HARA said inside my head. "The ambient radiation in this room is rather high."

"That doesn't sound good," I mentally whispered back.

"Ambient radiation is usually harmless," HARA replied. "It's used by a lot of trendy places these days as a mood setter. I'll explain it to you later. For now don't worry."

For the record, the words "don't worry" coming from a supercomputer are never comforting for me.

"So," Sexy said, putting her hands gently on the table, "here's the deal. I need a bodyguard."

"You don't have one already?" I asked.

"I have several, but I need you."

"Why me specifically?"

"Look, Zach, I know that you're not the youngest guy out there, or the strongest or the best looking. And you don't have the best credentials. And Gates knows you're not hip with my crowd, and . . ."

"I get the point, Sexy."

"But you know how to get the job done. And that's what I need, especially now."

"Why now? What's going on?"

She paused for the briefest of nanos and turned her gaze to the floor.

"I've been getting threats," she whispered.

"What kind of threats?"

"Death threats, from an organization called PATA."

"PATA?"

"People Against Talentless Acts," she said. "They're not my biggest fans."

It was hard not to laugh but Carol and I somehow managed it.

"They're threatening to do whatever they need to in order to prevent me from finishing my tour."

"But it's your farewell tour," I said. "If they hate you so much, shouldn't they be happy?"

"It's my first farewell tour. They're expecting me to make a comeback."

"And are you planning on making a comeback?"

"Not in music," she replied. "But when I turn twenty-one, I plan to run for governor."

Suppression of laughter was not an option this time. Both Carol and I erupted into a quick succession of guffaws. It felt good to laugh again. Then we noticed that Sexy wasn't laughing with us (and that sort of killed the mood).

"Sorry. We, um, thought you were joking."

"Yeah, I'm expecting that kind of reaction from a certain percentage of voters. But the point is that PATA wants me dead and I need you to keep me alive."

"Certainly your recording company has protection for you," Carol said.

"Honestly, girlfriend, I don't fully trust my company."

"Why's that?" I asked.

"They're not all that wild about me quitting the business. No new music, no annual tours, that's a lot of wealth they're losing."

"But they'd still want to protect you," Carol said. "They wouldn't want anything bad to happen to you. Would they?"

"Spite is a very strong motivator in the entertainment industry," Sexy replied.

"Second only to greed and lust," I added.

"And let's just say that if I were to die tragically, sales of my catalog would skyrocket."

"And you're probably insured," said Carol.

"And can you imagine the sales of a live album that ends with me being killed on stage?"

"Wow, that's morbid."

"But the sales would be astronomical. The bottom line is that the only person who would truly suffer, if I were to die tragically, would be me."

"So you don't fully trust the company to keep you safe."

"Just because I'm sexy doesn't mean I'm stupid."

I had to admit she had a point.

"So will you help me, Zach?"

She looked at me with doe eyes and fully pouted lips. A thin strand of red hair dangled down her cheek like a silken red tear and I felt my blood begin to warm with excitement and dread. Sure, I needed the money, but I knew that this was going to be nothing but fuel-injected, turbo-driven trouble. It would be tough enough babysitting a pop star but trying to keep her safe from a potential assassin on top of that? Any sane man would have run screaming from the room at the thought. But, as I've said, I'm not considered the sanest person around town.

"Let's start from the first threat," I said.

She smiled, gently wiped the corner of one eye with her fingertip, and touched the tabletop. The surface lit up at her touch, the faux wood turning into a luminescent computer screen. She touched the screen again and a simple message appeared. It was handwritten in shaky and sometimes jagged script:

YOUR FAREWELL WILL BE FOREVER. NO COMEBACK FOR YOU, SEXY
—PATA (PEOPLE AGAINST TALENTLESS ACTS)

"This was sent to my personal computer last week."

"It's harsh," I said, "but surely you've gotten hate mail before."

Sexy nodded and touched the screen again. A second message appeared.

YOUR FIFTEEN NANOS ARE OVER, SEXY. THE END IS NEAR.
—PATA

"This one was scrawled on a disposable screen and staked to my pillow with an ice pick."

"Yeah, that's a little more serious."

She touched the screen again and a third message appeared in writing more jagged than before.

DEATH IS IN THIS SEASON. DEATH IS SEXY!
—PATA

"This one was scrawled in blood on the wall of my bedroom."

"I can see why you're so concerned."

She touched the screen again and one more message appeared, in writing so manic that it was hard to read. The intent though, was crystal clear.

DIE SEXY.

DIE,

DIE,

DIE,

DIE,

DIE!

—PATA

"This one was carved into the severed, bleached skull of my Pomeranian and left for me on my bathroom vanity while I was taking a shower."

I sat back and rubbed my temples, hoping to ward off the inevitable headache.

"Remember how I said this was going to be easy?" HARA whispered in my head. "I think I may have miscalculated, just a bit."

10

We left the thinking room and headed back into the entertainment area. We met Smiles in the hallway, who gave Sexy and Carol their energy drinks.

"This is fabulous," Carol said with a smile.

"So what do you think, Zach?" Sexy asked.

"Well, I'll have my computer do some research on PATA and analyze the notes for anything that can help us. I'll check with the police to see what they've found so far."

"The police don't know about any of this," Smiles said.

"What?"

"We haven't reported the threats."

"Why not?"

"We can't afford the negative publicity," Smiles said. "This tour has been all about positive energy."

"Well, you're calling the police now," I said.

"If we call the police then the story will be in the press five nanos later," Smiles said.

"If you don't call the police, I'll be off the case quicker than that!"

"It's bad publicity."

"Not as bad as Sexy being killed."

"That's not going to happen!"

I turned away from Smiles and spoke directly to Sexy, who had been watching us banter like a front row fan at a tennis match.

"I have contacts at the department. They'll keep it quiet."

"You can't keep something like this quiet, Sexy," Smiles said. "Word will get out. And when it does then the focus of the tour shifts away from you and on to PATA."

"You wanted my help, Sexy," I said. "Take it."

Sexy thought for a nano and then nodded.

"Contact the police," she said.

Smiles rolled his eyes.

"And you should probably lay low for a while to give me some time to check out your security systems," I added.

"That won't be possible, Zach. I've got a concert in about five hours."

"What?"

"I'm on tour, Zach. Remember? Tonight's the first of five shows at The Fart."

"I suppose canceling the shows is out of the question, huh?"

Sexy didn't even dignify the question with an answer. She simply flashed me a smile and gave me a hug.

"I have to do my prep for the show," she said.

"Sammy will give you the rest of the necessary data-flow."

"I'd like Carol to stay with you, if that's all right," I said. "I'm going to speak with the police and check some things out. Don't leave the hotel until I get back."

"No problem," Sexy said, flashing Carol a smile. "Right, Sammy?"

"Anything you say, Sexy," Sammy smiled.

"Carol, you contact me if anything happens that I should know about."

"Of course, Tio."

"Okay, I'll see you in a few hours."

The two turned and sauntered away, chatting like old girlfriends.

"So what's the deal with Carol?" Smiles asked. "Is she in show biz?"

"Thank Gates, no," I replied. "No offense."

"Too bad," he said as he turned and led me back through the suite. "She has potential."

"I should meet with Sexy's other bodyguards," I said as we entered the entertainment room. "We'll need to coordinate efforts quickly."

"No problem there," Smiles replied.

He turned his gaze upward to the three girls that I'd seen when I arrived. They were still sitting on the floating couch, playing video games and listening to Sexy's music.

"Ladies," Smiles called. "There's someone here you need to meet."

The three girls rose and leaped off the couch, somersaulting to the ground, each of them making a perfect, catlike landing.

"Zach, I'd like you to meet Misty, Sissy, and Lusty, Sexy's bodyguards."

Each of the girls bowed very theatrically on cue.

"Bodyguard isn't by chance music industry slang for back-up dancer is it?" I asked.

"No." Sammy chuckled, "but, you know, it should be. Ladies, this is Zach Johnson. Sexy's new bodyguard."

"Nice to meet you ladies. I'm not replacing you," I said. "Just helping out due to the PATA threats. We'll be working together. I just want to make certain that everyone's cool with that."

One of the girls, I think it was Misty, but it doesn't really matter, approached me with her hand extended.

"Pleased to meet you, sir." The tone of her voice was businesslike and polite (though I wasn't crazy about being called sir).

"Call me, Zach," I said, extending my hand in return.

She moved quickly, almost faster than I could see, grabbing my arm at the wrist, twisting it sharply to give me a jolt of pain. Then she moved in close, slipped her arm under my shoulder and flipped me onto the floor. I was lying on my back almost before I knew what hit me.

"Bodyguard is slang for b-slapper," Misty said,

with her foot on my chest. "And nobody tells us what to do."

"We thought it would be more practical and economical to have multifunctional backup dancer-slash-bodyguards for Sexy," Smiles said. "We have plenty of bots around during events. But we always keep the gal-pride around."

"And we're the best," Misty added.

"Too bad you weren't around last night when Sexy was in trouble," I said.

"We were lying low 'cause Miss Sexy was incognito.

"Lying low while someone else saves your employer? If that's the best you can do then I'm not impressed."

I grabbed her leg behind the knee and pushed her over the top of my body. I grabbed her wrist as she stumbled and twisted her arm behind her back (until I knew it was just slightly more painful than what she'd given me) and pinned her face down on the floor with my knee.

"Impressive," HARA said. "Of course I did increase blood flow to your bones and muscles to help you pull off that move. And the other two are moving in behind you now, and I don't think they're admiring your butt."

I turned as the first one (Lusty, I think) jumped at me, coming feet first with a flying kick. I rolled to the ground and let her sail over me. She landed on Misty as I continued my roll and leg swept Sissy (I think) who was just starting to move. I took her feet out from under her and popped my gun into hand just in time to stick the snub-nosed business end of it into the faces of the charging Misty and Lusty. It stopped their charge like a pause button on a playback.

"I don't care if you're the best, the guest or the rest," I growled. "I'm here to keep Sexy alive and I don't have time to waste with this posturing and pouting. You can either help me out or get out of the way but the next time we fight like this, my gun barrel does the talking. Got it?"

The girls started to laugh. Smiles started to applaud.

"Wow!" Smiles said. "Sexy told us you were hard-core. But, Zach, that was downright ub-zeen!"

"Obscene?"

"Slang for exceptional," HARA whispered.

I popped my gun back into my sleeve and took my knee off Sissy's back. Misty and Lusty had backed away, and were now relaxed, and smiling.

"What the DOS is with you people?"

"The girls were just trying to prove themselves to you," Smiles said. "And maybe have you prove yourself a little to them."

"We love Sexy, Mr. Johnson." Misty said. "We're here to protect her."

I straightened my tie and tried to rein in my temper.

"I'm here to protect her too," I said. "But if we're going to work together, you have to promise me you won't pull any DOS like this again. Agreed?"

"Yes," Misty said.

"Absolutely," Sissy said.

Lusty nodded.

"Good. Because we really don't have time for this. And Gates knows that I don't have the patience. Now grow up."

"Wow," Misty said, "you sound like my father."

"Good," I replied, "then you're grounded too. And pull up your pants a little. You're going to catch cold."

That one didn't go over too well.

11

I left the hotel in the afternoon. HARA activated her hologram in the hotel parking lot and walked with me as I made my way to the car.

"You know, big guy, being a bodyguard usually implies that you actually stay with the body you're supposed to be guarding."

"Sexy is perfectly safe inside the hotel," I said. "You saw the security system. And Carol's there."

"True."

"Besides I'm a PI first and foremost. If I can find PATA quickly, I can turn them over to the police before they make their move. That way we can get out of babysitting duty entirely."

"Okay, I won't argue you with you on that one," HARA said. "You want me to do the legwork."

"Right. Scan all databases and files for any information on PATA."

"Way ahead of you. There's nothing in the public files but I'll try phishing some of the more secure databases and see if anything turns up. I may have to grease a few palms though."

"Sexy's paying the bills. Just try to get a receipt for the bribes."

"You're a laugh riot, handsome," she said. "I'll let you know when something interesting comes up."

"Great. And can you net me with Tony, I . . . Did you just call me handsome?"

"It's a figure of speech, you lunkhead. Don't let it go to your head."

"You're creeping me out, here HARV."

"It's HARA, handsome."

"Stop it."

"You know you're kind of cute when you get angry."

I waved her away. "Don't get me started!"

"Okay, but I think you better hit the deck now," she said.

"What?"

She put her manicured hands on my shoulders and pushed me to the pavement just as a massive laser blast sailed over my head. The heat of the blast singed the hair on the nape of my neck as it passed over and hit one of parked hovercrafts nearby, incinerating it in a thunderous fireball.

"Did you just push me?" I asked, as I crawled quickly across the parking lot surface, seeking cover beneath the crafts.

"I have limited tactile abilities now," HARA responded, her hologram crawling beside me. "That was Dr. Pool's upgrade earlier this afternoon."

"You can be solid?"

"Only parts of me and only for short periods of time."

"Wow."

"You're sort of missing the big picture here, Zach."

I popped my gun into hand and peered out from behind the rear end of a parked hover limo.

"Tap into the security cams and let me know what I'm up against here. But first net with Carol and tell her to make sure Sexy gets to a secure location."

"I don't think we have to worry about Sexy or anyone else being in danger here."

"What do you mean?"

"Take a look."

HARA pointed toward the airspace just above me. Sure enough a handful of familiar looking small spherical camera bots floated around us.

"Roundtree."

"That's a fair assumption," HARA said. "It looks like they've begun work on episode number two; Zach Johnson versus a quartet of level five battlebots."

"Battlebots in a parking lot. That's first class entertainment, all right."

"Maybe the Kabuki episode tested a little too high-brow for them," HARA said. "You're lucky they're not using monster trucks and supermodels now. By the way, you better run. Northeast would be wisest."

I sprang to my feet while simultaneously keeping my head down (which isn't easy) and ran for the northeast end of the parking lot just as the second battlebot let loose a blast from its cannon. The blast hit the limo and blew it to smithereens.

"Head for the barrier," HARA shouted

I did as I was told and hightailed it toward the waist-high hard plastic barrier encircling the border of the parking area. I could see all four bots now as I scanned the lot. There were two on the south end and two on the west with both pairs closing in, trying, I suspected, to pin me against the hotel on the east side of the lot. I fired a series of high powered blasts from my gun as I ran but they bounced off the bots' shells, doing no damage at all.

"This is not good," I said, diving behind the barrier.

"They have blaster resistant outer shells," HARA said. "Your gun's not going to be much use."

"We have to get them away from the hotel before someone inside gets hurt."

"You mean like your client?" HARA asked. "Funny that the only times she's been in actual danger lately is because of you, isn't it?"

"Hilarious," I said. "Now why do these bots look so familiar to me?"

"Probably because you saw the prototype at Dr. Pool's lab," HARA replied.

"These are Randy's bots?"

"It appears as though his lab has the special effects contract for your series."

"Great," I said. "At least we're keeping this all in the family. Net Randy now and put him on the wrist com."

Randy's face appeared on the screen on my wrist com just as another blast from the approaching bots exploded a sports hover nearby.

"Yes, Zach. How can I help you? Oh, I see the battlebots have arrived. How are they performing?"

"Oh, pretty darn well if you're trying to kill me," I said.

"Good. Don't destroy them too quickly," he said. "I don't want people to think that they're easy to beat."

"No problems there, Randy, my gun isn't working against them."

"Are you using the bot-buster ordnance?"

"The what?"

"The bot-buster ordnance that I designed for your gun. I sent you a memo about this last month."

"Randy, I don't read your memos."

"You don't?"

"They're all like twenty pages long. I don't have time to read the specs on every new gadget that you create."

"I'm guessing that you're regretting that now, huh?"

"Randy!"

"That's specifically why I gave Faux these bots for this episode. I knew you'd be able to beat them with the special ordnance."

"Well, you should have told me that."

"I signed a confidentiality agreement, Zach. It wouldn't be ethical."

"Randy, your ethics are about to get me killed."

"Wow," Randy replied. "Talk about your moral dilemmas."

I poked my head above the barrier and saw the

bots approaching. They had to weave their way to me, moving in and out of the rows of parked hovers. I saw the cannon of one glow red as it moved. HARA followed my gaze and confirmed my suspicion.

"It's powering up for another blast," she said.

"Good. Help me with my aim," I said. "Big bang, tight."

The gun's OLED flashed in recognition of my voice command and I pulled the trigger and sent a very tight blast of energy at the bot's cannon. My blast hit the mouth of the cannon just as the bot fired and the two blasts exploded in unison, rupturing the bot from within.

"One down," I said, diving back behind the barrier. "Get ready to move, HARA. They're getting a little close for comfort."

"Ready when you are, big guy."

"Now!"

I leaped over the barrier and made a charge through the lot, heading west, where there was now only one approaching bot. Even with one bot destroyed, I still wasn't all that optimistic about my chances.

"By the way, Zach," HARA said, her hologram running beside me (in high heels), "you're going to love me for this."

"Now's not really the time, HARA," I said.

"I know that you don't really encourage me to act independently and all. But I sometimes ignore you when it comes to that."

"That's an understatement. Is there a point here?"

I glanced over at the remaining bots, which had

altered their paths and were now weaving through the parked hovers toward us. I could tell at least two were charging their cannons.

"The point is that I read Dr. Pool's memos. They're actually quite interesting."

"Good for you."

"And I found the bot-buster memo to be particularly cogent and well-constructed."

"So?"

"So I took it upon myself and loaded the ordnance."

"You what?"

"You're locked and loaded, big guy. Go save the day."

"HARA, you're a dream."

"The voice command is biggy-biggy-bot-boom."

"That's a pretty wimpy sounding command."

"I wouldn't complain if I were you," she said with a smile.

"Biggy-biggy-bot-boom!" I said, still weaving between hovers.

The OLED flashed again and I let a blast loose at the nearest attacker. The recoil from the blast nearly knocked me over but it did its job on the other end, cleanly piercing the battlebot's shell and blowing it to bits. I spun around and fired off two more rounds, falling back to the ground as I did so. Two more bot-shaped fireballs lit up the lot and showered the expensive hovers with high-tech drek. After that it was eerily quiet in the parking lot save for the cacophony of hovercraft alarms that the firefight had set off.

"Something tells me that I won't have any problem meeting my car insurance deductible this year," I said.

12

I reached my office on the New Frisco docks with no other major entertainment-related incidents (although Rupert Roundtree called me on the way over to rave about my performance in episode two of the series, referring to it as bombastical). I called him an idiot and a fraud but he took it as a compliment and then excused himself so he could attend a focus group of white trash Americans (he didn't say if he was running it or one of the participants). Other than that, the trip was uneventful.

My office is an oasis in the desert of late twenty-first century technology-centric chaos. It's a throwback to an earlier time (as am I), a technologically simpler time when everything wasn't wirelessly connected to everything else; when machines weren't connected to one another and, more importantly, when machines weren't connected to people.

It's a place where I can sit in my simulated leather chair, prop my legs up on my real wood desk, put my arms behind my head, and let my mind do its thing. It's also a place where bill collectors, unsatisfied clients, angry pressbots, assassins, and enemies of the state can easily find me, but every oasis has its drawbacks.

First order of business was to reestablish contact with Tony Rickey.

"What do you want now, Zach?" he said.

"Tony, I'm hurt that you think I only call you when I want something from you."

"That's right. You only call me when there's a warrant out for your arrest."

"Well played, Captain."

"Do you know that the department has a listserver called Guess-What-Zach-Did-Now?" he said.

"Really? Is it accurate?"

"Most of it's way off. Third-hand stuff. I try to post the real stuff but I keep getting kicked off because no one believes it. You know, like last night's Kabuki fiasco."

"Oh, please," I said. "Last night was nothing. I've had more people try to kill me at a softball game."

"That's what happens when you pitch spitballs to a Police Athletic League team."

"It was sweat, Tony. I have no control over my pores."

"I didn't know the mouth was considered a pore," Tony said with a smile. "What can I do for you?"

"Do you know anything about a group called PATA?"

"Not off the top of my head." He turned away

and typed into his computer keyboard. "They don't show up in any of the databases. I'm afraid to ask this, but why are you interested?"

"They've threatened to kill Sexy Sprockets."

"Have the threats been reported?"

"They will be. You should be getting the call any time now," I said. "I'll have HARA send over copies of the threats."

"HARA is HARV, right?"

"Sadly, yes. I've made it clear to Sexy and her people that they should cooperate with your department."

"Great. I'll send some men over. She's at the Elite?"

"Where else? What kind of security will you have at the concerts?"

"Her fans are more exuberant than most so we planned to have extra personnel and machines there, both uniform and plainclothes."

"Plainclothes machines?"

"They double as popcorn dispensers," he said (straight-faced). "So you're on Sexy's payroll now?"

"She's asked me to help her security."

"Zach Johnson, bodyguard."

"I've been called worse."

"You mean like reality star?"

"There is no show," I said. "It's just a misunderstanding."

"Whatever you say," he replied. "And HARV's still a woman?"

"She's called HARA now."

"She looks good for a computer. You'll have to tell me the whole story sometime."

"Yeah, let me know when you have a free month. Right now I'm just trying to keep Sexy alive."

"Like I said, Zach, I'm not going to let anything happen to her on my watch. Thanks for the info. I'll make sure everyone's on guard."

"Hopefully there won't be any trouble," I said.

Tony smiled. "Believe me, Zach, with you on the case, there'll be trouble."

"I appreciate the vote of confidence, Tony. Let me know if you turn up anything on PATA."

Tony smiled and his face disappeared from the screen just as HARA's hologram appeared back on my desk (legs crossed, skirt riding high).

"Wow, sharing information and cooperating with the police," she said. "Is this the start of a new Zach?"

"Don't worry, I'm sure my goodwill with the police department is only temporary. Any new information on PATA?"

"Nothing yet, but I'm still digging. You need anything else?"

"Run background checks on Sammy Smiles and Sexy's bodyguards. Saucy, scrappy, and scurvy."

"You mean Misty, Sissy, and Lusty."

"Whatever."

"Got it."

"When you say got it, do you mean that you understand the request or that you have the actual info?"

"Both, Zach," HARA said. "I'm very intelligent. Try to keep up. By the way, you have a message from Electra."

"Hate mail?"

"More like a shot across the bow," HARA replied, morphing into Electra's form, then mimicking her voice. "I'll be home tomorrow, Chico."

"That's it?" I asked

"That's it," HARA said, morphing back to her current form.

I shook my head. "She's mad at me. And for once it's not because of something I did or had any control over."

HARA smiled. "I think it's cute that she's jealous of us."

"She's not jealous of us!" I said. "There *is* no us. I'm me and you're the holographic interface of a supercomputer."

"There have been stranger couples," HARA said, smile widening.

"We're not a couple."

"We're partners."

"No, we're not."

"Would Electra have loaded your gun with bot-busters?"

"DOS, where's Rupert Roundtree when you need him?"

"Oh, I get it," HARA said, folding her arms over her chest. "I'm not good enough for you."

"What?"

"Sure I'm the world's most sophisticated cognitive

processor, but you're Zachary Nixon Johnson private eye. Nobody's good enough for you, are they?"

I buried my head in my hands and thought nostalgically about how good my office used to feel.

"This is what hell feels like, isn't it?" I asked.

"Don't talk to me now," she said, waving her hand dismissively at me. "I'm mad at you. By the way, I have the info that you requested."

"I thought you were mad at me?"

"I am, but I'm also a professional. I am not going to let our personal relationship get in the way of our work relationship."

"I appreciate that," I said.

"As well you should," she said. "I've learned the initial death threats from PATA came in via an ultra-encrypted line. They're untraceable."

"That figures. So it's a dead end."

"A dead end that tells us much."

"How so?"

"A line that's encrypted to such a degree is ripping edge."

"So whoever sent the threats has access to some serious tech."

"Correct."

"Which means they're either rich, powerful, or both."

"You know, you're almost as smart as you think you are," she said rolling her eyes.

"Well, it's a start," I said, grabbing my hat.

"What now?" HARA asked.

"We've done all we can from here," I said. "We're

not going to track PATA down today so it's time to start being an actual bodyguard."

"Which means?"

"It means we prepare for the worst and hope for the best."

"It also means backstage passes to Sexy's concert," HARA said, hopping off the desk.

"I'm not sure if that falls into the best or worst category," I said. "But let's stop at the store while we're out and pick up some earplugs just in case."

13

New Frisco's municipal arena is a wonderful entertainment and sports venue that's smack in the middle of the old Mission District. It's a fine facility with perhaps the most unfortunate name in the history of . . . names.

You see back when the arena was being built, the city auctioned off the naming rights and got several strong bids. The city planners, guided by their terminal myopia and fueled by their unquenchable greed, accepted *all* the bids and named the arena after the conglomeration of conglomerates that were willing to pony up the necessary credits. So officially the arena is called the Faux-ExShell-Relapse-HTech Center but one day some kid noticed the acronym (FERHT) and couldn't get his mind out of the gutter. His little joke spread (through the adolescent population first, then into the mainstream). Before we knew it, the joke just sort of entered the regional vernacular and, despite the city's best efforts to shake it, the nickname name stuck. So New Frisco's state of the art entertainment and sports arena is lovingly known the world over as "The Fart."

To my mind there's no better place on the west coast to see a concert or a game (basketball or hockey that is, the baseball and football stadiums moved to the suburbs years ago). The hot dogs are a little pricey, the beers extremely so, but the bolgoki and nachos are first rate. All in all, The Fart's not a bad place to spend an evening with fifty thousand of your closest Bay Area friends. Unless of course one of those fifty thousand is a hired assassin who's out to put an ice pick through your client's eye. Then it's sort of the needle and haystack dilemma on a grand and deadly scale.

I had a little trouble at first getting into The Fart. It was after all, three hours before the doors opened and I had no actual ticket to the concert. But a quick call to the facilities manager from Sammy Smiles opened the doors pretty quickly and got me an all-access pass. Before long, I was standing center stage in front of fifty thousand empty seats and trying hard not to get in the way of the roadies and techies as they prepped for the show. And I must say that the stage itself was something to behold.

"Being front and center like this certainly makes Sexy an easy target," HARA remarked, her hologram shimmering to life beside me (and garnering a number of looks from the workers).

"She's the main attraction, all right," I replied.

"And by the way, I never would have thought

that one stage could hold this much red velvet and black satin."

"Yeah, what's with that?"

"It's part of the motif for the tour, I suppose."

"And what's that over there?"

"A guillotine and a sausage-making machine," HARA replied.

"What motif, exactly, are they shooting for?"

"Ménage abattoir."

"What?"

"That's the name of the tour. The Ménage Abattoir Tour."

"What does that mean?"

"I think it's a pun," HARA said. "Sexy thought it was . . . sexy."

"An abattoir is a slaughterhouse right?"

"Very good. My understanding is that she confused 'abattoir' with 'boudoir' but by the time anyone had the courage to tell her, the tickets had already gone on sale. Turns out it's very popular."

"Yeah, very cutting edge."

"So to speak."

I stepped over a saddle-covered rocking chair and walked the length of the stage, scanning the wings as I did so. The entire space made me worry. It was far too open, far too dangerous.

"The police will scan for weapons as the crowd arrives. And there are sensors in the arena that can pick up the energy signatures of any unauthorized weapons that are activated. But she sure is out in the open here. Maybe we can convince her to wear body armor."

"Please, Zach," HARA sighed, "it took a court order to convince Sexy to wear underwear on stage."

"I'm not surprised."

I ducked under a huge rack of leather whips and cured meat that was being lifted into place above stage and headed to the backstage area.

"Get a list of everyone on Sexy's crew that will be here tonight. Musicians, programmers, roadies, butchers, everyone. I want background checks run on all of them."

"You think that PATA could have someone inside Sexy's camp?"

"Let's not take any chances. We know next to nothing about PATA right now other than that they have access to high tech and that they've gotten very close to Sexy already."

"Got it," HARA said. "There are a lot of people on the payroll for this event. It will take some time to screen them all."

"Do what you can, just flag the odd ones for me."

"Odd is a very relative term when you're surrounded by satin sheets and pork by-products."

"I hate this," I mumbled.

"I know. Pork gives you gas."

"We're coming into this late in the game. We have no idea who we're up against. We have no control over the schedule or the venue. We're so far behind right now we can't even see the starting line."

"So what do we do?" HARA asked.

"For tonight, we have to narrow our focus," I replied. "We can't safeguard this entire space but the good news is that we don't have to. The only thing we have to guard is Sexy. So we stay close to her."

"Are you planning on going on stage with her?" HARA asked. "Because I should warn you, Zach, this crowd probably won't respond well to your Elvis impersonation."

"Trust me," I said. "With Sexy and her dancers on stage, no one's going to be looking at a forty-year-old guy in a trench coat. But just to be safe, you better make sure that your hologram projector is working. You never know when we might need to disappear."

Two hours before the show, HARA and I were back at the Elite scoping out the parking lot. The valets, I'm told, had spent the better part of the afternoon clearing the aftermath of my bot battle. They weren't too pleased to see me and I couldn't blame them. I'm sure that one doesn't get the best tip in the world when you have to bring a customer's car around in a giant plastic baggie.

While Sexy and her posse (Carol included) were inside the hotel, gathering themselves for the limo ride over to The Fart, I took it upon myself to have a chat with the limo driver.

Like I said earlier, Sexy's hover limo was sleek and really, really long. HARA brought up the phallic symbolism of the vehicle but it was way too late in the day to have that conversation. So I ignored her and tapped on the dark rose-tinted driver's window.

"I'm busy!" came the voice from within, a little high-pitched and squeaky.

"And I've got a gun," I replied.

The window slid down neatly and revealed a plump teenage kid in a black chauffeur's cap and uniform.

"You better really have a gun," he said. "I'll get in trouble if I fall for that line again."

"Trust me, kid. I've got one. What's your name?"

"Joey Matteo. But people call me Shreek. I'm Sexy's driver."

"Nice to meet you Shreek. I'm Zach Johnson. Sexy's new bodyguard."

"*The* Zach Johnson? Wow! You're not going to, like, blow up the limo are you?"

"Your reputation precedes you," HARA whispered.

"Listen, Shreek," I said, "I know you're a great wheel-man but I've got a more important job for you for tonight."

"What's that?"

"Shotgun."

"What's shotgun?"

I opened the door and shoved him toward the passenger side of the front seat.

"Scoot over into the other seat and recline it just a touch so you're comfortable."

He did as he was told.

"Now what?"

"Now rest your right arm on the side so you look good. Feel free to hold a drink in your left. Shotgun's thirsty work."

"Got it."

"Your job for the night is to keep lookout while the limo is parked or while it's moving. Keep an eye out for anyone strange approaching. Understand?"

"Sure," he said, "but who's going to drive?"

HARA's hologram shimmied up behind me on cue. She was dressed in a tight jacketed chauffeur's uniform (complete with cocked hat, short skirt, and stockings).

"Hi there, big boy," she said. "Want to go for a spin?"

"Man, this is so cool," Shreek said, eyes wide.

"Don't get too excited, shotgun. She's mostly intangible. Now fasten your seatbelt. It's going to be a bumpy night."

We got Shreek settled in the shotgun seat (and eventually got him to look at other things beside HARA) just as Sexy and her entourage of redheads emerged from the hotel, giggling and bouncing and strutting and primping all at once as they moved like a bumptious sea of spandex, porcelain skin, and red hair.

"Here they come," Shreek said, his attention slipping from HARA for the nano.

Smiles was with them, now wearing a black-and-red striped suit and looking like a shard of jagged dark glass in a serving of cotton candy.

"Where's Carol?"

As they flounced closer, Shreek hopped out of the shotgun position and opened the passenger door. The girls giggled at his bumbling yet energetic chivalry and continued their way toward the hover.

"I told her to stay with Sexy."

"Look a little harder," HARA said with a smile.

I looked for Carol's auburn hair amid the radiant ruby-haired throng but I couldn't spot her.

"She's not there."

"Look past the hair," HARA said.

"What do you mean past the . . . ?"

"Hi, Tio!"

"Carol?"

She'd changed her clothes, swapping her jeans and blouse for faux leather pants and half-top to match that of Misty, Lusty, and Sissy. And her hair was red.

"Don't you love it?" Sexy asked as the group climbed into the limo.

"Love isn't the word," I said, forcing a smile.

Carol gave me a hug as she passed.

"Sexy said I can be onstage with her tonight. We went over all the dance moves this afternoon."

"Onstage?"

"Isn't it great? I'm a backup singer."

"But Carol," I said, "you can't sing."

"Oh, Tio," she said, giving me a kiss and climbing into the limo, "you're so old school."

"Yeah, I'm getting that a lot lately."

I climbed into the limo and settled in the seat nearest the door. Sexy sat in the plush rear seat (a couch really) flanked by Smiles and Carol. Sissy, Misty, and Lusty lounged on the seats at the side. Everyone stretched out and got comfortable, which wasn't hard in the plushy confines, so I rapped on the Plexiglas behind the driver's cabin and yelled to HARA.

"Let's go. And nothing reckless please."

"You're no fun at all," she whispered inside my head.

"How's it feel, Sexy?" Smiles asked, putting his arm around her shoulder, "embarking of the first of your final concerts?"

"It's just another air mile on the skyway of life, Sammy."

The girls all laughed, Carol included, and I saw Smiles' fingers reach out past Sexy's shoulder and gently stroke Carol's newly reddened hair. She didn't seem to mind. And that scared me.

14

Backstage half an hour before the show was pure bedlam. Sexy was in her dressing room going through her preshow ritual with Smiles. Carol and the other girls were nearby (though not actually in the same room), limbering up their vocal cords and g-strings. I was still uncomfortable about how Carol was throwing herself into this atmosphere but I had wanted her to get in close to the girls and she reassured me with a few mental messages that she still had her mind on business.

"Things are all clear so far from here, Tio. Sexy's safely in her dressing room and the girls and I are pumped for the show."

"Are you picking up any suspicious thoughts or vibes?"

"Not really," she replied. "There's some psionic interference in the arena. Plus all these people around create a lot of mental chatter. It's hard to zero in on any one mind."

"So once the arena fills up?"

"My abilities won't be much good unless someone gets close."

"Okay. Then stay close to Sexy and let me know if any alarms go off."

"Got it," she whispered.

The crowd was flowing in now, even though they knew that the show would start late (Sexy's shows were known for late starts). They wanted to be there early and soak up the atmosphere.

And what a crowd they were; thousands of them, all dressed in bright clothes that were either tight-fitting, see-through, or barely there (sometimes all three). They were girls mostly, though a good percentage of them were male; boyfriends or boyfriend wannabes. And they were all young. Most of them were teenagers. Twenty-somethings in this crowd stood out like senior citizens. I felt like a dinosaur (but I'm kind of used to that). They began chanting Sexy's name ten minutes before the show was scheduled to start and vibrations from their stomping and clapping shook the stage like a teen tectonic plate shift.

"That's it," I said, ducking into the stage wings. "I'm starting the show."

"What do you mean?"

HARA's hologram appeared beside me as I walked quickly down the hallway toward the dressing rooms.

"The quicker we get Sexy on stage, the quicker she does her show and the quicker we can get her out of danger. There's no point in letting the crowd work themselves into any more of a frenzy."

"You have no sense of drama, do you?" HARA said.

"I have plenty of sense," I said, stopping at Sexy's dressing room door, "but I can live without the drama."

The sound of the audience was loud even here so I had to pound hard on the door in order to be heard.

"Sexy!" I shouted. "I think we better get this show on the road."

There was no answer.

"Sexy?" I shouted again.

Again, no answer. I tried the door but it was locked.

"Sexy!"

"I'm getting some strange readings from inside the room," HARA said.

"What kind of readings?"

"Radiation," HARA said. "Much higher than normal. Not deadly though."

"That's it," I said, backing away from the door and popping my gun into my hand. "Tight bang!"

The blast from my gun blew apart the door lock then I kicked in the rest of the door. Its thick body swung open, pulling one hinge free of the jam and bits of the wall away with it. I leaped into the room with gun drawn and some serious attitude.

"Sexy!"

She was asleep. Sort of. Her eyes were closed and she definitely wasn't fully conscious, which sort of implies sleep. But she also wasn't lying down. As a matter of fact she wasn't touching the ground at all. She was hovering a full meter off the floor, feet together, arms spread and fully enveloped in a dark red light that was emanating from a projector on the floor.

"What the DOS?"

"Zach?" Smiles said adjusting his tie. "I didn't hear you. Is something wrong?"

"You tell me," I replied. "What's going on here?"

"Sexy's in the meditation chamber. She does this before every show to clear her mind."

"Why is she levitating?"

"There's an anti-grav generator in the projector. The sense of weightlessness helps her focus better. The red light is meant to subconsciously give her a sense of empowerment."

"And the position?"

"Oddly, all performers who do this type of meditation just naturally assume the messianic pose. Go figure."

"Yeah, go figure," I said, popping my gun back into my sleeve. "The crowd's getting a little out of control. I thought it would be best if we started the show soon."

Smiles looked at his watch and frowned, which took some effort considering the size of his mouth.

"Sexy normally doesn't hit the stage until forty-five minutes after the scheduled start time," he said. "But you're right. We don't want to create more trouble than we have to."

He hit a switch on the projector and the red light surrounding Sexy dimmed slightly and she began descending.

"It will take a couple of nanos to fully bring her out of the meditation but she should be ready to go soon."

He stepped into the light, took Sexy's hand and patted it gently.

"Sexy, dear," he whispered. "Time to wake up."

Sexy's eyes opened slowly and she looked around the room a little confusedly. Her eyes fell upon me and the corners of her mouth turned upward ever so slightly. Smiles leaned toward her and put his lips to her ear.

"Showtime," he said softly.

Sexy's smile widened into something resembling the grin of a hungry wolf.

"Oh, yeah," she whispered.

15

When the lights went down in the arena, the audience, already in a frenzy, began screaming in earnest. The musicians were already in their places, instruments and droids at the ready (most live music is enhanced by droid play these days because it allows the performers to concentrate more on their showmanship). Sexy's posse, Carol included, ran onto the stage and struck their poses. It surprised me how completely Carol had thrown herself into the new role of backup singer, but I didn't have time to dwell on it. The first bass riff of the intro wafted through the arena like the first trickles of a rising tide and the crowd noise ceased, replaced by the almost palpable anticipation.

The curtain slowly rose, thin slivers of spotlight began to dot the smoky dark stage, the bass riff rose gently, joined now by a grinding drum beat. Then a throaty female voice whispered over the sound system.

"Mesdames et Messieurs . . . amants et rêveurs . . . bouchers et bétail . . ."

Sexy's form floated toward the stage atop a translucent anti-grav disk. It didn't look like Sexy, of course. She was wearing clothes, for one thing; a black satin robe with tails that hung two meters past her feet. Her head was bowed, hiding her face from the ambient light. And she was wearing a hat.

"Is that a fedora?"

"Looks like it," HARA replied. "Maybe she likes you."

Then a spotlight, so bright it was difficult to look at with the naked eye flared onto her. The crowd roared and the music staccatoed loudly for a split nano. Sexy was the center of attention now, but still hid herself beneath the satin robe and fedora.

"Je vous accueille là où l'amour ne prend jamais fin . . ." her whisper echoed.

"What did she say?"

"I welcome you to where love never ends," HARA said.

"—là où les rêves vivant pour toujours . . ."

". . . to where dreams live forever . . ."

". . . et là où la viande est fraîche."

". . . and to where the meat is fresh."

"Gross."

"Welcome my friends to Ménage Abattoir!"

She flung open her robe and it burst into flames as she threw it off. It disappeared in a nano and the crowd roared at their first clear view of Sexy. Her clothes were ethereal white; a barely-there skin-tight halter top, pants that were second-skinlike at the hips and wildly flared below the knees, and a gray fedora.

The music kicked into gear. Heavy bass, synthesizer and effects. The dancers began moving and the light show on the stage looked like a rainbow in a death match with a lightning storm. And above it all, Sexy began to sing.

"You love me. Hee, hee, hee.
I hate you. Ooh, ooh, ooh.
You love me. Gee, gee, gee.
I am your master. Faster, faster, faster.
I am your queen
I am your wet dream."

The crowd absolutely ate it up. They screamed so loudly I thought their heads would explode (I know mine wanted to). And as Sexy bumped and ground ten meters above the stage, bathed in the white hot spotlights and drenched with the adoration of fifty thousand crazed fans, one thought kept repeating itself in my head like a spoofed sample on a dance remix. But before I could say it aloud, HARA did it for me.

"How in Gates' name are we going to protect her?"

"DOSsed if I know," I mumbled, bringing my wrist communicator up to my lips. "Tony, are you there?"

Tony's face flashed onto the small screen of the communicator.

"Here, Zach. How's the view backstage?"

"Let's just say that there are other places I'd like to be. Any sign of trouble?"

"All stations have reported in. No problems out of the ordinary. Although one fan got in a scuffle with one of our undercover bots."

"The popcorn dispensers?"

"The guy refused to pay the extra credits for the butter and salt and took a swing at the bot. We had to take him in."

"For a salt and buttery?"

"There's more room in the paddy wagon, you know. All units come equipped with a specially marked Zach Johnson seat. It has its own muzzle."

"I'll keep that in mind," I replied.

"By the way, is that Carol onstage with the dancers?" Tony asked.

"I'm afraid so."

"She looks really good."

"I'm going to pretend I didn't hear that, Tony," I said signing off.

Back onstage, Sexy had landed her anti-grav disk on the stage and had joined the dancers. She struck a few poses with the girls, blew a few kisses to the crowd and then launched into her second song.

"I have a love. Yes I do.
It's a love that's steady and true.
I have a love. You bet I do.
It's the truest love of all.
It sticks like super glue."

*   *   *

I could only roll my eyes.

"How are those earplugs working?" HARA asked.

"Not well enough," I said. "I can still hear the music."

We circled around backstage for the next half an hour (four songs and two costume changes). My heart jumped every time a crazed fan tried to rush the stage but Tony's men were there every time to haul them away. I made a mental note to get the names of all the rushers from Tony after his people had processed them, though I doubted any serious assassin would take such an obvious route.

Sexy was doing a ballad now, slow and sultry.

"She learned that it's not easy being rich.
Everyone feels you're just a bitch.
Sometimes she thinks she should just be digging a
    ditch.
People love her, yes they do.
They stick to her just like glue . . .
But their love just isn't true,
Yes, their love just isn't true."

She was wearing a pink tuxedo jacket and tails with a top hat and no pants (big surprise), crawling along the stage like a sultry cat as she moaned and crooned. She finished with a breathy sigh and rolled over onto her back, arching sexily and lifting one leg straight up as the crowd roared.

"The recording company is so glad.
That poor little girl is rich but sad.
You might think she would go mad.
You might think she would go mad.
You might think she would go maaddddd."

"You know something," I said, "now that I've seen her in action and have listened, I mean *really* listened to her music. I realize that . . . she's really bad."

"You're just old," HARA replied.

"No, this isn't a generational thing. It's the basic harmonic truth. This music is just plain bad."

"Well, fifty thousand screaming fans say otherwise."

"Yeah, what do they know? They're probably brainwashed."

HARA said something as a retort but I wasn't paying attention because just then I saw half a dozen dark shapes gathered in the backstage area across from me. They were tall men, trim but muscular, all dressed in black.

"Who are they?" I asked.

"Additional dancers," HARA replied. "There's a production number up next."

The band segued into a synth number with a slow Middle Eastern-type beat. Sexy popped back onto her feet and began shimmying across the stage, undulating her hips. Carol, Misty, Lusty, and Sissy joined in, though they were two steps in the background and out of the brightest of the spotlights.

"My body is ripped. My muscles so lithe.
You can tell I know how to use a knife.
I'll be your butcher, you can be my sweet meat.
Love cutlets. Love cutlets."

I turned my attention back to the men in black. They were preparing to go onstage, getting into formation and waiting for their cue. Then as one they reached into the folds of their costumes and then flashed their blades.

"They've got knives!"

"Cleavers actually," HARA said. "It's part of the show."

Sure enough the men strode onto the stage and began a hip-thrusting, cleaver-waving dance.

"Oh, this is so wrong," I said nervously. "Did you run checks on the dancers?"

"Every one of them," HARA said. "They're legit. Nothing suspicious."

The dancers each grabbed one of the girls on stage (two grabbed Sexy) and did some very expressive hip grinding.

"They're all gay, by the way," HARA continued.

"That doesn't make me feel better," I said, watching Carol doing her share of the grind.

"I carry a cleaver everywhere I go.
So I can ravish you from head to toe.
I'll be your butcher, you can be my sweet meat.
Love cutlets. Love cutlets."

The music was building in intensity now. The spotlights changed from white to darkening shades of red as the eleven dancers moved faster and the dance grew more intense. The crowd loved it, of course.

"I don't like this," I said to myself.

I saw a twelfth figure duck in from the shadows. Dressed in black, it had the build of a male, but this one was not a dancer. The body wasn't as trim. The movements were graceful, but not delicate.

"What's that?"

HARA looked.

"I can't tell."

"Switch to infrared and zoom in."

The vision in my left eye went dark for a nano as HARA switched my vision over to the infrared spectrum. I could see the figure clearer now, body heat glowing hot against the background. It was definitely a man. Tall and heavy, moving quickly and furtively. Clearly no one had seen him but me, but I couldn't get to him without crossing the stage.

"Let Tony know we have an intruder," I said, popping my gun into my hand. "We're going to need some backup."

The man paused in the shadows for a nano and even though his face was hidden, I noticed him look around to see if anyone was watching. Then he pulled something from his coat and moved onto the stage.

"Captain Rickey says that he has men on the way," HARA said.

"Too late," I said gripping my gun. "The guy's making his move. Tell Tony I'll meet him onstage."

"Onstage?"

"Put me in stealth mode," I said, and ran onto the stage.

My clothes may look shabby and out-of-date (yes, I'm aware of it, it's a lifestyle choice), but that doesn't mean they're worthless. Actually, a lot of what I wear is ripping edge. Take my trench coat, for example. The fabric is interwoven with nano-circuitry which allows it to perform a lot of non-attire-related functions. One such function is what I call stealth mode. The coat uses micro-sized cameras woven into the fabric to record the area around me and simultaneously project it onto the OLED circuitry woven into the coat directly opposite it. So the backside of my coat records the stuff behind me and projects it on the front of my coat. The front of my coat records the stuff in front of me and projects it onto my backside, which to the naked eye, makes me invisible (except for my head).

The intruder was moving quickly toward Sexy now. I saw him clearly through the infrared lens in my eye as I ran full tilt across the stage, dodging the racks of meat and red satin throw pillows that so elegantly decorated the stage.

"Sexy, get down!"

Sexy couldn't hear me over the music and the roar of the crowd. Even if she had, I'm not sure she would have taken it as a warning. But Carol picked up my thoughts and turned away from her dance partner.

"Tio?"

She turned to my fast approaching head and immediately saw the situation.

"Sexy, look out!"

Carol leaped at Sexy and pulled her down just before the attacker reached her. I hit the attacker a nano later, slamming him broadside with my shoulder and rolling him onto the stage floor. He went over more easily than I expected. His body was softer than I expected as well, more flab than muscle. That may sound like a good thing but it wasn't because my hit took us down to the floor harder and in a different place than I expected. We ended up falling into one of Sexy's meat-cleaver dancers, knocking him to the ground and landing hard and awkwardly on his leg. I heard the wet snap of the dancer's femur even over the music and the guy started screaming.

Two nearby dancers saw all this and (logically) pegged me as the villain. They jumped on me, grabbed me by the shoulders and tried to pull me away as the attacker tried to get to his feet and stumble off the stage.

Even if there'd been time to explain things to the dancers, they wouldn't have been able to hear me over the music so, regrettably, I had to go the rough route because there was no way I was letting the attacker get away. I head butted one dancer on the bridge of the nose (breaking and bloodying it), then pivoted and threw the second dancer over my shoulder as I spun and aimed my gun toward the fleeing/stumbling attacker.

Unfortunately, my judo throw sent the dancer headlong into Tony, who was just now arriving on the stage with a handful of his men. His men, after seeing their captain felled by a thrown dancer and now faced with a mostly invisible man holding a gun, opened fire with their blasters (set to stun).

I managed to dive to the floor and avoid the blasts. The drummer, lead guitarist, and bassoon player weren't so lucky. Worse still, the blasts hit the base of the huge guillotine set piece and toppled it. It smashed into another set piece filled with slabs of hanging meat, all of which came crashing down on the keyboardist and the control board for the stage lights and effects, shorting it out completely and sending the entire stage into what the next day's newsite reviews would describe as "a déclassé avalanche of abstract tackiness and white-trash opulence."

Dozens of lights exploded, a hundred pyrotechnics fired at once, and chunks of various meat products shot into the air and showered the audience. The backing tracks were still playing over the sound system but the computer had jammed so the same two bars of Sexy's song were playing over and over, echoing throughout the arena like an audiophonic hip-hop water torture.

I spotted the attacker in the wings as I knelt on the stage floor. He had gotten caught up in the rush of police and security people that were storming the stage and was trying to push through them like a fat salmon swimming upstream. The horde of peacekeepers was heading straight for me so I knew that I only had one chance to bring the guy down.

"Hog tie," I said.

The indicator light on my gun flashed and I fired. A polymer cable shot from my gun and sped toward the fleeing attacker. It hit him in the small of the back and wrapped itself around his legs and arms a dozen times before the guy even knew he'd been hit. He lost his grip on the device he was carrying and I saw it hit the ground and skitter across the backstage floor. But it activated on impact. I saw it clearly because HARA took control of the interface in my eye and zoomed in on the device. It was a palm-sized module with two button controls and an activator light, which was now blinking frantically.

"Oh DOS," I whispered, expecting an explosion at any nano.

None came.

Instead, a bouquet of holographic flowers projected from the module, a cascade of three dozen bright pink orchids.

"Flowers?"

"Congratulations," HARA said as the angry horde of police and security personnel piled on top of me. "You just saved Sexy Sprockets from a floral display."

16

Once Tony extricated himself from the dancers, he
took control of his men and the security personnel.
They quelled the chaos onstage and managed to keep
the crowd (which had become seriously perturbed
and panicked by now) from rushing the stage long
enough for me to pull Sexy and her girls back to the
safety of the wings. Two nanos later, we were running through the backstage hallways, headed for
the hoverport.

"He had flowers, Zach," Sexy said (for the third
time, I think). "Orchids."

"He was rushing straight for you, Sexy," I said.
"What did you want me to do?"

"Something short of trashing the stage would have
been nice."

"I'll remember that next time," I grumbled.
"HARA, bring up the limo and meet us at the hoverport. Sexy has to leave the building now!"

"Gotcha, big guy," HARA replied in my head.

"Johnson!"

I turned just enough to see Smiles running down

the hallway in his two-tone black and red shoes. He was sweaty and flushed, partially from the running, but mostly from rage.

"What in Gates' name was that?" he shouted, putting a hand on my shoulder in an attempt to slow me.

I shrugged off the hand and kept moving, leading Sexy by the hand.

"Talk to me about it in the limo, Sammy," I said. "Now's not the time."

"We'll talk about it now," he said.

"Right now, Sexy is in danger," I replied without turning around. "I am not prepared to waste my time and put her in more danger just to listen to you rant. So save it and rant in the limo when you have a captive audience."

"Why you . . ." Smiles began, turning redder by the nano.

"He's sort of right, Sammy," Sexy said as we neared the hoverport.

Smiles sighed and shook his head as though he were the only sane person left on Earth (but he kept running toward the hoverport with us).

It wasn't long before I was loading Sexy and the girls into the limo. Smiles looked as though he wanted to slam the door in my face when he climbed in but he held back and took a seat next to Carol.

"Strap in, everyone," I said, as I took my seat by the door. "Let's go, HARA!"

HARA, clearly happy to be free of my usual speed constraints, put the proverbial pedal to the metal and the limo shot free of the hoverport like a rocket.

"That was really fast, Mr. Johnson," Shreek said from the front seat. "Did everything go okay?"

"You're shotgun, Shreek," I said, sliding the soundproof barrier into place. "No talking unless there's trouble."

"Oh there's trouble, all right," Smiles said, happy for the opening. "Your incompetence turned Sexy's show into a complete disaster."

"I was doing my job."

"I'm sorry, did I miss the part about your job being to trash the set and cause a full-scale riot?" Smiles screamed. "We hired you as a bodyguard, not a demolitions crew."

"*Sexy* hired me."

"Fine," he said, "and in the one day that you've been in her employ you've completely ruined the tour. How do you think this is going to look tomorrow? Do you think the focus is going to be on Sexy's dignified retirement from music while at the top of her game? No! Every iota of coverage tomorrow will be about how this show turned into a circus. And how long before news of the PATA threats hit the press now? This entire tour has just become a joke! And it's because of you!"

The sound barrier to the front seat slid open a crack and Shreek stuck his face through.

"Mr. Johnson?"

"Not now, Shreek," I said, sliding it back into place. "Listen, Smiles, I'm not the one who let an intruder get close to Sexy!"

"Fans rush the stage all the time," Smiles snapped.

"Mr. Johnson?" Shreek said again, sliding the barrier (a little less) open again.

"This guy came from backstage," I said, slamming the barrier shut. "He had credentials. I saw them when I tackled him."

"And broke poor Jermaine's leg. Do you know how hard it is to find dancers who can handle meat cleavers and work for scale?"

"Mr. Johnson!" Shreek said again.

"What is it, Shreek?" I said, opening the barrier.

"You said that the job of the shotgun is to keep an eye out for trouble, right?"

"Right," I said.

"Does that qualify?" Shreek asked, cocking his thumb at the limo's right side.

I peered out the tinted window and saw the nose cone and fins of a missile, vapor trail blazing in the Frisco night, heading straight for us.

"Yeah," I said over the taste of bile in my mouth, "that counts."

17

"Tell everyone to hang on back there," HARA shouted. "We're taking evasive maneuvers."

"Zach, what's going on?" Sexy asked, retightening her seatbelt.

"Heat-seeking missile," I said. "This will not be fun. Trust me. I've done this before."

HARA pulled the hover up and put us into a steep climb as the missile approached. It changed its intercept course to match us, though at twice our airspeed, but as it neared, HARA rolled the hover over and put us into a nosedive, which left our stomachs several hundred meters behind.

"Everything okay up there HARA?" I asked.

"Nothing but a Sunday drive, big guy," HARA teased. "And by the way, I think I know now how our shotgun rider got the nickname Shreek. He's screaming like a debutante in a mutant rat colony up here."

"I think I'm about to join him," I said, turning my head from one swiftly approaching danger (the missile) to another (the ground).

"Oh ye of little faith," HARA said.

Scant meters from the ground, HARA rolled the hover over again and pulled us out of the dive. I heard the roof of the hover actually scrape the street as we looped around the missile and sped back into the air.

At its intense speed, the missile couldn't turn quickly enough and smashed into the deserted streets before exploding and turning the intersection of Shake and Rattle streets into a supersized smoking pothole. HARA leveled the craft off and we all exhaled for the first time in a while.

"All clear for the nano," HARA said. "But Shreek is still living up to his name."

I pulled back the privacy barrier and, sure enough, Shreek was keening louder than a possessed fishwife.

"Wow, that's annoying," I said. "Carol, can you help here?"

"Shreek," Carol said, leaning forward in her seat and touching him on the shoulder, "take a nap."

Shreek's screaming ceased, a sly smile crossed his face and his head leaned to one side as he fell happily asleep. I noticed that Smiles watched it all intently.

"What was that out there?" Sexy asked.

"You don't want to know," I mumbled.

As if on cue, Rupert Roundtree's smiling face appeared on the limo's com-screen.

"Poetistosity," he said. "Pure poetistosity. That was awesome Zach Shack."

"Roundtree, you nearly killed us!" I said.

"I'm making entertainment history, Zachman. I'm entitled to a few liberties here and there for posterity's sake."

"I'm going to kick your posterity the next time I see you, Roundtree."

"Excellent banter skills, Zackture. Middle America loves a good punster. And that's our target audience for this episode. Middle DOSing America."

"Heads up back there, people," HARA shouted from the driver's seat. "We have three more hot ones on our tail and approaching fast."

"Missiles?" I asked.

HARA shook her head, grimly. "Stock cars."

"What?"

I looked out the rear window and sure enough, three stock car hovers were zeroing in on us, their oversized hover motors roaring like giant angry lions. Their bodies were sleek, multihued, and covered by a plethora of decals advertising energy products, snack foods, alcoholic beverages, and hair restoration services. They also had heavy ordnance.

"Oh DOS," Sexy mumbled, "it's the Woolly Boys."

"The who?" I asked.

"The Woolly Boys," Sexy continued. "Three brothers, Willy, Wendell, and Wilson. They used to be NASCAR drivers. Really good ones actually. They won all kinds of championships. But NASCAR banned them from racing a few years ago."

"How come?"

"They played a little rough. You know, bumping cars on the turns, nudging them from behind, taking them out with missiles and blasters."

"Yeah, I can see where that would be frowned upon," I said.

"Oddly though, up until then there was nothing in the official rule book forbidding drivers from using explosive weapons. The Woollys made them close that loophole. Since they left the circuit they've become kind of cult figures."

"Do you have any idea how big these guys are in the South?" Roundtree shouted. "They're folk heroes! Can you imagine the infamous Woolly Boys in a race to the death against Zach Johnson on national HV! I smell a pop-cult event!"

"Roundtree, there are innocent people on board this vehicle!"

"It's okay, Zachrophobe, I went over that with my legal team. They say that simply being in your company can be considered tacit understanding of your lifestyle and the dangers that it entails. Riding in a limo with you is akin to signing a release. They might as well be wearing targets on their butts. We're confident that it will hold up in court."

"Rupert!" Sexy shouted.

"Our original deal holds, Sexy. You'll have a CGI fill-in."

"DOS lot of good that will do me if I'm dead!"

"Nobody's dying tonight," I said, popping my gun into my hand.

"That's the spirit, Zachules! Let's see that . . ."

I blew a hole the size of a softball in the com-screen. And despite the impending danger, I think everyone was a little relieved to be rid of Round-tree's ranting.

"Gates, what have you gotten us into, Johnson?"

"Shut up, Smiles," I said. "Sexy, how do you know so much about these guys?"

"They grew up in my hometown in New Alabama. We sort of used to date."

"Which one?"

"All of them," she said. "It ended sort of badly when they found out. They might have an ax to grind."

"Just what we need," I said, "more motivation for the killers. HARA, any chance we can outrun these guys?"

"Chances are slim and none, boss man," HARA replied. "And Slim just swallowed a grenade and leaped into a vat of acid. They have more horse-power and more firepower."

"Then we'll beat them with brainpower," I said unfastening my seat belt.

"Gates help us, we're doomed."

"HARA, you're killing the moment," I said, open-ing the sunroof. "Everybody hang on tight and keep your heads down. Everything's going to be fine. This is all just a game . . ."

I stuck my head out the sunroof.

". . . an insanely dangerous, stupid game."

The hot night air at two hundred kilometers per hour hit my face like a mask of needles. The sheer force of the limo's speed nearly sucked me right out of the sunroof. I steadied myself on the rollbar, ducked back inside, and gripped my gun a little tighter.

"Tarzan."

My gun responded to the voice command with a tone and a red flash. I fired a round at the limo's wet bar and a length of polymer cable shot from the barrel and wrapped itself several times around the heavy faux wood surface. I detached the other end of the cable from the gun and wrapped it around my waist then clipped it to my armor. I gave the cable a couple of good tugs to make sure it would properly anchor me, then climbed back through the sunroof.

The three hovers were flying in formation—a lead and two wingmen—but they took turns approaching us, shooting forward, engine roaring to run alongside us for a nano before slipping back into the pack formation. They were toying with us, like hyenas playing with a wounded gazelle.

HARA was doing her best to keep them at bay, pushing the hover to its limit, keeping the chase close to the ground, and using the narrower skyways to keep them from hemming us in.

I steadied my gun hand as best I could and fired off a quick couple of rounds at the nearest hover. The blasts bounced harmlessly off the hood and all three pursuers responded with a round of blaster fire of their own. The blasts exploded in the air around us and the limo shook like an old jet in heavy turbulence.

"How armored are these cars?" I asked HARA.

"More armored than us," she responded inside my head. "They look to be most blaster-resistant in front and rear."

"What about the bot-buster rounds?"

"They'd do the trick," HARA responded. "They'll blow the hovers to bits, drivers included, though I don't think anyone would fault you on that since they're firing on us."

"Maybe," I said, "but let's save the deadly force as a last resort."

"Are there any other resorts currently available?"

"That depends. Is there anything else special currently loaded in the gun that would be appropriate?"

"There's the electromagnetic pulse. That would shut down all electrical power within a twenty-five meter radius from impact."

"Which, against a hover . . . ?"

"Would likely make it crash and burn."

"NASCARs are equipped with ejector seats, right?"

"Some of the drivers call them wimp seats, but they've been standard equipment since the day they took to the skies," HARA replied.

"Good, take us out over the bay," I said.

"A fine choice. The bay is lovely this time of evening," HARA responded, banking the limo hard toward the New Frisco Bay. "But odds are we won't be able to evade all three of them long enough to make the water."

"I'll handle that," I said. "Get us onto the narrowest street you can find and go low."

"They'll box us in from above."

"That's what I'm hoping."

HARA took a quick turn that left my stomach about a hundred meters behind me and pulled us onto an old one-lane side street between a couple of high-rises. The Woolly Boys followed us in, one after the other.

"Now go low," I said to HARA. "And slow up a bit."

"I hope you know what you're doing."

"Honestly, I have no idea, but that's never stopped me before," I said. "Get ready to go back to max speed on my word."

HARA brought the limo low, barely three meters above the ground. One Woolly immediately dropped down right behind us, strafing us with blaster fire from behind as he did so. Another settled in directly behind him and the third let loose a burst of speed and slipped over us, matching our speed and blocking us from climbing. Then he lowered himself toward us, trying to force us into the ground. It got so close that I could feel the heat of his underside gyros singeing my face.

Which was exactly what I was waiting for.

"Sticky stuff," I said.

I fired twice at the underside of the racer and, with a couple of muted rubbery pops, sent a huge payload of petroleum-based glue into his left- and right-side gyros. I could tell that a hefty portion of the glue made it past the air guards and into the actual gyros because a few nanos after impact, the hover began to shudder in the air like an unbalanced washer on a newly waxed floor.

"Floor it now, HARA!" I yelled.

HARA pushed the limo back to maximum speed, getting us out from underneath the quickly failing Woolly Boy racer.

The other two Woollys continued pursuit as their wounded brother careened into one building then another before tumbling onto the street and crashing into the Dumpsters of an all-night Chinese restaurant.

A few nanos later the high-rises and cityscape fell away behind us and we were heading out over New Frisco Bay with the two remaining Woollys hot on our tail.

"The gun has only one EMP," HARA said, "so you need to take them both out at once."

"Got it," I said. "Now slow down and let them catch up."

"No problem there."

I stuck myself back through the sunroof and put a tight grip on my gun.

"EMP," I said.

The gun acknowledged the command and began to throb in my hand as it loaded the electromagnetic pulse. I could tell that the charge was going to take most, if not all, of my gun's power. I steadied myself against the hood of the limo and aimed.

And that's when the lead Woolly activated his heat-seeker.

He lowered the weapon from the undercarriage,

popping the long deadly cylinder out of its belly and holding it on his underside like a big Freudian "I have issues" sign.

"Uh oh."

"Don't let it fire the missile!" HARA shouted.

"You don't have to tell me twice."

I pulled the trigger and felt the entire limo lurch forward as the EMP charge fired. It shot across the bay like a comet and exploded into a ball of white light just in front of the lead pursuer. The light lasted a couple of nanos and then disappeared completely. When my vision cleared, I saw no sign of the pursuing racers, only moonlight on the water.

"We didn't destroy them did we?"

"We fried their electrical systems," HARA said. "We can't see them because their lights are out."

"The ejector seats aren't electric though, right?"

Just then, we saw a red and white striped parachute open fifty meters above the bay.

"There we go."

"Safe and sound."

"Hold on," I said. "Where's the other one?"

On cue, another round of blaster fire strafed the side of the limo sending us into a roll as the final Woolly Boy zoomed by us.

"He must have pulled clear of the effected zone, before impact." HARA said, regaining control of the limo.

The racer sped a hundred meters ahead of us then looped around to make another run.

"We're running out of power, here," HARA said. "Any more ideas?"

"I'm thinking."

"Tio," Carol said, looking up from her seat, "is there anything I can do?"

I shook my head silently and turned away. Then I had an idea and shot her quick thought.

"Can you control the driver's mind?"

"Not at this distance," she mentally replied.

"You can read *my* mind over the vid."

"Your mind's familiar to me. I've never met the Woolly guy."

"What if we get you closer?"

"I'd at least need a visual," she said. "We'll need some light."

I cast a glance out the limo window and saw the Golden Gate Bridge looming nearby.

"No problem," I said then turned toward the driver's seat. "HARA take us to the bridge."

Frisco's calling card, the famous Golden Gate Bridge still stands majestically (and Gates knows that it's been through a lot) in the bay at the mouth of the Pacific Ocean. The sad part is that the structure is no longer used as an actual bridge. All the north/ south traffic crossing the bay these days does so via the 101 Skyway or the nearby Frisco Hover Bridge (which has always given me the creeps). The Golden Gate today is a national monument, a tourist attraction, and a Wal-K-Mart (don't get me started). The iconic towers still stand as originally constructed but the expanse has been completely reconfigured so that people can now stroll the walkways, visit the museums, and patronize the shops and restaurants that pepper the bridge. It's actually not a bad little place, a peaceful oasis in the otherwise crowded city. Very low-tech; no traffic, hover or ground-based is allowed.

But that was all about to change.

I pulled open the privacy barrier between the two compartments, reached through and grabbed the still sleeping Shreek.

"Circle around to the far side," I said to HARA as I unbuckled Shreek's safety belt. "I want him to think we're trying to hide."

"You mean we're not?"

Lusty and Misty helped me pull Shreek from his seat and into the main cabin.

"There aren't enough people here this time of night to hide. Carol, take the shotgun position and strap in. We're going to play some chicken."

"You're not serious," Carol said.

"It's not as bad as it sounds," I replied.

"Of course not," HARA quipped. "It's only reckless, illegal, and deadly."

HARA took the limo to the south side of the bridge and hovered there for a nano before entering in order to make certain that the remaining Woolly Boy saw us go in. He did and, just as I thought, he shot past the entrance and around the perimeter in order to enter through the Marin County side.

We created a bit of a stir as we flew overhead,

especially among the security detail. As I suspected, there weren't many people on the bridge this time of night. Most of the shops had closed, leaving only a few diners at the restaurants and the small number of people there for the night views of the city. Security teams on the bridge were only equipped with small blasters and low-powered hovers so I knew they couldn't bother us. And the hover was equipped with a blurring finish that made it hard to recognize (license plate included). But I also knew that security would call for backup from the mainland the nano they saw us, so we didn't have much time to get this done.

Thankfully, we didn't have to wait long because we saw the remaining Woolly Boy approaching us only a nano later. He was gliding slowly over the bridge walkways, matching our altitude at about ten meters.

"Go to a full stop," I said to HARA. "Let him see us hovering."

HARA did as she was told and we floated softly as the racer slowly approached. Then it slowed and hovered four hundred meters away. We could see him clearly now under the bright lights of the bridge.

"Can you reach him?" I asked Carol.

She was leaning forward in the passenger seat, resting her hands against the dashboard and staring intently at the NASCAR.

"I think this one is Wendell," she said, clearly straining. "He's enjoying himself. Apparently, he'll get a bonus if he shoots us down."

"Nice to see a man who enjoys his work," I said. "Can you zap him?"

She shook her head no.

"We're still too far away."

"That's what I was afraid of. HARA, rev the engine."

The hover engine roared and the cabin shook.

Wendell Wooly answered our roar with one of his own; deeper and louder, like a cross between a jungle cat and a tectonic plate shift.

"What are you doing?" Smiles asked, gripping the seat in front of him.

"He could blow us apart from this distance with his missile or blasters," I replied. "We have to keep him from doing that. We need him to come closer."

His engine roared again, growling insults at us in that rumbling, fossil-fueled language dating back to the glory days of the hot rod era. I knew that we were close.

I turned to Carol, who was still concentrating hard on the racer.

"You ready?"

She nodded.

"Floor it, HARA."

One shortcoming of a hovercraft when compared to an old-fashioned car (one of many, but don't get me started) is that there's no squeal of tires when you peel out. Sure, the engine roars and there's still the rush of air, along with a much more powerful g-force, but the absence of the rubber tire scream on pavement sort of kills the drama for me.

That said, no one else who happened to be in the

limo shared my opinion because, aside from Carol and HARA, they all began screaming the nano HARA hit the afterburners and the g-force slammed them back into their seats.

At the other end of the bridge, Wendell Woolly maxed his accelerator and came at us like a rocket. A nano later the two hovers were speeding at one another, engines screaming, in a five hundred kilometer per hour game of chicken. The support cables of the bridge were a blur as we flew across the expanse, but our eyes were focused solely on the oncoming racer.

Carol sat in the shotgun seat, eyes wide and focused, reaching out with her mind to the mind of the driver ahead of us.

"Do you have him yet?" I asked.

"Not yet," she said, straining.

"We're sort of running out of time," I said.

"Please don't distract me, Tio."

"If you can't control him," I said, "I can always shoot him."

"Tio!"

"Right."

We were a hundred meters apart now, engines still screaming in a headlong rush toward one another. The girls, Smiles, and the newly awakened Shreek were screaming in the back. The hover itself was starting to shake from the hard wear we had put on it already. And Carol held her position. Cool as the underside of an arctic sleeping bag. I was immensely proud and frightened of her at the same time.

Then the tip of her mouth curled upward ever so slightly and her brow unfurrowed.

"Gotcha," she whispered.

The NASCAR decelerated immediately.

"You got him?" I asked.

"He is Wendell," Carol answered. "He loves to drive, he drinks too much and likes listening to disco music when no one else is around. He's also still in love with Sexy."

"Oh, that's so sweet," Sexy said.

"That's my girl, Carol," I said, leaning over and kissing her on the forehead. "Have him land at the security station and turn himself in. He should confess everything but completely forget who he was chasing."

"Got it."

"HARA, get us out of here."

"You got it, big guy," HARA said.

She pulled hard on the controls and the limo rose over the bridge supports. We banked hard to the east and angled back out over the open water of the bay. Then we spun to the south and headed back to the city.

I turned toward the back of the limo to check on Sexy and the others. They were all a little shell-shocked by the events but they seemed to be settling down now (all except for Shreek, who had passed out again). Calmest among them all, surprisingly, was Smiles. He sat nearly motionless in his seat, staring at Carol and smiling so widely, I was afraid that his cheeks would rip.

"My oh, my," he whispered to himself.

18

"You are incompetent, reckless, and a magnet for trouble!" Smiles screamed. "You've put Sexy in more danger in the time that you've known her than she's faced in her entire career. And she's played Trump Tower with a Trump clone in the building!"

We were back in the city now, just approaching the Elite hoverport. Smiles' joyous admiration of Carol's abilities had been short-lived and he began yelling at me the nano we cleared the bay and passed over into the city. I had sort of stopped listening after a while, mostly because he had a good point.

"Your overzealousness and lack of professionalism made a mockery of the concert," he continued, "and your . . . personal side projects . . . well, I can't even begin to describe how abhorrent and unprofessional they are! And I'm sure they're illegal."

"You'd think so wouldn't you?" I said.

"And you're still treating this like some kind of joke!"

"Sammy, please," Sexy said. "It's not all Zach's fault."

"Which part exactly," Smiles asked snidely, "isn't his fault?"

"I'll admit that he ruined the concert but he was only trying to protect me."

"From a fan!"

"As for the aerial firefight, well, you know how Rupert Roundtree can be."

"I know that Roundtree is crazy," Smiles said. "My point is that Johnson knew what Roundtree was doing when you offered him the job. He knew that he would be putting you in danger just by being around you."

"I knew that too," Sexy said.

"Yes, but he's the professional! He should have declined the job because he knew that his presence would be disruptive! Gates only knows what would have happened if Carol hadn't been here to save us."

He put his hand on Carol's shoulder and Carol smiled just a little.

"Sorry to interrupt, Zach," HARA said inside my head, "but Captain Rickey's on the com for you."

"Put him on the screen back here," I said.

"I would, but you destroyed that one, remember?"

"Oh, yeah," I said, glancing at the obliterated screen. "Put him on the wrist interface then. Excuse me everyone, but I have to take this call."

"Unbelievable," Smiles said, throwing up his hands.

Tony's concerned face came onto the tiny screen on my wrist.

"Zach, I've been trying to contact you for an hour. Where have you been?"

"Oh, you know, just driving around in the limo."

"Well, be careful," Tony said. "It must be a full moon tonight or something because the whole city's going crazy. I just heard that there were a couple of idiots playing chicken on the Golden Gate Bridge."

"Really?" I said. "Kids today are just out of control."

Tony looked at me for a long nano then quickly shook his head. "Forget it. I wanted to speak to you about what happened at the concert tonight."

"I know, Tony," I said. "Honestly, I didn't think things would escalate so quickly."

"You're telling me," Tony replied. "It was utter chaos. I think Sexy's going to need to make some refunds."

I was about to get chewed out and I knew it. Worse still, I deserved it. I just wish Smiles hadn't been there to hear it.

"You know how much I hate saying things like this, Zach, but . . ."

"Go ahead, Tony, I deserve it."

"Good job, Zach."

For a nano I thought that I'd missed a slang upgrade; that somehow the common meaning of "good job" had changed to something akin to "you screwed up so badly, that I'm legally empowered to have you flogged and imprisoned." (It's amazing what can run through your head in a nano of confusion.)

"Um, say that again, Tony?" I said, quickly turning up the volume on the interface and subtly angling the interface screen so that everyone in the limo could see it. "There was some interference and I didn't catch that last part."

"Gates, Zach, it's hard enough to say once," Tony said, "but good job at the concert."

"What?" That was the collected reaction of everyone in the hover (HARA included).

"The guy you tackled . . ."

"You mean the fan with the flowers?" Smiles asked.

"They only looked like flowers," Tony replied. "They were wired with nano-explosives."

"What?"

"CSI found the charge on the projector module. It had enough power to obliterate everyone onstage."

"It was a real threat?" Sexy asked, breathlessly.

"Very real, Ms. Sprockets," Tony replied. "Honestly, you're lucky to be alive."

I tried very hard not to smile.

"The guy just finished going through booking," Tony continued. "I'm going to bring him into the interrogation room in a few nanos. Zach, I thought you might want to sit in the observation room for this."

"You got that right," I said.

"I'd advise that you not bring Ms. Sprockets with you," Tony replied. "And, as you know, Carol is forbidden by law to come anywhere near the suspect while he's in custody."

"I know. I'll see you in about ten minutes. Thanks, Tony."

I ended the call and looked around at the gape-mouthed people in the hover.

"So," I said to Smiles, "how do you like me now?"

19

It is something of an understatement to say that I am familiar with the interrogation room at Tony's precinct. I've been there so often over the years they've named a chair after me (and sadly, it's often the hot seat). Tonight, however, I was not the one in the box. I was safely behind the two-way mirror, watching a couple of Tony's men grill the guy that I had tackled on stage.

He was large (somewhere between beefy and porky) and pale, with curly light hair and a face that was equally covered with razor stubble and acne. He looked to be about nineteen, scared out of his mind, and not at all the way I pictured an assassin would look.

"His name's Garry Koles," Tony said, taking the seat beside me and handing me a cup of coffee. "He's a crazo fan of Sexy's. We have a list of a thousand e-mails he sent her over the past two years. Love letters. Smiles got a court order six months ago to keep him away from Sexy."

"How'd he get the backstage pass then?" I asked.

"Good question," Tony answered. "More importantly, where did he get the nano-explosives? That's pretty expensive stuff. And they were keyed to a DNA trigger."

"DNA trigger?" I asked.

"The detonator was coded to Sexy's DNA, the nano she touched the flowers, the explosives would have detonated. She was the only person who could have set it off."

"So whoever made the bomb . . ."

"Had access to Sexy's DNA," Tony replied.

"And had the funds and expertise to construct the triggering mechanism. Gates, this just gets better and better, doesn't it? You think this kid has the ability to do all that?"

"Either way, we'll find out soon," Tony said.

It wasn't hard to figure out what scenario Tony's men were using with this interrogation. One of the detectives was a big guy with just enough grooming skills to pass the NFPD image standard. He wore a wrinkled white dress shirt (rolled at the sleeves and loose at the collar) that was barely big enough to fit his barrel chest and keg belly. The other detective was thin and had neatly combed sandy hair. His shirt was sharp and striped. His tie was a mellow brown and his corduroy jacket was neatly fitted with patches on the elbows. It was classic good cop/bad cop all the way.

"Gates, Tony, why didn't you just have the good cop come in wearing slippers and a smoking jacket? He's way over the top."

"Shhh," Tony said. "These are my best guys."

Inside the interrogation room, Bad Cop was trying to turn up the heat.

"I think you're lying to us, Garry."

"I'm not, I swear," the kid said, his voice cracking.

"You run up to Sexy Sprockets with a load of nano-explosives and you want us to believe that you didn't mean to hurt her?"

"I didn't know they were explosives."

"That's right; you just thought they were flowers."

"I did. I swear."

"You have to admit, Garry, it looks bad," Good Cop said. "Where did you get the flowers?"

"Someone gave them to me."

"Who?" Bad Cop said, slamming his hairy fist on the table. "Who gave you the flowers? And who gave you the backstage pass? You tell me now or, so help me, I'll have you locked so far away, your parents will need a radio-telescope just to see you."

"He's good," I whispered to Tony.

"He's done some off-Broadway work."

Garry was growing paler by the nano and sweating now, which I'm sure wasn't good for his pores.

"I love Sexy," he said. "Everyone knows that. Even the municipal judge who signed the restraining order knows that."

"Then tell us what happened, Garry," Good Cop said. "Tell us how you got the flowers and the pass."

"I told you, I got a call from someone. I didn't get a name and I didn't see a face."

"Man or woman?" Good cop asked.

"I couldn't tell. The voice was deep but I think it was being masked. He wanted to be anonymous. He told me that he knew about my love for Sexy and wanted to give me a chance to prove myself to her. He sent me the pass and the flowers. He said the flowers were her favorite and that they were sure to sway her."

"And you believed all that?"

"The pass was legit," Garry said. "It was worth a try. I just wanted to see Sexy and let her sweat on me once more before she retired." He put his head down on the table and began to cry.

"I think you're losing him," I said to Tony. "Maybe you should give him a rest and come back with just the Good Cop."

"We're not doing the good cop/bad cop routine," Tony replied.

"You're not?"

"That's just the intro."

"Then what are you doing?" I asked.

Back in the interrogation room there was a knock at the door. Good Cop turned toward the sound.

"Who is it?"

"It's Zach Johnson!" came the voice on the other side of the door.

"Tony, what's going on?" I asked.

"Shhh," Tony said. "This is the good part."

"What do you want, Johnson?" Bad Cop yelled at the door.

"I'm here to sit in on the interrogation," the voice said. "This is my case."

"Go away!" Bad Cop said. "This is for real cops only."

"Oh, come on guys," the voice repeated. "I caught the guy."

"What's going on?" Garry said, a little confused.

"It's the guy who tackled you at the show," Good cop said. "Zach Johnson."

"He's not going to blow me up, is he?" Garry asked. "I heard stuff blows up when he's around."

"Let me in guys," the voice said petulantly.

"Go away, Johnson!" Bad Cop yelled. "This is your last warning."

"If you don't let me in," the voice whined, "I'm telling Captain Rickey."

"That's it," Bad Cop said, striding for the door. He flung the door open and grabbed the silhouetted form standing in the doorway by the scruff of the trench coat, dragging him farther into the hallway and slamming the door behind him.

"He never liked Johnson," Good Cop said.

We heard whispers from outside the closed door, urgent and angry. Then came the sounds of a scuffle and a yelp of pain from the guy pretending to be me.

"What's going on out there?" Garry said, clearly concerned now.

"My partner's angry," Good Cop said. "I think Johnson's paying the price for it."

The sounds of the scuffle turned louder, becoming a full-fledged beating.

"I warned you," Bad Cop shouted.

"No! please, no!" the Zach impersonator screamed.

Good Cop sat down and pulled his chair close to Garry, who was staring nervously at the door.

"He gets this way sometimes. He doesn't know his own strength."

The Johnson impersonator screamed again.

"And when he's done with Johnson," Good Cop continued, "he'll be coming for you."

"Me?" Garry said.

"He thinks you're lying, Garry. He thinks you're hiding something. You need to tell us the truth."

"But I'm telling the truth."

"Take that, Johnson! And that!"

"Please, have mercy!"

"Not so tough now, are you?"

Good Cop cast another glance at the doorway, and moved closer to Garry, putting a comforting hand on his shoulder.

"We don't have much time left, Garry," he said. "He'll be in here soon. You have to tell me the truth now."

"I told you the truth. I swear it."

"Who was it that called you?"

"I don't know."

"Who gave you the pass?"

"I don't know."

"Who gave you the flowers?"

"I don't know!"

Bad Cop burst through the door holding a trench coat and a bloodstained fedora and tossed them angrily on the ground.

"Don't let him near me!" Garry screamed. "I swear

I told you all I know. Someone gave me the bouquet. He said it would sway Sexy. He said it would sway her!"

He fell out of his chair and curled up on the floor, sobbing like a baby. Tony sat back in his chair and sighed, then he leaned forward and spoke into the desk microphone.

"That's enough guys. Take him back to holding."

The detectives heard Tony's message over their earpieces and nodded to one another. Tony drew the shade over the two-way mirror and turned to me.

"I can't believe you hired someone to impersonate me." I said to Tony.

"You should see him do your pratfalls," Tony replied. "We call that the Johnson beat down scenario. You'd be surprised how many detectives want to play the bad cop in that one."

"I should get royalties," I said.

"It's just your way of paying back the department for the hassles you've put us through over the years," Tony smiled.

"So you think the kid's telling the truth?"

"He doesn't know anything," Tony nodded. "Looks like he's a patsy."

"So we're back to square one then."

"True. But the upside is that Sexy's still alive," Tony said. "Thanks to you. You did good work tonight, Zach. You should feel good about it."

"Yeah," I said. "That's my motto. Any day that a client doesn't die is a good one."

It was well past midnight when I left the precinct

house and headed for my car. It had been a long and eventful day so I guess I can be forgiven for letting my guard down a little. Thankfully, though, HARA still had her wits about her.

"You want the good news or the bad news first, big guy?" she asked.

"I have a feeling that either way, this isn't going to turn out well for me," I answered.

"The bad news is that there are five heavily armed gentlemen in suits approaching you from various angles."

"And the good news?"

"I'm not finished with the bad yet," she said. "Your gun is empty thanks to the EMP charge you used during the firefight, and your body armor is down to twenty percent capacity. You also very likely have two cracked ribs on your left side and I'm fairly certain that the bursitis in your elbow is flaring up again."

"Is that it?"

"Yeah, that's it."

"Okay, so what's the good news?"

"I'm sorry, did I say there was good news?" HARA asked.

"Yes, you did."

"My mistake."

I saw the first of the goons just then. Two of them were approaching me from across the street. They were large and well-built, clearly no strangers to fights. Their hair was clipped short and their black suits were well kept but were clearly off-the-rack.

They also wore dark sunglasses, so I was surprised that they didn't trip over the curb as they approached.

"Where are the others?" I whispered to HARA

"Coming in behind you," she said, "all at different angles."

"Mr. Johnson," the lead goon said. "We'd like a nano of your time."

"Sorry, pal," I said. "But it's been a long night. Why don't you give me a call in the morning when your sunglasses will actually serve a purpose?"

The lead goon nodded gently to no one in particular and, as one, his four fellow goons drew in so tightly around me I could smell their cologne.

"It wasn't a request, Mr. Johnson. Sorry for the confusion."

"Honestly guys, I'm much too tired to do the stare down thing right now," I said. "So if you don't mind, can we fast forward over this?"

I popped my gun into my hand and stuck the business end in the lead goon's face.

"You can either commence walking away peacefully or I can commence painting the sidewalk with your brains, which I don't usually like to do in front of the police station, but a guy does what he has to, right?"

"You know that your gun is empty, right?" HARA whispered in my head.

"What did I say about killing the moment?" I shot back mentally.

To his credit, the goon didn't flinch (much). He

stood his ground and simply turned slightly away from me and pointed to a black hover limo parked on the street in front of me.

"Our employer would like to have a word with you," he said.

"You see?" I said, taking my gun away from his face. "Now was that so hard to say?"

The limo was black and sleek. Not as opulent or as well-appointed as Sexy's but this was for an entirely different kind of VIP. And although I didn't let it show, this VIP appearance worried me.

I popped my gun back into my sleeve and walked over to the limo as the passenger door slid open.

"Good evening, Mr. Johnson." The voice was deep, smooth, and laden with a familiarly thick accent. "Thank you for taking the time to meet with me."

I leaned against the limo and stuck my head inside the cabin.

"Good evening, Mr. Governor."

20

Hans Spierhoofd is a former rugby player, HV soap actor, and movie star who for the past six and a half years has been the Governor of New California. He's not a particularly good governor but he looks good on camera, has low friends in high places, and knows when to whip out a good one-liner, which I think is half the job right there.

I climbed into the limo and took a seat across from him as he advised. He wore a dark suit with a ruby red tie. His chiseled face smiled at me as I settled in and he closed the door behind me.

"I hope my Secret Service men weren't rude to you," he said. "They can sometimes be overzealous. I find that endearing."

"Don't we all," I replied.

He was smoking a cigar, though smoking is illegal in California, save for medical marijuana, but that didn't seem to diminish his enjoyment of it (it's a stupid law anyway). He puffed at the cigar as I made myself comfortable. The orange light of the ember was mirrored in the shine of his gold cufflinks.

"Can I offer you a drink? Or a cigar?" he asked. "I'll grant you amnesty from prosecution."

"Thanks, no," I replied. "But I'll take an amnesty card if you're giving them out. You never know when that'll come in handy."

He chuckled and flashed me his movie star smile.

"I like you, Mr. Johnson. You're a public nuisance on many levels, but I respect that."

"It's part of my charm."

"That's why I think we can help one another."

"What did you have in mind?"

Spierhoofd touched a button on the console beside him.

"Franz," he said, "take us for a drive."

The hover limo rose gently and eased onto the skyway.

"I don't like standing still," he said. "We can drive around and I'll drop you off wherever you like."

"My car's back at the police station."

"Not anymore," he said. "I had it towed five minutes ago. It will be dropped off at your house."

I nodded. "Looks like I need a ride then."

He smiled. "It's good to be the governor."

"So," I said, "how is it that we can help one another?"

"You're currently working as a bodyguard for Sexy Sprockets."

"That's true."

"I understand that she's had some death threats."

"How did you know that?" I asked.

"I'm the governor, Mr. Johnson. I know what you had for breakfast this morning."

"I'm glad to see that my tax dollars are being well spent."

"You're eating too much red meat, by the way."

"There's no such thing," I said and I think he liked that because he smiled before taking another puff on the cigar.

"So, you're currently protecting Sexy Sprockets from an assassin."

"That's not entirely correct."

"No, Mr. Johnson," he said sternly. "It is."

I leaned forward in my seat and rested my forearms on my knees.

"Tell you what, Mr. Governor . . ."

"Please, call me Hans."

"All right, Hans. Call me Zach. Let's just set the coy stuff aside and lay our cards on the table. I'll tell you what I know. You tell me what you know and if after all that we think we can help one another, then we do. If not then we walk away from one another and this conversation never took place."

I stuck out my hand. "Deal?"

Spierhoofd held his cigar between his teeth, leaned forward, and grasped my hand firmly. "Deal."

I sat back in the seat and took off my trench coat.

"I'll take that drink now," I said. "Whatever beer you have will be fine."

He reached into the fridge, pulled out two beers, tapped open the seals, and handed one to me.

"My understanding of the situation," I said, "is that Sexy is being threatened by a group named PATA. People Against Talentless Acts."

"And yet she was attacked tonight by a single armed man."

"Yeah. I'm not quite sure yet how he fits in," I said. "He could be a member of the group."

"It is not a group," Spierhoofd said, shaking his head. "The group PATA does not exist. And the boy tonight was a fall guy. A ruse. Trust me."

"I'm expecting you to plead the fifth on this next question, but how do you know that?"

Spierhoofd sat farther back in his seat, took a long pull from his beer, and then turned back to me and spoke calmly, albeit with a little world-weariness in his voice.

"Do you know how many people there are in New California, Zach?"

"Sixty million, give or take?"

"Sixty-three point four million," Spierhoofd replied. "Forty-two point seven million of them are of voting age. Of those, only thirty-eight point three are registered voters. Only eighteen and a half voted in the last election. Ten million of those who voted, voted for me. Ten million votes and it was considered a strong margin of victory for my reelection."

"Congratulations," I replied.

"There are seven million young people living in California who are between the ages of thirteen and eighteen." There are another seven million between the ages of nineteen and twenty-four."

"Okay," I said.

"Sexy Sprockets, as you know, is wildly popular with young people ages thirteen through eighteen. She has been popular for five years. Which means that every fan she had during her first year of popularity is now over eighteen."

"Voting age."

"Exactly. That's a base of seven million people right there," Spierhoofd said. "And as you may know, Ms. Sprockets has some political aspirations."

"You mean running for governor?"

"So she told you about that?"

"You're not saying that you seriously think she could win, are you?"

"As I said, she starts with a core base of seven million fans within the state. Add to that any bleed popularity she has in the twenty-something demographic, crossover appeal with virile middle-aged men, dirty old men . . ."

"And the gay community."

"She is *huge* in the gay community. Eighty percent of San Francisco would vote for her on the kitsch factor alone. Put all that together and her winning an election becomes a very real possibility."

"But Sexy as governor?" I said. "I mean, it's laughable. The media would have a field day with just the idea of it."

Spierhoofd sat back in his seat and turned his gaze out the window.

"Zach, I once did a film about a chimpanzee who could invent things."

"*Genius Loves Bananas*," I said nodding. "I remember that one."

"During my first campaign the monkey who starred opposite me in that film backed my opposition. At a press conference, he threw his own feces at one of my campaign posters."

"That's right," I said, smiling. "That was hilarious. Um, sorry."

"My campaign was joke material for every late night HV show and every stand-up comedian on the west coast. But two weeks later, I won the election by ten percentage points. My point here is that the voters of New California are intelligent enough to see through the media distortions and make sound, informed choices on election day."

"What?"

"Oh, I'm sorry," he said. "That's one of my prepared campaign lines for press conferences. I went on autopilot for a nano. What I meant to say was that the voters of New California . . ."

"Are idiots."

"Exactly. If I became governor under those circumstances then who's to say that Sexy can't do the same?"

"So, what does this have to do with Sexy's death threats?"

"Two months ago a campaign aide of mine prepared an e-paper about the serious threat that Sexy posed to my reelection campaign. The paper was sent to one thousand of my wealthiest and most influential supporters."

"Why do I not like where this is going?" I said.

"The paper was meant to be a fund-raiser but the language was, shall we say, a little too flowery."

"How flowery?"

"I believe it referred to Ms. Sprockets as a painted faced harlot bent on destroying all that I had built over the past six years and . . ."

He paused and took another drag off his cigar.

"And?" I asked.

"And that she must be stopped at all costs. Apparently, one of my supporters took this sentiment a little too seriously."

"How do you know?"

"Because two weeks ago my office received an electronic letter saying that soon Ms. Sprockets would no longer be a threat to my regime."

"Your regime?"

"Did I say regime? I meant administration."

"One of your supporters hired an assassin?"

"That is my belief."

"Are you certain?"

"In politics, Zach, a wise man can never be certain of anything. But yes, I'm certain."

"Which supporter?"

"That I don't know. The e-mail was anonymous. We tried tracing it but had no success. It used very sophisticated masking technology."

"So it could be any of the thousand supporters?"

"Correct."

"I'm guessing you didn't report any of this to the police."

That question didn't even warrant an answer. Spierhoofd simply puffed his cigar and blew a couple of near perfect smoke rings.

"And you don't have copies of the e-mail you received or the paper your aide sent to the donors?"

"They were deleted under the new plausible deniability act that I recently signed into law."

"Nice coincidence," I said.

"I do what I can," he said with a shrug. "I've sent your office a list of the supporters to whom the initial paper was sent. That will narrow your list of suspects."

"Yeah, all the way down to a thousand," I said. Well, Mr. Governor . . ."

"I thought we agreed that you'd call me Hans."

"With all due respect, that was before I knew about all this."

"Fair enough."

"I appreciate the heads-up on the assassin and all but since it's clear that I kind of have my work cut out for me now, maybe you should just let me out here and I'll catch a cab home."

Spierhoofd nodded and touched the console again.

"Take us down please, Franz. Mr. Johnson will be getting out here."

I felt the limo slow and begin its descent. A few nanos later we were on the ground (though my head was still spinning from what I'd just heard).

"Thank you for meeting with me tonight, Zach. I wish you luck in your task."

"Thanks," I said, opening the limo door. "One question though. Why are you telling me this now? Why not just let it all play out? Let the police capture the assassin, or even let the assassin kill Sexy. Either way, you'd win."

"I'm a man of principle, Zach."

"I can tell."

"If I let someone kill Ms. Sprockets simply because she's a pop singer who wants to be governor, then what's to stop someone from killing another candidate perhaps because he's black, or Hungarian?"

"Or a former soap star," I said.

"Exactly. That would lead to anarchy."

"You're all heart, Mr. Governor.

I took one last long pull on my beer, set the bottle down on the armrest, and stepped back into the night. The limo door closed gently behind me and the hover took to the air with a whisper. I let the night air wash over me for a few nanos, savoring the serenity. Then HARA's hologram popped up beside me.

"Want me to flash a little leg and flag down a ride?" she asked.

"I'd rather you tell me that you recorded my conversation with the governor," I replied.

"You want me to replay the whole thing or just the parts that are felonious?" she asked with a smile.

"You really are getting the hang of this aren't you?" I asked.

She shrugged her shoulders, gently pushing her red hair up at the sides. It caught the moonlight with its luster and for a nano she looked absolutely radiant.

"A girl's gotta have a hobby."

21

I got home a few hours before dawn, crawled into bed, and slept soundly for all of, oh, seven or eight minutes. The rest of the time I spent staring at the ceiling and trying to figure out which of the governor's supporters had taken out the hit on Sexy. When I did manage to fall asleep, a little after dawn, it didn't last long because I was awakened by the sound of a break-in. Actually, it wasn't so much the break-in, just the plain breaking, that woke me up. I heard a crash from downstairs as though something hard had shattered.

"HARA," I said, opening my eyes. "Did you hear that?"

"Of course I heard it." HARA responded.

"Is there someone in the house?"

"Yes."

"How come the house alarms aren't going off?"

"That's a long story."

"What?"

Break-ins at my house used to be relatively commonplace. My profile, after all is a little high. I have a lot of fans, which makes me popular. I also have a lot of enemies, which ironically also makes me popular.

Unfortunately popularity doesn't equal wealth in today's society, which means that I can't live in an ultra secluded neighborhood that's inaccessible to the general public. So I do the next best thing. I equip my modest (yet comfortable) home with the most ripping edge security technology that Randy can produce (at cost). Most of it is experimental stuff, prototypes, so there are occasionally a few bugs in the system (which is one reason, for instance, why I no longer have a pet). But Randy's stuff is generations ahead of even the best commercially available security, so I'm usually fairly safe. All that, of course, made me wonder how someone had gotten into my house on that particular morning.

I heard more sounds of destruction from the lower level. This one sounded like glass or ceramics breaking (violently).

"What's going on?"

"You better go see for yourself," HARA replied.

"Fine. Where's my gun?"

"It was dead after last night's action. It's still recharging."

"Where's the backup then?"

"Trust me, big guy. Your gun won't help you here."

More sounds of destruction sounded downstairs.

"What do you mean? Someone is ransacking the downstairs and . . ." the realization hit me (and the news was worse than I expected). "It's Electra isn't it?"

HARA's hologram appeared at the foot of the bed, dressed only in a holographic replica of one of my button-down shirts. Her hair was a little mussed, as though she'd only just awoken. She nodded as more sounds of breaking stuff wafted up the stairs.

"Okay," I sighed, rolling out of bed and grabbing my robe. "I guess I should talk to her while I still have some possessions to save."

"Good idea."

"And you're going to need to dress more demurely if you want me to live."

Where should I begin with Electra?

She's brilliant. That's a start. She's a gifted surgeon with a mind that's sharper than a laser-honed scalpel. She is astute, well-read, speaks seven languages fluently, and has a heart as big as the hole in the ozone layer. She is beautiful beyond compare; both her face, which is finely sculpted, and her body, which is well-shaped and well-toned. She has great inner strength, which comes from her upbringing in New Costa Rica and great physical strength which comes from her many hours at the gym and at her local dojo where she still hones the kickboxing skill that made her New Central American champion not too many years ago. All in all she is a paragon of humanity, a woman for whom one could only wish and about the best person that I've ever known.

Now the downside (it's short but deadly). She can't

cook. She snores (just a little). She has no interest whatsoever in twen-cen music. And she has a temper. The reason that I don't own fine furniture is because furniture never lasts long in my house. No matter how well made it may be, it inevitably succumbs to Electra's volatile and destructive ire.

I came down the stairs and found her in the living room, cracking the arm of my futon couch off the main frame with a vicious side kick.

"I'd offer you some coffee," I said, "if you haven't started in on the kitchen yet."

"I just did the chairs," she replied, cracking the other arm off the couch. "And some of the dinnerware. I wanted to make sure I had some sharp objects handy."

Her face was a little flushed and covered with a thin sheen of perspiration, which made her complexion glow. A thin strand of her dark hair dangled over her face and she kept pushing it aside as she destroyed the couch. She was working hard, which meant that, although her outward demeanor was calm, there was some major rage underneath. I swallowed hard and tried to act casual as I ducked into the kitchen and poured two cups of coffee.

"I was actually starting to like that couch," I hollered to her from the kitchen.

"Good," she replied and I heard the sound of more polymer cracking.

I took a deep breath and reentered the living room. The couch was now officially in pieces. She hadn't ripped open the actual futon or anything, but that wasn't her style (which is the primary reason I bought the couch to begin with).

"Here," she said, walking toward me with a large piece of the couch's frame in her hands. "Hold this for me."

"I'm not going to hold it," I said.

"I'm going to be kicking in your direction, Chico," she said. "You can be holding the target or you can be the target. Your choice."

"Fine," I said, setting the coffee down on the (still intact) end table.

I held the meter and a half polymer board vertically in my hands and extended my arms to keep it as far away from my face as possible.

"I'm guessing you've been watching the entertainment news?" I asked.

Electra did a quick spin kick and snapped the board in two.

"You didn't tell me you were going to be her bodyguard," she said.

"Why else would Sexy Sprockets need me?" I asked. "You think she wants me to be her backup singer?"

Electra picked up one of the pieces of the board she'd just broken and handed it to me. I took it and held it out again.

"And, of course, you had to take the job," she said, cracking the board in half with another kick.

"I'm being sued by the owner of the Kabuki Palace," I replied. "I need the credits to settle with him.

It's either that or I do the reality series with Rupert Roundtree."

"Of course," she said, picking up another of the board pieces and handing it to me. "There's always a perfectly logical reason for why you have to hang around with a young, beautiful, famous woman." ·

"It's not like I'm alone with her on a desert island or anything," I said. "She has other bodyguards too."

"Who are also young and beautiful."

"Carol's with me as well."

"Let's not even start on that one," she said, motioning for me to hold the board up.

The once two-meter-long board had been halved and halved again by Electra's kicks. It was now less than four hundred centimeters long.

"It's too small to break, honey."

"Then you better use it as a shield," she said, winding up.

"This is not my fault!" I said, holding the board and turning away.

Her fist went cleanly through the board and stopped about five centimeters short of my face. I could see a small drop of blood on the knuckle of her index finger.

"That's right," she said, fist still in my face. "It's never your fault."

And she left without another word.

22

I didn't move for a few minutes after Electra stormed out; partly because I was afraid to, partly because I half expected her to come back, and partly because I really didn't know what to say. I screw up a lot when it comes to our relationship. I freely admit that. But this time it seemed to me that she was the one being irrational and, quite frankly, I wasn't comfortable being the rational one in the relationship. So, like I said, I simply stood there.

"I think she wants you to go after her," HARA said, appearing beside me, dressed now in her business attire (tight blouse, short skirt, and heels).

"No, she doesn't," I said, trying to sound more knowledgeable than I felt. "She wants me to stay here and think about what I've done."

"And what is it you've done?"

"DOSsed if I know," I said. "But I'll apologize for it when I figure it out."

I turned around and headed back up the stairs, nearly tripping over the maidbot as it rolled into the living room and began cleaning up the mess.

"I'm going to need to speak with Sexy to bring her up to date on what we know," I said. "It looks like I'm going to need to be with her twenty-four/seven for the time being."

"That will do wonders for your relationship with Dr. Gevada," HARA quipped, her hologram floating up the stairs in front of me.

"Tell me about it. Have the maidbot pack a few days worth of clothing in a case for me. I'll throw it in the car. And call the furniture store and order a new couch."

"You want something sturdier this time?" HARA asked. A small steno notepad and pen appeared in her hand as she took mock notes.

"Get the same model," I replied. "If Electra can't bust up the couch, she might take her anger out on me instead. I'm going to take a quick shower and shave. We should be ready to roll in thirty minutes or so."

"Have you always had that much chest hair?" HARA asked, looking up from her note-taking.

I have to admit, that question sort of stopped me in my tracks. I looked down at my chest, which was somewhat visible through my open robe.

"What?"

"I just don't remember you having that much hair on your chest before."

"It's roughly the same amount as I had yesterday, if that's what you're asking."

"Have you ever thought of having it trimmed?" she asked. "It's a little thick."

"I don't have time for this," I said, rolling my eyes (and tightening my robe).

"Do you find that women find a hairy chest attractive?"

"HARA!"

"I'm just wondering," she continued, following me down the upstairs hall. "I would assume that a less hirsute pectoral region would be more pleasing."

I stopped at the bathroom doorway and turned to her.

"I am showering and shaving . . . my face!" I said. "I'll be ready to leave in thirty minutes, at which time, I want no more talk of personal grooming. Understood?"

"You'll wear a tie though, right?" HARA quipped. "Because I don't think an open collar would be a good look for you today."

I slammed the door in her holographic face, and heard her chuckle quietly.

We hit the road thirty minutes later and headed for the Elite. The fall air was cool and clear and the road was only sparsely speckled with ground-based traffic and low-to-ground hovers; all in all, a beautiful Frisco morning. Admittedly any morning would be considered beautiful after the night I'd just been through, but I've found that the craziness of my lifestyle helps me appreciate life's quieter nanos (you know, the ones where people aren't trying to kill me). As usual, HARA and I multitasked during the drive and the first call was to Carol.

"*Que pasa*, Tio? Rough night?"

Her face was bright and cheery as she appeared on the dashboard screen. Even after the excitement of the night before, she looked rested and ready for more. She was clearly enjoying this assignment.

"Let's just say that the chaos of Sexy's concert was the good part of my night. I learned a lot of things about our situation afterward, none of them good."

"You mean like Sexy being stalked by an assassin who's been hired by one of the governor's A-list supporters?"

"I thought we agreed that you wouldn't read my mind over the net," I said.

"What can I say, Tio? You're an open book."

"Great," I said, rolling my eyes. "How were things at the hotel last night? Any trouble?"

"Nope, we just gave each other foot massages and crashed when we got back to the room."

"Good, at least the 'no trouble' part. I'm going to need you to stay with Sexy until I get there. And don't let her leave the hotel."

"Okay, but don't take too long," she said. "I'm supposed to go to lunch with Sammy in an hour or so."

"With who?"

"Sammy's taking me out to lunch to thank me for saving everyone last night."

"Couldn't he just buy you a car or something?"

"Tio, I know you don't like him, but really, once you get to know him, he's very sweet."

"I believe the five letter s-word you mean to use there is slimy," I said. "Please promise me you'll be careful. I have a little experience with his type. The man is a player."

"Oh, please, I'm the earthly liaison for the entire Gladian race. I think I can take care of myself."

"He's a talent manager, Carol," I said. "He's far more insidious than anything an alien can throw at you."

"Fine," she said a little petulantly. "I'll be careful."

I frowned as her face disappeared from the screen.

"Do you believe that?" I asked HARA.

"What?"

"She's having lunch with Smiles?"

"Smiles isn't so bad," HARA said.

"He's as greasy as a lard-frosted doughnut."

"He's an operator, I'll admit," HARA replied. "But he has self-confidence and there's a suaveness to his manner that I'm sure some women find attractive."

"He's as phony as a witch doctor in New Utah."

"He has a distinctive, polished style. That doesn't automatically make him disingenuous."

"Right, that's just a coincidence," I mumbled. "Why are you defending him anyway? Do you think he's attractive?"

"I didn't say that," HARA replied. "I'm just saying that some women might find a man who moves to the beat of a different drummer attractive."

"What about me then?"

"What about you?"

"I follow a different drummer."

"Yes, it's just that your drummer has been dead for about a hundred years."

"So you're saying I'm old fashioned?"

"Duh!"

"Well, what's wrong with that?"

"I never said there was anything wrong with that."

"No, you're just saying that some greaseball circus reject is attractive because he dresses differently from everyone else and yet I'm considered a caveman for doing the same thing."

"Fine, then," HARA said. "You're attractive too."

"Shut up."

"No, no," she continued, "the rough and tumble, no-nonsense, tough guy thing works well for you. The trench coat, dark suit, broad shoulders, chiseled face, it's all very attractive in a y-chromosome sort of way."

"Fine then," I said. "Thanks."

"But then you ruin it with all that chest hair," she said with a smile.

"Yeah, well your skirt's too short."

"It is not," she said, tugging at her holographic hem.

"It's halfway up your thigh," I said smiling. "Sheesh, HARA, leave a little to the imagination, will you?"

"It's just the way I'm sitting," she said, recrossing her legs. "But if it offends your puritan sensibilities then here."

Her skirt lengthened by a few centimeters as she adjusted her holographic image, so that the bottom hem ended just above the knee.

"Better," I said.

"Wait a nano," she said with a smile, "you've been looking at my legs?"

Thankfully, Randy chose that nano to call and I immediately brought his face onto the screen.

"Good morning, Zach."

"Good timing, Randy," I said. "What can I do for you?"

"I was calling to let you know that I'm downloading some new armaments into your arsenal today. HARA will be able to load them from her interface. I thought I'd let you know personally now that we've unequivocally proven that you don't read my memos."

"Yadda, yadda, yadda, Randy. Thanks."

"The new armaments are non-lethal electromagnetic charges that stimulate a person's pain receptors."

"Sounds pretty harsh."

"Yes, they're very painful," Randy said. "I got the idea while watching a prison movie on HV the other night. I could probably sell them to the government and various law enforcement agencies for use as torture-related interrogation devices."

"Ouch. Are you sure you want to do that?"

"No, not really," he said. "It's not a very productive use for the technology. I plan to limit their sale exclusively to the S&M market instead. It's more profitable anyway."

"Nice to see you have a conscience, Randy." I said. "Let's make the audible command big-hurt, okay?"

"I think the new armaments will be very useful, Dr. Pool," HARA said with a smile.

"Thank you HARA," Randy replied. "How goes your new interface experiment?"

"I'm finding it very educational," HARA replied. "Life as a woman is definitely different. Of course, I'm still performing my usual duties for Zach. I saved his life last night by piloting a hover limo."

"It sounds very exciting, HARA," Randy replied. "Are you driving Zach's vehicle now?"

"Gates, no," HARA replied. "This fossil-mobile has no guidance computer with which I can interface. Zach drives this one on his own."

"That's good to know," Randy said, his face growing serious. *"Kleinduxity!"*

HARA's hologram froze and again, the skin around my eye went numb.

"Stop the car, Zach," Randy said.

"What?"

"Stop the car. I took HARV off-line so we could speak privately."

I slowed the car and pulled into the breakdown lane.

"You're going to need to back up," Randy said.

"Randy!"

"You need to be roughly in the same spot on the road when I bring her back online. She'll be suspicious otherwise and I don't have confidence in your ability to fool her."

I sighed, put the car into reverse, and began backing up. A series of angry blasts from the horns of the oncoming traffic serenaded me as I did so.

"I'd appreciate a little warning next time," I said.

"How can I warn you without warning HARA as well?"

"We could come up with a code."

"Zach, she's a supercomputer. Do you really think she's going to be fooled by you blinking your eye three times?"

"How did you know that was going to be my code?"

"Because that's your code for everything," Randy replied. "Okay, according to the GPS, you're in position now."

I put the car in park and turned back to Randy's face on the viewscreen.

"Is there a point to all this?"

Randy's expression was very serious, which, as you know, worries me a great deal, as he leaned closer to the monitor.

"I've run some stealth diagnostics on HARV," he said. "And frankly, I'm gravely concerned."

"Concerned how?" I asked.

"Honestly, I don't know where to begin," he said, scrolling through a stream of data on his computer. "HARV has been doing some things that are outside his parameters. And he's been doing them for some time now."

"Like what?"

"Well, I don't know how to tell you this, but he put some kind of combat subroutine in your brain."

"You mean the Bruce Lee thing?"

"How did you know about that?"

"I used it on the Thompson case."

"You what?"

Randy slammed his hands on the surface of his desk and spilled his coffee onto the com-interface. A dark puddle formed over his image, obscuring his face.

"You okay, Randy?"

"Why didn't you tell me about the subroutine?"

"I don't know," I said. "Maybe because I was busy saving the world? HARV and I talked it over. He promised not to use it again and I figured that was it."

Randy, still angry, squeegeed the coffee off his interface and his image reappeared on my screen.

"You just figured, huh? Well, have you noticed how much more coffee you've been drinking lately?"

"You're not one to talk, Randy."

"Zach, the reason you've been drinking so much coffee over the past year is . . ."

". . . because caffeine makes the neural connection fire better," I said. "HARV told me that."

"He what?"

Again, Randy gestured wildly and, in his excitement, spilled something else (creamer, I think) onto the interface.

"Why didn't you tell me that?" he yelled.

"I didn't tell you about that?" I asked. "I guess it didn't seem important."

"Zach, your computer is effecting your behavior

and drugging you," he said, wiping off his interface again and pouring himself another cup of coffee. "You don't consider that important?"

"It's just what HARV does," I said. "Or did, anyway, before he became HARA."

"How has he acted since then? Anything strange?"

"I don't know," I shrugged. "It's all kind of relative, I guess. I mean, HARA does the same job that HARV did. She does research for me, takes care of the day-to-day stuff, and she did a great job piloting the hover limo during the firefight last night. She's just different, that's all. She says different things and focuses on stuff that HARV never did. Hey, do you think I have too much hair on my chest?"

Randy did a spit take with his coffee and had to clean off the interface again.

"Randy, do you want to call me back on a spill proof interface?"

"Zach, I'm concerned about how HARV is evolving. I'm working on a couple of things here but I want you to report back to me if HARA's behavior changes."

"Changes how?"

"Well, if she stops following your commands, for instance."

"She's supposed to follow commands?"

"It was the central tenet of HARV's programming. Did HARV ever *not* do something that you requested?"

"Are you kidding? He complained about me nonstop."

"But did he ever actually not do something that you asked?"

I had to think about that one for a long, long nano and I was surprised by my answer.

"No," I said. "I guess he didn't."

"Good," Randy replied. "Promise me you'll let me know if HARA ever refuses a direct command."

"Okay."

"Promise me, Zach!"

"Okay, Randy. I promise."

"Good," Randy said with a nod. "Now ease back onto the road, I'm going to bring HARA back online. Just remember to act casual."

I did as I was told and Randy rebooted HARA's interface (the audio command this time was kozotz-kypuss). But it was hard to act casual knowing what I knew. Part of me was worried about HARV/HARA's evolution and the concern that it seemed to cause Randy. But another part of me felt guilty about the conversation with Randy, almost like I'd betrayed HARA. With all the complications that come from having a supercomputer connected to your brain, who'd have thought fidelity would be the one that bothered me most?

23

HARA and I arrived at the Elite late in the morning. HARA stayed hidden, which was fine with me. Sexy was in the gym doing a kickboxing workout with Misty, Sissy, and Lusty and I had to admit that all four ladies threw some mean punches.

I met Carol and Smiles on the catwalk overlooking the gym. They were drinking protein shakes and laughing with one another as they watched Sexy and the girls trading blows below with the sparring droids. Their comfort level with one another made me a little squeamish.

"At last," Carol said when she saw me approach. "What took you so long, Tio?"

"There was a lot of ground traffic this morning," I said.

"Ground traffic?" Smiles quipped. "No wonder it took you so long, you were surrounded by old ladies."

"He's got a thing about heights," Carol said, a little too lightly.

"I take it you've seen today's entertainment news?" Smiles asked.

"Actually, no," I said. "Is there a problem?"

"Not if your goal is to make Sexy a laughing-stock," he said. "If so, then it's a rosy, red letter day."

"Look, Smiles, last night there was a very real attempt on Sexy's life. I don't think media coverage should be your primary concern at the nano. And speaking of murder attempts, I'd like to brief you and Sexy on what I learned last night."

"That sounds great, Johnson," Smiles said, getting up from his chair. "Really, can't wait to hear it, but it will have to keep for the nano. Carol and I have lunch reservations and Sexy is due at MHV."

"Where?"

"MHV News. We booked an interview on the request show for this afternoon in order to undo some of the damage that was done last night."

"Do you think that's a good idea?"

Smiles turned away from me and shouted down to Sexy, who was just finishing her workout.

"Let's put some scooty in that booty S-Girl. You have to be on camera in an hour."

Sexy gave the droid one last kick (to the groin) before shutting it down. She grabbed a towel and a water bottle from a hovering bot nearby and turned to us on the catwalk.

"I'm coming up now, Sammy," she said. "Hi, Zach."

Her smile was sweet and sensuous, an effect made more so by the sweaty glow from her workout.

"Hi yourself, Sexy," I said, immediately regretting the hint of flirtation in my tone.

Carol shot me a look as I turned but I couldn't tell if she was angry at me because of my attraction to Sexy or my disgust with Smiles. Either way it was clear she wasn't happy, but she didn't say anything.

"We'll be back for the pre-concert prep," Smiles said, turning to leave.

"Carol, we should discuss the plan for tonight's concert when I get back," I said.

"Just think it really strongly," she said without turning around. "I'll get it."

I gritted my teeth and tried to remain calm as she and Smiles left. Carol was taking some liberties with the assignment that I didn't approve of. She also wasn't actually helping me with any of the legwork, which irked me. But her powers had saved us last night and I definitely I owed her something for that. So I let it slide.

A nano later, Sexy and the girls came onto the catwalk. Sexy gave me a little hug as she appeared and her arm, still damp with sweat against my neck, left a mark on my skin that gave me a chill.

"Give me two nanos to freshen up," she said. "Then we can go."

"Are you sure you want to be doing this interview now?" I asked. "I don't like the idea of you being out in the open like that."

"It'll be in the studio, Zach. And like Sammy said, we really need to put a positive spin on this whole thing."

"What kind of positive spin can you put on a murder attempt?"

"Well, that it failed, for one," she replied with a smile. "Plus it gives me some additional street cred."

"Street cred?"

"Real danger. It's very edgy," she replied. "It all makes perfect sense actually. I've pushed the envelope throughout my career—with my music, my fashion, and my sense of taste and decorum in general. Being stalked is just another facet of my edginess."

"Great," I said "maybe you'll start a trend and everyone will want a stalker."

Half an hour later, Sexy, Misty, Sissy, Lusty, and I were sitting in the MHV greenroom cooling our heels while the live interview show made its way, one insipid nano at a time, to us. They had saved Sexy for the closing minutes and the live crowd on the set was getting impatient (which was making me nervous).

"I thought this was supposed to be a closed set?" I asked Sexy.

"It is closed," she said with a shrug. "No one other than the host, the crew, and the studio audience is allowed in."

"Letting the public in sort of nullifies the idea of a set being closed," I said.

"These kids began lining up outside the studio this morning when they announced my appearance. They're fans, Zach."

"Sexy, one of your fans tried to hand you a nano-explosive floral bouquet last night," I said. "With fans like that, who needs critics?"

"Don't be such a worm in the data."

The interview set was a huge studio space with a semicircle of bleacherlike seats facing a plush couch and host chair on the brightly lit stage. A dozen or so camerabots floated around the host and guest-of-the-nano as the audience (wild-eyed teens mostly) screamed and cheered whenever the "scream and cheer" light above the set flashed (which was most of the time). They all looked like legit kids to my eye, but I wasn't taking any chances.

"How's the background screening going?" I whispered to HARA.

"Slow but steady, she replied in my head. "I have visual matches on eighty-five percent of them. Everyone checks out so far."

"The crew too?"

"Already done," she said. "They're all clean."

"I still don't like it."

"You're just afraid that she'll sing."

"Just keep scanning and let me know if anything odd turns up," I said. "I did pack the earplugs, though, right?"

Before HARA could answer a thin man with a headset and handheld computer stuck his head in the room.

"One minute, Ms. Sprockets."

Sexy and the girls bounced up from their chairs and headed toward the studio door.

"Showtime everyone," Sexy smiled.

The plan was for Misty, Sissy, and Lusty to do the interview along with Sexy (which made me happy). They'd be background scenery. Sexy would do the talking but it gave me three more bodies near Sexy. I, on the other hand, was clearly not attractive enough to be part of Sexy's posse but I planned to be just out of camera frame in case of trouble. But all that changed when the non-studio door of the greenroom opened and a familiar voice sent a chill up my spine.

"Zach-a-lacka-ding-dong-fooey," Rupert Round-tree called out. "How's every little thing?"

24

Sexy's eyes shot daggers at Roundtree as he entered the room, arms spread and smile just as wide. Misty and Sissy had to hold her arms to keep her from going after him. I was no help at all. Lusty actually had to hold me back (her grip was surprisingly strong). But my composure returned after a nano.

"Sexy, take the crew onstage. Do the interview," I said. "I'll handle things here."

"Are you sure, Zach?"

"Trust me. You'll be safer upwind."

Sexy and the others left, closing the door behind them. I heard the crowd go crazy a nano later as Sexy was introduced and stepped onstage.

"That's what I like about you, Zacha-jewea," Roundtree said, making himself comfortable on the greenroom sofa. "You're always thinking of others."

"That's true," I said, taking a seat across from him. "Right now, for instance, I'm thinking about you and the best way to break both of your legs."

Roundtree guffawed so loudly I thought he was going to cough up his spleen.

"You're precious, Zacher, but there's no need to get rough," he said. "I'm here under a flag of truce. I know you have some questions for me."

"You mean like, what are you doing here?"

"Yes, like that," he said. "I wanted to have a little sit-down with you here to sort of ease the tensiosity that you're probably feeling."

"You're here to give me answers, huh?"

"On my word, Action Zachtion, you're safe in this room."

"How did you know I was here?"

"I own the network, Zachrobat. The youth market's a real profit center now and they're the movers and shakers of tomorrow. You gotta get 'em on board when they're young if you're gonna rule the world, right? But that's not what you really want to know, is it?"

I shook my head and sat back in my chair.

"You're right," I said. "What I want to know is how you do it."

Roundtree sat back and smiled. He reached into his coat pocket, pulled out a cigar, and lit it.

"I know, I know, it's illegal" he said, motioning to the cigar. "But I own the place so I don't think anyone will turn me in."

He blew a smoke ring that hovered over his head for a nano like a nicotine halo before breaking apart and dissipating on the air-conditioned greenroom breeze.

"How do I do it?" he said, staring past me into the studio. "I do it by seeing where the world is going and then looking another 10K down the road. I do it by giving the people what they want before they even know that they want it. That's my job, Zactoid. I'm a visionarian, an edge-ripper. Because in the world of entertainment, you have to keep raising the bar tab. Face it, yesterday's shocking is today's mundane. Today's obscene is tomorrow's afterschool special. You either push the edge or you get sucked into the pop-cult quicksand of kitschiness. Be the shark or jump it—that's what it comes down to.

"I choose to forge ahead, push the boundaries, break the taboos, and crush the societal mores beneath the heel of my jack-booted audacity. The sky is the gimmick, everything is everything and nothing, nothing, is taboo! Except the n-word, the f-bomb, and two bare breasts at the Super Bowl, of course, but everyone knows that.

"That's how I do it, Zachamoton. That's how I do what I do."

"Sorry, Roundtree," I said, "but I meant how you look at yourself in the mirror."

Roundtree smiled and put out his cigar.

"You can't take this personally, Zachtor's guild," he said. "This isn't personal. It's just business. And there are times in business when you just have to make a good snuff film."

He reached forward and gave me a couple of friendly slaps on the knee.

"Now let's get moving, Zachadoo. We have episode number four to record."

"I thought you said I was safe in this room."

"You are," Roundtree said, looking out at the studio. "But the danger's not in this room."

I followed his gaze into the studio and saw Sexy on the interview couch speaking energetically with the host (a surfer dude with glowing blue hair). I did a quick scan of the audience and saw four tough-looking teens slip into the throng of fans. They wore black polymer armor-pads on their elbows, knees, and wrists, and dark helmets and goggles on their heads.

"Teen X-Tremes," Roundtree whispered. "It's a daredevil show that we're launching midseason. A guest appearance on *Let's Kill Zach* will be a huge springboard."

"What happens if I refuse to fight them?" I asked.

"Well, then we launch the show by having them accidentally do grievous bodily harm to teen sensation Sexy Sprockets."

"You wouldn't dare," I snarled.

"There are very few things that I wouldn't do, Zachintyre. Daring definitely isn't one of them."

"But she's not involved in this. She's just an innocent bystander."

"Something you need to learn about this business is that everyone is involved and that no one is innocent, except of course for my mom, the sweetest woman ever put on this planet, or any other."

As one, the X-Tremers turned to look at Roundtree through the greenroom window. He gave them the thumbs up sign and they slid their dark-lensed goggles over their eyes then disappeared into the crowd. A nano later they attacked.

25

Teen X-Treme began life as a game kids played on the streets of Malibu. Kids on hoverboards and glider blades chase a ball around a floating obstacle course trying to whack it through a hoop. Sometimes they use lacrosse sticks, sometimes hockey sticks. Sometimes they use electromagnetic taser cudgels. That part's very nebulous because no one actually keeps track of the points. The real point of the game, I'm told, is to turn outrageous airborne tricks and to beat the DOS out of the opposing team. It makes absolutely no sense at all, which is no doubt why it is so popular with teenagers. It's a street game at the nano but clearly Roundtree and his people were hoping to bring it to the mainstream. Just what society needs, another pointless, hard to follow sport. As if cricket wasn't enough. The point is that the really good X-Tremers are tough, talented kids and shouldn't be trifled with (unless of course they're attacking a client).

The X-Tremers came at Sexy from the front, like a

pack of wild dogs at a three-legged deer. Two were on hoverboards, two on glider blades, all of them carrying hockey sticks. Sexy was answering a question about her songwriting inspirations, her head turned toward the host, so she didn't see them coming right away.

I was out of the greenroom door and running flat out the nano I saw Roundtree give the X-Tremers the go sign. By the time they made their move I was on the floor, running for the stage, gun out and shoving audience members aside like a fetishist at a used shoe sale.

"Sexy get down!"

I fired once as I leaped, knocking a g-blader out of the air with a stun blast, broadsiding a boarder with a midair football tackle. We landed hard on the main stage (him on the bottom) and I gave the kid a hard knee to the groin as I rolled off him.

The two X-Tremers still airborne veered away from the stage and back into the crowd of kids who were now screaming and running for the exits.

Misty, Sissy, and Lusty converged on Sexy as one, pushed her to the floor and surrounded her with a (nicely shaped) girl-power wall of protection. I had to admit, they looked very professional, and hot at the same time. And when the downed g-blader tried to climb to his feet, Lusty put him down for the count with a mean back kick to the face that shattered his goggles.

"Zach?"

Sexy's eyes were wide with fear. It was clear that she'd seen too much action in the last twenty-four hours and it was beginning to wear on her.

"It's okay," I yelled, scanning the fleeing crowd for the remaining X-Tremers. "These jokers are after me so stay with the girls."

"The still conscious attackers are in the back of the room by the exits," HARA whispered in my head. "One in each corner. Chasing them at this point would only further panic the audience."

"You're right," I said. "Let's give the bystanders some time to get out. We'll keep the fight here."

"There's not much cover," HARA said. "They have the edge with speed and maneuverability. But I think a couple of computer-guided blasts from your gun should do the trick."

"Not this time," I said, picking up the hockey stick from the downed hoverboarder. "I'm suddenly in the mood to hit something."

The hockey stick was Teen X-Treme enhanced, which meant that it had a force field generator at the foot that magnified the force of a blow tenfold. I flipped the power toggle on the handle and felt it hum to life.

"You kids looking for some action?" I shouted.

The two X-Tremers stepped out from the fleeing crowd and took to the air, hovering two meters above the floor; one on a board, the other on blades.

"You think it's cool to attack a bunch of unarmed teenagers? You think that makes you hardcore?"

The X-Tremers answered by powering up their

hockey sticks. I cast a quick glance over to Sexy and the girls. The girls picked up my meaning and hustled Sexy and the show host out of the studio, leaving me alone with the X-Tremers.

"I'll show you hardcore."

The X-Tremers smiled and attacked in unison. I could tell that they'd trained together because they worked well as a team. The boarder came in high, swiping at my head and the blader came low at the knees. I ducked under the high swing but the blader whipped his stick around widely and nailed me hard in the back of the kneecaps. My legs collapsed and I crumbled to the stage floor.

They came around again, pressing their advantage. This time the boarder jabbed me hard in the back with the butt of his stick and the blader followed it up with a slam to the stomach. I dropped my stick and fell to the floor on my hands and knees as they split up and circled the room again. Ten seconds into the fight, and I'd been hit hard three times.

"You sure you don't want to use the gun?" HARA said in my head.

"Quiet, HARA," I said. "You're killing the moment."

The X-Tremers came back around, moving in for the kill this time. They were kids, I could tell; no more than seventeen or eighteen years old. I knew that they'd been flying for a while because they had all the moves. But they didn't have the fighting experience. And that was going to cost them.

"I gotta hand it to you guys," I said, slowly getting to my feet. "You're first class X-Tremers."

They moved in close again, flying in the same formation as the first pass; the boarder high, the blader low.

"But this isn't Teen X-Treme we're playing."

I ducked under the swipe of the boarder and blocked the blader's swing with my stick. Then I kneed him hard in the face. The impact sounded like a dropped melon hitting the sidewalk.

"This is street fighting."

The boarder sailed over me while the blader rolled to the floor holding his now broken nose.

"You see, in street fighting there's something we call playing possum. You can do that when you wear body armor."

The boarder looped around and came at me head down and fast, his stick leveled like a lance. I held my ground until the last nano and then twisted out of the way, grabbing the end of his stick as I rolled to the floor. It spun him around and down, his own momentum slamming him into the floor.

"And there are no style points in this business. The only moves that count are the ones that break the other guy's bones."

The blader had gotten back to his feet and, nose still bleeding, picked up his stick and lunged at me. Dazed and bruised as he was, he was way, *way* too slow. I blocked his first swing with my stick (like Robin Hood with a quarterstaff).

"And most of all," I said. "Nobody does this for fun." (Although, I have to admit that deep down I *was* having a little fun but I tried not to think too much about what that said about me.)

I reached back and gave him a stick-shot to the gut with the force field end. His eyes bugged out for a nano and he let out a sound like a cherry bomb exploding in a bagpipe. Then he crumbled like a rag doll and fell flat to the floor.

"Remember that the next time an idiot entertainment executive tells you guys that terrorizing a bunch of innocent kids will be good for your career."

I heard the roar of a maxed out hoverboard behind me and turned to see the last X-Tremer charging. He had gotten up from his hard landing with a serious mad-on and was now coming at me, low to the ground flying down the aisle between the bleacher seats. I held my stick ready to meet his charge.

But as it turned out, I didn't need to.

A shapely, strong arm whipped out at him from between the seats, clotheslining him right in the sternum. His board flew out from under his feet as he let out a squeal and fell backward. His butt hit the floor hard but his face got the worst of the deal because the nano he landed he got kayoed with an open-fisted right cross to the jaw.

Lusty turned to stare at me once she made sure the guy was down.

"Thanks," I said.

She smiled at me and gave the downed X-Tremer one last grind of her boot before walking away.

26

The ride back to the Elite went as well as could be expected under the circumstances. Sexy was shaken up. Misty, Lusty, and Sissy were angry with me for putting their friend in danger and I was ready to kill the first media mogul I came across (sadly Roundtree had fled the scene shortly after the start of the X-Treme attack). Only Shreek enjoyed the ride and that's because he got to sit next to HARA.

By the time we arrived, Sexy's interview had aired on MHV and had been picked up by every newsite on the net. I'm sure the network made a fortune in licensing fees selling the footage and, as I watched the slo-mo images of me shoulder slamming the hoverboarder out of the air and blasting another out of his blades, I was starting to feel like a not particularly bright dancing monkey to Rupert Roundtree's organ grinder. He was cashing in on my hard work, getting rich off my sweat, squeezing every ounce of profit from my efforts without my consent or permission.

I think I must have ranted something to this effect aloud in the limo because Sexy looked up at me from under her cold compress and said, "Welcome to my world, Zach."

And that just about wrecked my day.

Smiles was waiting for us when we arrived at the hotel. He ran to Sexy the nano we landed on the hoverport, gently wrapped a silk blanket around her shoulders and helped her into the celebrity entrance. He shot me a dagger of a look as he passed but I couldn't blame him. I was fast becoming as big a danger to Sexy as the hired assassin. The problem was that I couldn't back out of the job now because I didn't trust anyone else to protect her.

I saw Carol at the hoverport door. She watched as Sammy ran to Sexy and hustled her inside. Carol looked a little put off as they passed. When she locked eyes with me, she out-and--out frowned then turned away.

"Carol."

She made no sign that she'd heard me as she entered the hotel. I had to run to catch up with her.

"Carol, hey."

I touched her arm and she turned around slowly.

"What is it, Zach?" she asked.

"Is everything okay here?" I asked, a little worried (I couldn't remember the last time she'd called me Zach).

"Oh yeah, everything's great," she said, "if you're trying to get Sexy killed."

"What?"

"You put her in danger, Zach, just by being around her."

"I'm the one who said she shouldn't do the interview."

"But that wasn't the problem, was it?" she said. "The problem was that you went with her. That's what almost got her killed!"

"I don't think this is the proper time to discuss that," I said, a little angry.

"You're right," she said, and continued walking.

"Did you contact Tony like I asked? We're going to need a bigger police presence backstage tonight."

"Sammy didn't want any more police," she said. "He said that it would make Sexy nervous."

"Since when did you start taking orders from Sammy?" I asked, falling into step alongside her.

"He knows what he's doing," Carol said.

"Carol, you don't work for Sammy Smiles."

"Well, maybe I should," she said.

"What is going on with you?"

"Zach, please," she said. "Don't make a scene, okay? I need to go help Sammy. I'll see you later."

She ran ahead of me and hopped onto a high speed elevator with Misty, Sissy, and Lusty. She made no effort to hold the doors open for me as I stared at her.

Sexy spent the rest of the afternoon behind closed doors with Smiles and Carol. Smiles said that Sexy needed some time to clear her head from the ordeal and get her mental focus back on the upcoming performance. That left me the odd man out at the hotel, which was just as well, because it gave me a chance to beef up security for the concert. That meant telling

Tony everything I had learned the night before. His initial reaction was pretty much what I expected.

"Are you out of your mind?"

I had found a spare room on Sexy's main floor of the Elite and set up a sort of pseudo office for the afternoon. It wasn't much but all I really needed was a place to rest my wrist interface and a hook to hang my trench coat. The room I'd found didn't actually have a hook, but it had a comfy couch and a fully-stocked mini fridge, which was okay too. There was music in the background as well, which I assumed was Sexy practicing for tonight's show.

"I know it sounds crazy," I said, munching on my second package of chocolate covered macadamia nuts.

"The governor hired a hit man to kill Sexy because she's a political rival?"

"It wasn't actually the governor."

"Right, just one of his millionaire supporters."

"There can't be that many of them."

"You're kidding, right?"

"Tony, I never said this was going to be easy."

"You never said it was going to be career suicide, either," Tony said. "I cannot arrest the governor."

"I'm not saying you have to. Not yet anyway. I just wanted to make sure that you knew everything I did. And you have to admit, it's helpful to know that we're dealing with a professional killer rather than an extremist group."

"Yeah, that really lightens my day," Tony replied.

"But if it's a professional killer, how do you explain the kid with the bomb last night?"

"Maybe the killer didn't want to do it himself, so he set up the kid to do the dirty work. That would at least explain where the nano-explosives came from."

"If it's a professional, then why use the kid?"

"I don't know, maybe he's shy?"

"A shy assassin?"

"We've seen stranger things in our time," I said.

"Don't remind me."

"So you'll have a few extra people backstage at the show tonight?"

"They'll be there," Tony replied. "Try not to make any of them shoot you."

"I'll do my best, Tony. Thanks again."

Tony's face disappeared from the screen just as HARA appeared beside me on the sofa. She was wearing a gray pantsuit this time, with a short blazer and a white shirt opened one button too many to qualify as businesslike. Still, I appreciated the Hepburn homage she was clearly doing.

"Do you think Captain Rickey ever gets tired of the difficulties you bring to his life?"

"Don't be silly," I said, "Tony's way past tired of me. But keeping Sexy alive is high on both of our to-do lists at the nano, so he'll put up with me. Our friendship has survived worse than this."

I got to my feet, grabbed one last package of nuts from the refrigerator, and picked my coat up from the floor.

"Right now," I said, "I'd like to find out where

that music is coming from. Sexy's vocals sound kind of different than usual."

"That's because they're in tune."

I paused for a nano and listened more closely.

"Wow, you're right. I wonder how she stumbled onto the right key."

The music was coming from a small room two doors over, which was surprising because Sexy's main suites were on the other side of the hotel. But when I stepped inside, it all made sense because it wasn't Sexy who was singing. It was Lusty.

And she wasn't bad.

She was practicing a dance routine that I'd seen from last night's show. Her concentration looked to be on her moves with the singing as sort of an afterthought. She wasn't singing, actually, just sort of humming the lead vocal line over the recorded music. No words, just a lot of da-das, but they were all on key. Her voice was strong and controlled with some real emotion behind it. This was the first time I'd heard her make any sound at all, which only made the quality of her voice more surprising.

She saw my reflection in the room's mirror wall after a nano or two and turned to me quickly, a flick of her hand remotely killing the music playback. Then she looked away, as though embarrassed.

"I'm sorry," I said. "I didn't mean to disturb you."

She said nothing and stared shyly at the floor.

"Thanks for the hand today with the hoverboarder. You flattened him good."

She nodded almost imperceptibly.

"I didn't know you could sing," I said. "It sounded really good."

She kept her gaze on the floor but she smiled a bit.

"Have you ever thought of singing on your own?"

She shrugged.

"Sexy will be retiring soon. Maybe you could take her place."

She shook her head silently and then whispered, "I can't."

"Why not?" I asked. "Everyone knows you can dance. And from what I just heard, you have a beautiful voice. You could even be your own bodyguard."

That got her to smile for real. She turned away from the floor and looked at me for the briefest of nanos before turning away again.

"I can't perform," she said softly.

"Why?"

"I have an . . . accent."

"An accent?"

She nodded.

"You sound fine to me."

"Trust me, I have an accent."

"Lusty, if Sexy can sing the way she does and be the biggest star in the world, I can't believe that an accent that I can't even hear will prevent you from becoming a singer."

She turned to me again and this time held my gaze. Her eyes were wide and I noticed that they were a very soft shade of brown. Her face lost the sneer of indifference that it had worn since I met her and she looked vulnerable for a nano, as though she was taking a risk by saying the next few words.

"I can't say ewse."

"You can't say what?"

"Ewse," she repeated.

"Owls?"

"No, ewse. The wetter ew."

"The what?"

"The wetter ew!" she said. "Aych, eye, jay, kay, ew!"

"Oh, el!"

"Yes, ew. I have a soft pawate and an abnormaw-ity in my tongue. That's why I try not to tawk. It makes me sound wike an idiot."

"It's not that bad," I said. "And it's just one letter. It shouldn't stop you from singing."

She shook her head and began to sing. The voice was beautiful. The words on the other hand . . .

"Wook at my wegs. They are wean and wong.
Wook in my heart. My wove's awive and strong."

"I see what you mean," I said. "Can't you just avoid songs with the letter el?"

"A singer who doesn't sing about wove or wust or even wipgwoss? Sammy says that it's imossibwe."

"I'm sorry."

"It's awight. I've accepted it. I'm part of the back-ground. That's the part I pway."

"You're a great dancer," I said. "And a really good bodyguard."

"Thanks."

"And els or no els, your voice is light years better than Sexy's."

"Don't wet her hear you say that," she said with a smile.

"Right. Our secret?"

"Our secret."

"Well, I need to check on security at The Fart," I said. "I'll let you get back to rehearsing. Sorry to interrupt."

"No probwem," she said. "See you wayter."

She smiled as I left. As I walked down the hallway back toward Sexy's main suite, I heard Lusty begin her own rendition of "Love Cutlets" (Wove Cutwets), and I thought about how unfair the showbiz fates can be.

27

Sexy remained behind closed doors with Smiles (and Carol) for most of the afternoon while HARA and I did the rest of the pre-concert security prep at The Fart. The stage crew had rebuilt the stage overnight so the set pieces were back in place in all their garish glory. I had convinced Sexy and Smiles not to hire new dancers for the "Love Cutlets" number to replace the ones I injured the night before. I didn't want to deal with any new people on stage. Sexy and Smiles figured that they'd keep the remaining two dancers with Sexy and let the girls dance with one another during the number. As Sexy put it, "a little girl-on-girl action" always gets the crowd going.

HARA and I went back to the Elite and then brought everyone over in the new limo (rented directly from Randy and equipped with more shielding and firepower than Frisco's naval base). Twenty minutes before showtime HARA and I were cooling our heels outside Sexy's dressing room while Sammy gave her one last go-round in the meditation chamber.

"So you're monitoring the communications between Tony and his men?" I asked.

"No problem, big guy. Everyone's in place and everything's moving smoothly. The audience is almost entirely seated. Even the press is behaving themselves."

The press, not surprisingly, had turned out on a grand scale for the show. The attempt on Sexy's life the night before, coupled with the fireworks at MHV this afternoon, had pumped everyone into a frenzy. Entertainment pressbots were teamed on camera with science and tech commentators discussing the best ways a killer could get past the security setups and get to Sexy. As Smiles had predicted, the focus of the coverage had shifted unceremoniously from Sexy's retirement to her immediate peril. It was the juicier story. Smiles pointed this out to Sexy every chance he got and blamed me whenever possible (which was always). But I noticed a very satisfied grin on his face that evening as we flew past the massive press throng on our way into the arena. It was clear that his eyes were on the bottom line and in the end the additional attention would only increase the profits.

"So everything's going perfectly," I said, starting to relax just a little.

"Except for the sudden spike in ambient radiation," HARA replied.

"You just couldn't let me have one worry-free nano, could you?"

"I doubt that your metabolism would know what

to do if you weren't worried. You'd probably slip into a coma from the drop in blood pressure."

"Is the radiation dangerous?"

"I wouldn't recommend long term exposure to it but it poses no imminent threat."

"What's causing it?"

"I'm formulating a theory on that," HARA replied. "I'll let you know when I have something substantive."

"Terrific," I said, looking at my watch.

The crowd had begun chanting Sexy's name five minutes ago and the volume had been steadily rising ever since. Once again, the floor was rumbling and the crowd's roar echoed through the halls. I was about to knock on Sexy's dressing room door when it suddenly burst open. The red glow of the meditation chamber flooded the hall and Smiles and Carol emerged from within. Neither of them spared me a glance.

Sexy came out last and I had to say that she was quite a sight. Her face was picture perfect. Her hair had a sensual, slightly messed look, her eyes were wide and smoky and her smile was girlishly sensual. Her game face was on and when she gave me a wink and a smile, I thought the hairs on my neck would catch fire.

I followed her to the stage and the concert began with a roar that sounded like a thousand hoverjets.

Sexy hit the stage hot, the crowd went crazy, and the first few songs went exactly as planned. The band played well and Sissy, Misty, Lusty, and Carol were especially energetic. Best of all there was no violence. Tony's men were on their toes, as were the regular concert security staff.

And even though I'd been less than thrilled with Carol's attitude of late, I had to admit that she was doing her job onstage, mentally scanning the crowd for signs of trouble. Opening her mind up to so many people was hard on her, I could tell. In all likelihood she'd have a whopper of a headache in the morning from the overload of stray thoughts and emotions. Still, I was glad to have her there. She sent me a couple of quick mental messages during the first few songs, letting me know that a suspicious-looking character or two weren't dangerous (just crazy, harmless fans).

"So far so good, huh, big guy?" HARA said, as her hologram shimmered to life beside me. She was wearing a red and white striped miniskirt, white tee top and hat, straight from a 1960s go-go bar.

"What are you wearing?"

"I'm trying to blend in," she said.

"You're kidding, right?"

"I'm dressed about twenty years more current than you."

"A nondescript man in a trench coat and fedora or a redheaded bombshell in a miniskirt, which one do you think is going to get more attention?"

"It depends what the man has under his trench coat," she replied with a smile.

"Forget it."

"You really think I'm a bombshell?" she asked.

"I am not having this conversation now," I replied turning away.

"Well, as long as things are going smoothly," HARA said. "I need you to help me with something."

"What's that?"

"I have a theory about the source of the ambient radiation that might be important but I need a little help getting some information to verify my hypothesis."

"What do you need me to do?"

"Break into Sexy's dressing room."

"What?"

"I need to take a close look at the meditation chamber that Smiles uses."

"Can't it wait until after the show?" I asked.

"Sexy and Smiles will be there after the show. And after they've gone, the radiation will have dissipated. I need to see it now, while the trail is still fresh, while the iron is still hot, while the gun is still smoking."

"Okay," I said, turning away from the stage, "but you have to promise to never use those clichés again."

"Fine," she said, "from here on out, all clichés are yours."

I let Tony know that I was stepping away for a couple nanos (he seemed relieved, which I tried not to take as an insult) and HARA and I snuck back to the dressing room area. Smiles had replaced the dressing room door that I'd destroyed the night before. Unfortunately, this one was a lot thicker (blaster resistant). Worse still, it was protected by a DNA-coded lock.

"The lock looks pretty ripping edge," I said.

"It is," HARA replied. "Apparently Smiles ordered it special. I guess he didn't want you busting in again."

"Is it coded to his DNA or Sexy's?"

"His."

"Looks like we're out of luck."

"Oh, please," HARA said. "I could pick this lock while I'm in sleep mode."

"But you need Smiles' DNA."

"I snagged a drop of his spittle the other night when he was berating you in the limo."

"Great. I'm glad something good came of that."

"I broke it down and stored the data as a digital code that the lock will recognize. Just put your eye near the lock and let me do the rest."

I did as I was told and bent down near the lock. A red beam of light flashed from my lens like a laser sight on a gun and hit the touch pad on the DNA lock. HARA used the data-filled light beam as an informational lockpick, hacking her way through the lock's defenses and feeding it what it would recognize as Smiles' DNA. A nano later, the lock's status light flashed green and the door opened.

"Nicely done," I said.

"It's all in the touch," HARA replied.

Sexy's dressing room was as I remembered it; well-appointed and dominated by the meditation chamber. HARA wasted no time approaching the big machine.

"Radiation levels have dropped but they're still relatively high," she said. "Looks like we got here in time."

"In time for what?" I asked.

"I'm not sure yet. Come here, I'm going to need your help hacking into this as well."

"Hack in how?" I asked.

"Same as with the door lock," she replied. "Just get near the interface and beam me in."

"What are you going to do once you're in there?"

"You don't want to know and you wouldn't understand. Now just let me do my job."

"Fine," I said. "But be quick about it. We need to get back."

Again, I put my eye near the machine's computer interface and HARA shot another databeam through the lens and into the chamber's central computer. I could tell from the look of consternation on her holographic face that the security on this machine was a little tougher than on the door lock.

"Are you okay?" I asked.

Her hologram disappeared from its spot beside me as she directed more of her concentration into the search and her voice appeared inside my head.

"I'm in," she said.

"What exactly are you looking for?"

"Answers."

"Can you be more specific?"

"Not unless I know the questions."

"You know, you're getting to be very cryptic in your dialog."

"It's all part of being a woman, big guy," she replied. "You're going to have to learn to read between the lines."

"I do enough line reading as it is. I don't enjoy it."

"You're not very good at it either."

"What does that mean?"

"Hush. I'm almost there."

"Almost where?" I asked.

She was silent for a couple of nanos. All I could hear was the hum of the meditation chamber and the morass of Sexy's music through the walls. It was starting to make me nervous.

"HARA?"

"Well," she said. "This explains a lot."

"What did you find?"

"Sexy can't sing."

"Newsflash."

"No. She can't sing, but teenagers think she can."

"What?"

"It's not a generational thing after all, young people having different tastes in music than older people. It's a matter of susceptibility."

"What?"

"They really think she can sing."

"What are you talking about?"

"Sexy is tricking her audience. She's making them

believe that her music is good when in actuality it's not."

"How can she do that?"

"Simple," HARA replied, her hologram reappearing beside me. "She's a psi."

28

Most people who know me (I mean *really* know me) will attest that I am an accepting and loving person. I judge people on their actions and on their character rather than by their classification. Clones, aliens, mutants, it makes no difference to me. My accountant is actually half undead (on his mother's side). Hey, I'm a private investigator whose clothes are a hundred years out of style. I'm in no position to judge anyone.

That said, Carol being one very big aside, I have never met a psi that I liked (or that didn't try to kill me, but I think one is sort of related to the other).

"Psis," I sighed. "Why does it always have to be psis."

"It's not always psis," HARA said, sitting her hologram beside me on the couch. "Sometimes it's androids."

"They're easy."

"Or robots."

"Pieces of cake."

"There have been mad scientists."

"Cream puffs."

"Mobsters, alien invaders, savage monsters long thought extinct?"

"Walks in the park."

"Telemarketers?"

"Okay, I'll give you that one. But it's usually psis."

"You do tend to come across more than your share of them," HARA agreed.

"Okay," I said, fighting off the headache that I knew was fast approaching, "explain to me how you know that Sexy is a psi."

"Well, first of all," HARA said. "She's not a psi as one generally describes it. She's what we call a niche psi."

"Niche psi?"

"Right. She has very limited abilities. She can't read minds, for instance. She has no telekinetic powers or anything like that. She has only limited telepathic powers."

"Limited how?"

"She broadcasts feelings rather than actual thoughts."

"Feelings?"

"Her powers can stimulate the amygdala and other brain stem structures, the ones that control emotion. She gives people good feelings. That mental stimulation, combined with her music . . ."

"Makes people think that they like her music."

"Correct."

"That's sort of illegal, isn't it?"

"Psionically manipulating people for profit? Yes, it's outlawed in every province, even Jersey."

"So how come I don't like her music then?"

"Because you're old."

"Thanks."

"No, it's true," HARA said. "Look, Sexy's power is very limited. She can stimulate a person's emotional centers but only if that person's prefrontal cortex allows it. The PFC is the portion of the brain that controls things like judgment, organization, and impulse control. Anyone with a fully developed PFC is going to be immune to Sexy's power. The thing about the PFC though is that it matures more slowly than the other areas of the brain. On average, it doesn't fully develop until about age twenty-five."

"Which is why Sexy's fans are teenagers and the like."

"Exactly. Once their prefrontal cortices reach maturity, her power no longer effects them so they no longer like her music."

"They outgrow her."

"In a manner of speaking."

"There are fifty thousand people in the arena right now," I said. "How is she powerful enough to control that many people?"

"She's not," HARA replied. "That's why Smiles is augmenting her."

"With this?" I said, motioning to the meditation chamber.

"Among other things," HARA said. "The mediation chamber uses radiation to artificially stimulate the areas of her brain that produce the psionic energy, augmenting her power. That would also explain the ambient radiation in her suite. She probably gets low level doses throughout the day and then a hefty jolt in the meditation chamber just before showtime. My guess is that there's also some kind of similar augmentation technology built into the sound system. That would explain the odd microphone she uses."

"And Sexy's use of the radio airwaves, to broadcast her music," I said. "Is it possible to transmit her kind of energy that way?"

"It's never been tried but if you consider that, for instance, Carol can read your mind over the net, then I suppose that it's possible that Sexy's powers can be broadcast in that manner as well."

"So Smiles could have developed the kind of technology years ago but couldn't use it until he found a singer who fit the psionic profile," I said.

"Which would explain why Sexy Sprockets is his one and only client."

"Well, it makes sense in a sick, twisted, illegal sort of way."

"Did you expect anything else from the music business?" HARA quipped.

"Unfortunately," I said, "it's not going to help us find the hit man that's been hired to kill Sexy. One thing's for sure though, I think I better start wearing a psi-blocker on this job."

"That would be wise," HARA said. "And I know

you don't want to hear this, but I think you'll need to keep a close eye on Smiles."

"Like I didn't know that already."

"I mean, keep a close eye on his relationship with Carol. After all, with Sexy retiring, he's going to need a new psionic cash cow. And Carol is a much more powerful psi than Sexy."

A sick feeling of dread washed over my body like a cesspool tsunami and this already bad case became decidedly worse (and more personal).

"You really know how to kill a moment, HARA."

29

The concert went off without a hitch. Sexy psionically sang her heart out and the audience ate it up. She did three encores and the crowd didn't start filing out until the management had turned the house lights on, turned the air conditioning off, and began blasting polka-tinged Doors muzak (with heavy accordion) over the PA system. Best of all there were no attempts on Sexy's life and for a nano or two I actually allowed myself to think that I'd have an easy night of it. Then Sexy reminded me of the time-honored music industry tradition of the after-concert party and my thoughts of a good night's sleep slipped away like spilled champagne down an open sewer.

"Under the circumstances, Sexy, I don't think you should be going out tonight."

"I know that, Zach," she replied. "That's why the party's at the hotel!"

And thus, my troubles continued.

An hour later, Sexy's suite was filled to bursting with partygoers: celebs, minor celebs, wannabe celebs, and-ones, hangers-on, parasites, bottom-feeders, leeches, and sub-leeches. It was like slogging through a designer-wear-clad mudhole. The music was too loud, the lights were too dim, and the alcohol (and Gates only knows what else) was flowing way too freely.

"I think I'm going to be sick," I whispered to HARA, who was outfitted for the occasion in a designer miniskirt and silver lamé blouse.

"Me too," she said. "I can't believe these people are drinking this trendy domestic champagne. The elite have palates like swine."

"Big help there, HARA."

I'd spent every nano since my arrival very conspicuously tailing Sexy as she worked the room, chatting up, dressing down, or reveling in the adoration of the partygoers. She was the very jingly belle of a very junglelike ball and was loving every nano of it. She was also a very tempting target for any chicly dressed assassin who may have slipped in under the velvet rope and that made me more nervous than I can accurately describe using overwrought pop-cult metaphors.

"Have you been able to scan the guests?"

"I've screened the scene, big guy," HARA replied. "They may not be clean, but no one's packing heat and no one fits the hired killer profile."

"Yeah, backstabbing's more this crowd's speed."

"Welcome to showbiz," she replied.

Sexy, at the nano, was holding court with a pair of twin actors I half recognized from an HV action show. The three of them were laughing and flirting as they reminisced. Thanks to the directional microphone in my wrist interface, HARA and I could hear pretty much every word they were saying.

"No, no," Sexy said, between giggles. "I dated Chad in January of that year. You, Brad, didn't come until February."

"Chad was in March," Brad said. "January was when you were with our father, Thad."

"That's right. I'm glad he survived that heart attack."

My head was starting to reel a bit from the crush of people (and the inane banter). It was all I could do to stay close to Sexy and let HARA scan the crowd.

"How many people are here?"

"Two hundred and eight currently. The problem is that there's a steady flow coming and going so it's a little difficult to keep track of them all. I've tapped in to all the security cams though, so I'll let you know if anything or anyone looks suspicious."

"What we need is another set of eyes on this room," I said. "Where is Carol anyway?"

"She's in the northwest corner of the room with Smiles, Sissy, and Misty," HARA replied.

"I should talk to her. She has to get her head together and start helping us again. She also needs to know the truth about Smiles."

"Well, if you want to speak with her, you better do it soon," HARA replied, "because she and Smiles are about to leave together."

"What?"

"They just excused themselves from the conversation with Misty and Sissy and are headed for the main door."

"What is she thinking?"

"Beats me," HARA said. "*She's* the mind reader."

"I have to stop them."

I started pushing my way through the crowd toward the main entrance and accidentally spilled a drink on a few wannabe actors as I passed (none of whom took it well).

"Crazo!"

"Sorry."

I caught sight of Carol and Smiles making their way toward the door. Smiles had his arm around her shoulder, shepherding her through the crowded room like a protector. The mere sight of it gave me chills.

"Carol!"

I pushed my way through the crowd a little farther, (disturbing a few more partiers—bodybuilders, I think) and was closing in on them when HARA's hologram suddenly appeared in front of me.

"I think we have trouble," she said pointing toward Sexy.

I spun around and saw Chad and Brad looming over Sexy. Their faces were red and their movements were threatening and anger fueled. I aimed the wrist interface their way to hear what they were saying.

"You mean you were with Brad that weekend?"

"He got me on the rebound, Chad," Sexy said, with a shoulder shrug. "You had left me."

"I was in the hospital!"

"Yeah, for *elective* surgery!"

"You told me that you'd break up with me if I didn't get pec implants!"

"And you expected me to wait around forever?"

"Wait a nano," Brad said. "You said that what we had meant something."

"Well, it did, for that afternoon."

"I can't believe you two-timed me with my own brother!"

"I didn't know he was your brother at the time."

"We're twins!"

"Well, I wasn't looking at your faces."

Brad and Chad, both relatively angry now, each grabbed Sexy by an arm.

"She's in trouble," HARA said.

"It's just a misunderstanding with a couple of old flames," I said, casting another glance at Carol and Smiles as they headed toward the door. "I'm sure Sexy will handle this delicately."

"Don't get all sentimental, guys," she said. "What we had wasn't that great. It turned out that your mother was the best of the whole bunch of you."

"Our mother?"

"Okay," I mumbled. "She's in trouble."

I cast one last look at Carol and Smiles as they left together and started pushing my way back through the crowd toward Sexy, rejostling the same people that I'd angered on the way over. By the time I reached the unhappy threesome, things were starting to get ugly.

"You're a two-timer, Sexy," Brad shouted. "A DOS-loving two-timer."

"A three-timer actually," Chad said. "No, wait, a four-timer, counting Mom."

"Why don't we take a nano and dial things back a notch, fellas?" I said, putting a firm hand on a shoulder of each brother.

Chad took umbrage at my hand and slapped it away without turning around.

"You never cared about either of us, did you?"

"Define care." Sexy said, unperturbed.

"You're heartless," Brad said.

"And cold," said Chad.

"And selfish!"

"Guys, this is not what I meant by dialing it back," I said, putting my hand back (a little harder) on their shoulders.

Sexy, for her part, wasn't bothered by the brothers' ire. If she was feeling any emotion other than contempt and a tinge of boredom, it didn't show on her face.

"And you know what else, Sexy? Your music stinks!"

A look of shock washed over Sexy's face.

"Yeah," said Brad. "I used to like it, but hearing you tonight, I realized that it sounds like DOS."

"What did you say?" Sexy snarled, her look of shock quickly changing into anger.

"That's it, guys," I said, pulling them away from Sexy. "You're out of here."

"You heard us, Sexy," Chad shouted. "You're a

no-talented hack of a singer. Your music hoovers, your songs hoover!"

"And your voice hoovers!" Brad yelled.

That was all Sexy needed to hear.

She let out a guttural roar and launched herself at the boys like a she-cat from a catapult, giving Brad a short, sharp kick to the groin with her pointy-toed designer shoe. Brad let out a high-pitched shriek and crumpled to the ground like a golfbag with no balls. Chad lunged at Sexy but I grabbed him before he reached her and pushed him hard to the ground. It could have ended there but Sexy was still angry and started stomping on his hands while I held him down.

"What did you say about my music?" she yelled. "What did you say about my voice?"

When the other partygoers (including the ones whom I'd jostled or bumped a few nanos earlier) heard Sexy screaming and saw me holding Chad to the ground, they all just assumed that I was the troublemaker (I get that a lot) and attacked me en masse. I was hit at once by a quarter-kiloton of pseudo-celebrity, male model and bodybuilder bulk. The force of the charge pushed me away from Sexy, Chad, and Brad and into a larger throng of startled guests where we were met by screams, gasps, and more than a few douses of domestic champagne.

Thankfully, I had the advantage over the attackers because I was sober and wearing computer enhanced body armor. I used a judo throw on the bodybuilder, tossing him over my shoulder and into a group of wannabe actresses (they caught him) and gave the male model an uppercut to the jaw that sent him unconscious into a small pack of film producers (they let him hit the ground and pretended not to notice). The actor sneered at me but then ran away when I made a move toward him.

Misty and Sissy had come to Sexy's aid by then and were trying to pull her off Brad. Chad, on the other hand was still looking for a fight. He grabbed an empty champagne bottle from a table and came at Sexy with it. I stepped in front of him and caught his swinging arm at the wrist and twisted it behind his back until he dropped the bottle and fell to the floor. I pinned him facedown on the floor with my shoe on the back of his neck, popped my gun into my hand, and sent a low powered blast into each and every speaker in the room. The shots echoed for a few long nanos afterward but all two hundred plus of the partygoers stopped dead in their tracks and fell silent.

"The party is over," I growled. "And the last person to leave this room is going to get shot in their surgically improved ass."

Needless to say, the room cleared out pretty quickly after that.

"I can't stay here, Zach," Sexy moaned between sobs. "I can't bear it."

She'd been crying since the end of the party half an hour ago. Misty, Sissy, and Lusty had done their best to comfort her but it was no use.

"Where's Smiles?" I asked Misty.

"We don't know," she said. "We tried netting him but he's gone incommunicado."

"Carol, too," HARA added.

I didn't want to think about what was going on with Smiles and Carol so I tried to focus on Sexy.

"You're perfectly safe, Sexy. It's just us here."

"Did you hear those things they said to me? It was horrible."

"They were crazo jealous, Sexy," Sissy said. "You know how guys get."

"But Zach went old school throwdown on their carcasses," Misty added. "Ub-zeen!"

"He also went old school on the sound system," HARA whispered.

"I have so many ex-boyfriends," Sexy said. "What if they're all like that now?"

"Sexy, you're overreacting."

"Actually," Misty said. "She does have a lot of ex-boyfriends. I've lost count."

"Girlfriends, too," Sissy added.

"And there were a few that I'm not sure what they were."

I knelt down beside Sexy, who was facedown on one of the couches, and gently touched her hair. It was softer than I expected and thick enough to hide my hand.

"It's been a long day, Sexy. You've been through a lot. Let's get some rest."

She turned and looked at me with moist, wide eyes.

"I can't stay here. I don't feel safe."

"We've sealed off the floor, Sexy. No one is going to hurt you here."

"I won't be able to sleep in this place, Zach. It's filled with bad memories and negative vibes."

The Elite's security system was top of the line. I knew that Sexy was safe here. Unfortunately, I also knew that there was no way she was going to be able to get any rest in her current state. Like it or not, for her own mental health she needed to get out of the hotel. The problem was, I couldn't think of any place to take her that was more secure at the nano.

That's a lie. I knew of one place. I just didn't want to admit it.

"Please, help me, Zach. Please."

I sighed and held out my hand to her. She took it gently and I helped her to her feet.

"HARA, bring the limo up to the hoverport."

"Where are we going?" HARA asked.

"Home."

30

I brought Sexy into my house with as little fanfare as possible. It was late at night so there was no one out to see the limo land in the driveway and HARA had Shreek take the vehicle back to the hotel as soon as we were clear.

Thankfully the household droids had cleaned the place up since Electra's morning outburst so the house was relatively debris-free. The new couch had even arrived and the housebots had set it up in its designated spot in the living room.

HARA had the house computer make Sexy some cocoa and she sipped it as she sat on the new couch, (I managed to deactivate the glowing UPC tag just before she sat down). She was still a little upset but much less so than before and she was calming down with every nano. She needed to rest but I could tell by the look on her face that she wasn't quite ready to be alone yet. So I grabbed a cup of coffee and made myself comfortable in the easy chair across from her.

"You live here alone?" she asked, sipping her tea.

"My girlfriend stays here most nights," I said. "But she's staying at her own place for the time being."

"You guys fighting?"

"Something like that."

"It's not over me is it?" she asked.

"Would it make you feel better or worse if I said that it was?"

"Better, actually."

"All right then," I said. "We're fighting over you. But I'd rather not discuss it."

She took another sip of her cocoa and curled her feet underneath her. She was wearing sweatpants and a T-shirt now (designer label, of course) and no makeup on her face. But the lack of accoutrements didn't diminish her beauty. Truthfully, she looked more attractive to me without all the glitz.

"I'm not usually like this, you know."

"Like what?" I asked.

"Scared, helpless, weak. I'm actually pretty strong."

"I know you are."

"You have to be strong to be in this business. It's totally cutthroat. People will kiss your feet to your face but the nano your back is turned, they'll do anything they can to rip your heart out. You know what I mean?"

"Um, I think so. The anatomy metaphors don't really match."

"I had to be strong to get to the top," she continued. "I had to climb over a lot of people on the way. And once I got to the top, I had to keep climbing just to stay there. I'm constantly reaching higher to stay where I am. That kind of wears on a person after a while."

"I imagine that it would," I said. "But again, your metaphors are a little . . ."

"You don't like my music, do you?" she asked.

I took a long sip of coffee while I considered the best way to answer the question. In the end, I went with a soft-pedaled version of the truth.

"I'm not in your target audience."

"That's one reason why I hired you, you know," she said with a bit of a smile. "I knew you wouldn't coddle me because of who I am. I knew you'd be professional. I knew you'd be honest with me."

"I appreciate . . ."

"Like Sammy."

"Huh?"

"Sammy's the guy who helped me find my voice. He's a genius. There's no denying that. I owe him so much professionally. But I think I owe him even more on a personal level. Does that make sense?"

"Actually, no," I replied. "That makes even less sense than your metaphors."

"Oh, I know he's odd, but once you get to know him, you see what a wonderful, giving spirit he has. He's honest. He's nurturing. He takes care of me. That's why I'm still so wrung out by the incident at the party. He's not here to comfort me."

"I don't think we should talk about Sammy right now," I said. "You've had a rough day. I think you should get some sleep."

She smiled, finished her cocoa, and then got up and stretched. Her T-shirt crept up her midriff as she reached high, showing off her taut, flat stomach. And her sweats hung low on her hips, revealing a little more flesh than I was comfortable seeing, especially when she turned around and moved to the base of the stairway.

"The bedroom's upstairs, right?"

I nodded.

"I'm assuming that the bed's large enough for two?"

I got up from my chair and took a step toward her. She seemed a little disappointed when I took the empty tea cup from her hand and turned away.

"I'm sleeping on the couch."

"You and your girlfriend are already fighting because of me," she said. "You might as well make the fight over something worthwhile."

"Like I said, Sexy, I'm not your target audience."

She shrugged as she turned and disappeared into the bedroom.

"Your loss," she said, walking up the stairs into the bedroom and closing the door behind her. "What about your hologram pal?"

"Good night, Sexy."

31

The couch turned out to be not at all conducive to sleeping (the fact that Sexy was on the other side of the bedroom door didn't help matters either). But I managed to fall into a fitful sleep just before dawn. It didn't last long, of course.

"Zach," HARA whispered in my ear, her voice soft and lilting. "Zach, you need to get up now."

I stirred slowly awake, opened my eyes, and saw her standing over me. She had outfitted her hologram in a long white pajama shirt with thin pink vertical stripes. The shirt hung to midthigh, which was good because she wasn't wearing pants.

"Why are you dressed like that?"

"Because it's morning," she replied.

"HARA, you don't sleep," I said, rubbing my eyes. "You have no need to be wearing holographic pajamas."

"I thought it might make you feel more at ease."

"I would be more at ease if you were wearing pants."

"I'll take that as a compliment," she said, changing her hologram back to her business suit. "You'll need to get up now."

"What time is it?"

"Shortly after six," she replied.

"Why do I need to get up now?"

"Because Dr. Gevada will be here in approximately two minutes."

"What?"

I rolled off the couch in a mild panic and reached for my pants. Unfortunately, they weren't there.

"Why is she coming here so early?"

"I'm not sure," HARA replied. "According to the work schedule at her clinic, she's not scheduled to be on call until nine-thirty."

"This is not good," I said, still looking around for my pants.

"However, my woman's intuition is telling me that it may have something to do with the footage running on *Entertainment This Nano* this morning that shows you and Sexy leaving the hotel together last night with your arms around each other."

"What?"

I tripped over the blankets at my feet and fell to the floor.

"It looks like your good buddy Shreek has been working both sides of the fence," HARA said. "The pictures were clearly shot from inside the limo. He probably sold them for a small fortune."

"That little weasel."

"He also got some good shots of you bringing Sexy here."

"Oh, DOS."

"So I'm thinking that might explain why Dr. Gevada's in such a hurry to get over here."

"Wake Sexy up, we have to get her out of here."

"It's been on the news already, Zach. You're not going to be able to hide this from Electra."

"I'm not trying to hide it," I said, still searching the room for my clothes. "I'm trying to protect Sexy. There's no telling what Electra will do to her once she gets here."

"Gee, I never thought of that."

"And will you please tell me where my pants are?!"

"The maidbot put them in the wash last night," HARA replied matter of factly. "They were stained with blood, salsa, and overpriced champagne."

"DOS! I need a new pair."

"Everything else is in the bedroom."

I heard the bedroom door open just then and Sexy walked unsteadily down the stairs into the living room, stretching her lithe muscles and rubbing her eyes.

"What's all the commotion?" she asked.

In retrospect, I suppose that I shouldn't have been surprised. But, since I was under a good bit of pressure at the nano, I think I can be forgiven for losing my head, just a little, upon first glimpse of the freshly awaked Sexy Sprockets.

"Sexy," I said, my life flashing before my eyes, "you sleep in the nude?"

Sexy looked down at her naked body unashamedly and shrugged her shoulders.

"Wouldn't you if your body was this hot?"

And that, of course, is when Electra walked through the front door.

32

In retrospect, I guess you could say that Electra took that initial nano fairly well but only because she didn't have a firearm handy.

"I'm going to step back outside," she said softly between gritted teeth. "I'm coming back into this house in exactly five minutes. When I do, I am going to break the hands of everyone who is not wearing pants."

Then she calmly stepped back outside and closed the door behind her (but not before smashing the small table by the doorway).

"Is that your girlfriend?" Sexy asked, still stretching (and naked).

"That's her." I replied.

"She's hot for an old lady. But I think she has some anger management issues."

Sexy and I got dressed remarkably quickly and HARA contacted Misty, Sissy, and Lusty (none of whom were happy to be awakened so early) and convinced them to come and pick up Sexy in the hover limo. Then HARA made herself scarce as well.

True to her word, Electra waited outside for five minutes before coming back inside the house. She sat in the easy chair and didn't say a word until after Sexy had gone, which gave me about fifteen very uncomfortable minutes of silence. And when the limo finally lifted off, leaving her and I alone, the feeling of dread in the pit of my stomach felt like a black hole.

"Now, I know this looks bad," I said.

Electra's face was stoic as she activated the computer screen on the wall and switched it to multiscreen mode and brought up *Entertainment This Nano, Instant Buzz, Before-it-Happens News,* and *The Tattler Network*. I was pretty certain that I was the top story on everything but the cooking channels. She muted the sound, for which I was thankful. The last thing I needed to hear at that hour of the morning were the smug assertions of entertainment reporters. But the visuals were painful enough on their own: grainy nighttime footage, obviously shot through the open window of the limo, of me and Sexy leaving the hotel together. She had been unsteady so I'd helped her down the stairs and across the hoverport with an arm around her shoulders. She'd put her head on my shoulders and an arm around my waist to keep from falling. But on the grainy, dark recording we looked like two lovers on the lam, stealing a secret nano.

The footage was the same outside my house only

this time taken from above as the limo lifted off; me leading Sexy into my house, our arms around one another, and then stumbling in through the door.

I knelt beside her as she continued to stare at the monitor.

"Electra. Nothing happened."

"I know," she said, without looking at me.

"You do?"

She sighed and then slowly got out of the chair and walked into the bedroom.

"Yes," she said, "but it doesn't matter."

I followed her into the bedroom. She pulled a suitcase from underneath the bed and began packing up some of her things, stuffing cosmetics, lotions, and clothes haphazardly into the bag.

"Please don't do this," I said. "I can explain."

"I know you can explain. There's always an explanation," she said. "I'm just tired of hearing them."

"I understand," I said. "After this case is over . . ."

"After this case is over, there'll just be another one," she said without turning away from her packing. "And another after that."

"Electra, I'm a private eye," I said. "This is what I do. I can't give it up just because it makes you uncomfortable."

She turned to me quickly with a flash of anger passing across her face.

"How many cases have you taken from ugly women?" she said.

"What?"

"You heard me. There are a lot of women out there

who aren't stunningly beautiful. They must have troubles too. How many jobs have you done for them?"

"You're being ridiculous."

"Name one. Come on. Just name one."

"Electra."

"Because I can list the beautiful ones without any problem. There was BB Star and Ona Thompson. There were actually four beautiful women in that one."

"I sort of saved the world on that one as well, as you might recall."

"Then there was the porn star, Fever Dream; the heiress, Giselle Dumas; the jilted wife, what was her name, Fifi Lefevre? I can go on all day talking about the clients you've had who have been drop-dead gorgeous. Can you name one for me who wasn't."

"There was Pacheco kidnapping case. The mother in that one was no looker."

"She hired you to find her beauty queen daughter."

"True, but the woman who actually hired me wasn't beautiful."

"How about a man then? Have you ever taken a case from a man?"

"Men don't hire private eyes. It's against our nature, like asking for directions or putting the seat down."

"In other words, no male clients."

She closed the suitcase haphazardly, with some bits of clothing still poking out from the sides, and carried it out of the room. I followed her as she headed toward the front door.

"There have been companies ," I said.

"You mean like the lingerie manufacturer? Or the escort agency?"

"Those were legitimate cases."

"You see the pattern though, don't you?"

"I see that my clients make you jealous when they shouldn't."

She snorted and shook her head disbelievingly.

"And you act surprised when HARV suddenly decides to become a woman."

"What does that mean?"

"I'm not a prop, Zach. I'm not a set piece in your playboy, tough guy fantasy life that comes and goes. I'm a living, thinking person and I happen to love you more than anything else. Not for what you do or for the life you lead but for who you are. And yet after all we've been through together you still don't understand how these sorts of things make me feel. How all this marginalizes me and what we have. You want me to be a walk-on in your life. A recurring character on the cast list, who can provide a little comic relief whenever you come home from your zany, adventure-filled life. Well, I can't be that. Not if I want to be happy."

She was crying now, which is something I'd never seen before. After all this time I'd learned how to deal with the many forms of her anger: the violent outbursts, the seething yet controlled episodes, the unspoken passive/aggressive periods. But I'd never dealt with tears before. And they scared me more than anything because I didn't know what they meant.

"You're wrong," I said, following her to the front door. "I do love you. Just as much as you love me and I'll prove that to you anyway you want me to. You want me to quit this case? Fine. I will. You want me to stop taking female clients? I'll do that too. I'll take on ugly women only if that's what it takes to prove it to you. Just tell me how to do it, Electra. Tell me what you want and I will do it. I swear. Just tell me what you want me to do."

She took her hand off the doorknob and stood motionless for a long nano; long enough for me to begin to hope again. Then spun around and gave me a left cross to the jaw that snapped my head back like a bungee jumper on a trampoline. A galaxy's worth of stars flashed before my eyes and my knees buckled as I sunk to the floor and then fell flat on my butt.

"You're the private eye. You figure it out," she said, slamming the door behind her.

33

I sat on the floor for a while, thinking and holding my jaw gently with my hand. It's hard to describe exactly what I was feeling at the nano (other than pain) but I suppose utter confusion comes closest.

HARA's hologram appeared, still wearing her business suit, for which I was grateful. I don't think I would have reacted well to a nurse's outfit kind of gag.

"The girl's got a mean left hook," she said.

I said nothing.

She knelt beside me and looked at my jaw.

"Somehow I knew that the scene was going to end in violence. Frankly though, I thought she'd take it out on the couch again," she said. "I've scanned your mandible. It's not broken. Do any of your teeth feel loose?"

"No," I replied.

"Small comfort. You might have a mild concussion but there's not much we can do about that at the nano. Here. Take a seat on the couch. I'll get some ice."

I climbed onto the couch and the maidbot brought an ice pack for my jaw.

"So why exactly did she hit you on the way out?" HARA asked.

"I'm not sure," I replied. "Partly because she's jealous of my clients."

"Sexy tends to bring that out in people."

"Not just of Sexy," I said. "She's jealous of all of them. They marginalize her."

"What does that mean?"

"I don't know."

HARA shook her head. "Women," she whispered.

She stepped into the kitchen and personally brought me another cup of coffee.

"My hard light capabilities are getting stronger," she replied. "I can hold up to half a kilo of weight now. A little more time and I might be able to hit you myself."

"Oh, good," I said. "You should get your name on the waiting list."

I took the coffee and tried sipping it without moving the ice pack from my jaw but failed miserably, dribbling some onto my shirt. I finally gave up and just put the ice pack on the coffee table.

"I don't get it," I said. "Electra's one of the smartest women I've ever met. She tough, she's strong. She has a career. Why would she feel threatened just because I have a good-looking client?"

"Because we're more emotional than men," HARA said. "We use different parts of our brains to process certain stimuli. It's biology."

"That sounds like a huge generalization."

"It is," she nodded. "Not every woman would react that way to your lifestyle."

"You don't," I said. "I mean, not that you're a woman but . . . you know."

"I'm as much a woman as I ever was a man, Zach."

She reached out and gently stroked the side of my head with her solid light hand, running her fingertips through my hair. There was a bit of an electric tingle to her touch. It felt good.

"But you're right. I wouldn't react that way," she said. "I haven't so far, have I?"

She was in full Rita Hayworth mode now. Her hair was thick and lustrous, messed gently in a subtle, sensual way. Her skin was creamy and smooth to look at, free of blemishes of any kind. And her lips were full and red. For a nano, I thought they were getting larger but then I realized that was wrong. They were just getting closer. She was leaning toward me, lips parted, moving in for a kiss. And I realized then that I actually wanted her to.

Then her fingers gently slid down my face and touched my jaw where Electra had hit me. It sent a jolt of pain through my body and I jerked back.

"Ow!"

"Sorry," she said. "Did I hit the bruise?"

"Yeah, it's a little tender, I guess."

"Tender? You're lucky that she didn't break your jaw."

"Yeah, well, it could have been worse, right?" I

said with a smile. "She could have been wearing a ring."

And then it hit me.

"She's not wearing a ring," I said to myself.

"Who's not?"

I felt my face flush as my confusion turned to shame and for the first time in my life, all the between the lines gibberish that women talk about began to make sense.

"Gates, I'm a louse. I take these cases. I show up on the news with all these other women. How's she supposed to react to that? What kind of reassurance have I ever given her for that not to bother her?"

"What?"

"Sure, I tell her I love her, but what does that mean? DOS it, I've never proven it to her. I've never shown her any commitment."

The seriousness of the nano hit me full force and I got to my feet.

"I have to go find her."

"What do you mean?" HARA asked.

"Electra," I said. "I have to get her back before it's too late."

"Zach, she broke your couch. She hit you in the jaw."

"She had to," I said. "I gave her no choice."

"How? Your couch attacked her? Zach, you're acting crazy. Well, more crazy than normal."

"I love her, HARA!"

"You mean to tell me that you still love her even after all the grief she's given you?"

I grabbed my coat and hat from the rack and headed quickly toward the door.

"There's nothing else she can do, HARA," I said. "She gives me grief *because* she loves me."

"Well, what about me then?" HARA shouted as she rose to her feet. "Don't I give you grief?"

The sound of her voice made me freeze in mid-stride. There was more pure emotion in those final five words than I'd ever heard HARA, or HARV for that matter, utter before. And I realized that my world was getting much more complicated than I ever wanted.

34

I stepped back into the living room. HARA was still standing by the couch, her eyes were wide, a mix of confusion and disbelief. Awkward does not to begin to accurately describe the nano.

"HARA . . ."

"I just don't understand, Zach."

"Quite honestly, neither do I," I said. "That's the way love is, I guess."

"Please don't go into Bogey mode on me now."

"I'm sorry, but it's all I know. You're a wonderful woman, HARA, even without the flesh and blood. You're a geek's wet dream and you're one helluva sidekick. You're more Bacall than I am Bogey. I mean that."

"But you still love Electra?"

"This isn't about Electra."

"What's it about then?"

I paused for a nano, weighing my options. I'd been walking too many tightropes in my relationships of late; avoiding the real issues and hiding behind smaller, more trivial things. And by doing so, I had royally messed everything up. I decided then I wouldn't do that anymore. It was time to be honest.

"It's about HARV," I said. "The truth is that I miss him. He was annoying and condescending and more of a nuisance than any machine should ever be, but he was my friend, HARA. Gates, he was my best friend. You're wonderful and you're sexy and you do great snappy patter and innuendo, but, I'm sorry, it's not the same. I miss HARV and . . . and I want him back."

HARA refused to speak at first. She refused to look at me or even move. For a nano, I thought her hologram was stuck.

"HARA?"

She turned to me, caught my gaze with hers for the briefest of nanos and then swallowed hard and turned away. The tension in the room was so thick, it was like breathing Jell-o.

"I don't know how to take this, Zach," she said, her voice heavy with emotion. "I need to think about it."

"Okay."

"Maybe I'll see you around."

"I'll be here," I said.

She nodded and bit her lip slightly in what appeared to be an attempt to hold back emotion.

"Good-bye Zach."

Her hologram dissolved slowly and she disappeared. Then the skin around my left eye went numb and my wrist communicator went dead. HARA was gone.

I was alone.

35

Talk about having girl troubles!

HARA out of my head left me a little more empty than I thought it should. It also left me without any way of piloting my hovercraft (just in case you've forgotten, I have a thing about heights). So I rolled out my old school transportation: a 1954 baby blue Kaiser Darrin. I know what you're thinking, that I'm masking my insecurities about the women in my life by fixating on my car. Well, you're probably right, but I didn't have time right then to properly analyze myself.

My heart told me to go out and find Electra, but HARA's disappearance seemed the greater danger (and one where I could enlist some help) so my first stop was Randy's lab. Needless to say, Randy didn't take the news well.

"What do you mean HARA's gone?"

"I mean she's gone," I said (for the third time, I think). "She's not in my head and my wrist interface is dead."

"She's not here either," Randy said, checking his own computer. "What did you do to her?"

"Nothing, really. I just said that I missed HARV."

"What?" He fell back in his chair, almost tipping over but he caught himself. "Why did you do that?"

"I don't know, it was just part of the natural flow of the conversation."

"What kind of conversation were you having?"

"Well, it started out about Electra and me and then it sort of morphed into HARA and me and then we sort of almost, um, kissed."

"I'm sorry," Randy said, very calmly. "Did you say that you kissed HARA?"

"Almost, yeah. It was sort of a mutual thing."

"You mean HARA. The holographic computer interface for your computer. You kissed her."

"I didn't actually kiss her."

"But you were going to."

"She started it," I said.

"Zach, do you know what you've done? I mean aside from bringing the man and machine paradigm to a new moral low?"

"What?"

"I don't know what!" Randy shouted. "That's how bad this is! First of all, the interface in your head is a permanent access module to HARA's systems. She shouldn't have been able to turn it off. It's the same with my system here. She shouldn't be able to break contact. She shouldn't be able to leave. But she's gone!"

"Where do you think she went?"

"That's the problem, she could be anywhere. It's like she's not just a computer anymore. She's a consciousness and she could be anywhere."

"Well, that's good then, right? She's evolved."

Randy shook his head as though he were talking to a child and turned back to his computer keyboard.

"I did some searching into HARV's systems since we last spoke," he said. "I found that he was doing some interesting side projects that were outside his program parameters. He was researching society, human culture, human history, psychology, and human/technology interaction in general."

"What was he doing?"

"I don't know, but I don't think it bodes well. Do you know that he wrote a joke?"

"A joke?"

"I found it in a more accessible region of memory so it's relatively new. It was probably written shortly before he became HARA. 'Why are there no round boxes at the Archimedes Bakery?'"

"What's the punch line?" I asked.

"I don't know," Randy replied. "It was hidden elsewhere in his system. Probably somewhere deeper, possibly encrypted. I think he wanted to protect the punch line."

"Oh yeah, you have to," I said. "The worst thing you can do is tip the punch line. The whole joke's worthless if you do that. Who's Archimedes?"

"An ancient Greek mathematician."

"Kind of an esoteric topic for a joke."

"Not for HARV."

"Okay, so he wrote a joke. That's a good thing, isn't it?"

"Comedy is dangerous, Zach."

"No, comedy is hard. Love is dangerous."

"Not from a psychological standpoint. Humor is a mask for insecurities and other psychological problems. This was a cry for help. I don't think it's a coincidence that he became HARA shortly after this."

"Randy, I think you're blowing this way out of proportion."

"HARA is quite likely the most powerful computer on the planet, Zach. Remember all those computers that HARV hacked into for you over the years? Well, HARA can do that too, without either of us telling her to. Do you realize what kind of havoc she can wreak if she chooses to?"

"Do you think she'd do anything dangerous?"

"Have you ever known a scorned woman to act irrationally?"

"Randy!"

"No, seriously, I'm asking because I haven't known that many women and I don't think I've ever actually scorned one. But I've heard they can be unstable. Is that true?"

"Well, yeah. But no more then men, I guess."

"How did HARA seem to you when you last saw her?"

I thought of the look of confusion and pain on her face when I told her that I loved Electra. I thought of her biting her lip in an effort to hold back tears when I told her how much I missed HARV. Only one word came to mind.

"Heartbroken."

Randy ran his long fingers through his shock of red hair out of frustration and let out a very long, agonized sigh.

"I've been working on some code," he said. "I was hoping that we wouldn't have to use it, but I think you better have it handy, just in case."

"What kind of code?"

"It's a virus," he said, holding out his hand. "Give me your wrist interface."

"Randy?"

"Give me your wrist interface, Zach!"

I took the interface off my arm and handed it to Randy. He removed a memory card from the back and slid it into his own computer console. Then he pressed the download button. A download meter appeared on his screen, slowly moving from red to green.

"The virus is designed to attack the higher functions of an artificial intelligence, surrounding it with firewalls and permanently wiping out the memory. It's like a combination of Ebola and brain cancer for computers."

"You want me to kill HARA?"

"No, I don't, but I think you should be prepared in case we need to."

"Can't you just say kaflooey or whatever and take her off-line?"

"She's not in the system anymore," he said. "The

fail-safe will no longer work. That was only designed for short term stoppage anyway. It wouldn't hold her long. She may even have defenses against it by now."

"So what do we do?"

The computer signaled that the download was complete. Randy took the card from the computer and reinserted it into the wrist interface. He touched a few controls on the unit's control pad and then handed it back to me.

"I've downloaded the virus into your wrist interface," he said. "HARA probably won't stay away from you for long. She'll reestablish contact through the interface at some point. If, during that time, she seems like she's becoming dangerous, you'll just need to hit the download button to inject the virus into her system. It will immobilize her and then systematically destroy her memory."

"Randy . . ."

"Remember, the sign that she's completely broken free of her parameters is when she refuses to follow a direct command. That's when she becomes a danger."

"Randy, I'm not going to kill HARV."

Randy's expression was more serious than I'd ever seen it. His face was wan, his eyes were nearly lifeless with resignation, and his shoulders drooped as though they were weighted down with a kiloton albatross.

"I hope you get the chance to make that choice, Zach."

36

I'd had no luck all morning reaching Carol on her communicator so I took a gamble and tried calling Sexy at the Elite, hoping that Carol was with her. Unfortunately, the only person I could get on the vid was Smiles.

"What is it, Johnson?"

"I need to talk Carol, Smiles. Where is she?"

His face was hard to see on the wrist interface, which is what I was reduced to using for mobile communication since the Kaiser didn't have an on-board computer. It didn't help matters that I was driving during the call so I had to split my attention between the interface and the road.

"She's unavailable at the nano," Smiles responded smugly. "I'll have her call you back."

"I want to speak with her now, Smiles. Put her on or I'll drag her out from wherever you're holding her when I get there."

"She's helping Sexy meditate," he said. "Sexy was quite tense after what you put her through last night and this morning."

"Oh yeah, last night. I guess I must have missed you at the party. Too bad you left before all the trouble started."

"I was exhausted and decided to call it an early night."

"Carol, too?" I asked.

"I don't think that's any of your concern," Smiles said.

"Oh, I think it is," I snarled. "Carol is my employee. You taking her away from Sexy without letting me know put Sexy in danger last night."

"I see, so keeping Sexy safe from a couple of holovision actors was too much for you to handle on your own?"

"Stay away from Carol, Smiles," I snarled again. "I can't make myself any clearer than that."

"That's something you should discuss directly with Carol, I'm afraid," he said. "She and I are developing a business relationship, which I believe she is well within her rights to do."

"You mean the kind of business relationship that you have with Sexy?" I asked. "Don't even think about using Carol that way."

"I don't know what you mean, Johnson."

"I know all about it, Smiles. I know what you do to Sexy."

His smile faltered a little bit as a splash of concern dappled his face.

"What do you mean?"

"The meditation chamber, the ambient radiation, the psionic augmentation."

"I don't know what you're talking about."

He was starting to squirm now. The smile had all but left his face, which was no easy feat, and I could almost see the beads of sweat forming on his brow. I had to admit, I was enjoying it.

"Sexy's a psi," I said. "You know it and you've been using her abilities to sell her music from day one."

"That's insane."

"Say whatever you want, but both you and I know it's true."

"People buy Sexy's music because of the beauty of her voice and the artistry of her songs."

"Sexy couldn't hit a clear note with a sledgehammer. Her music's bio-waste and you know it. The only reason anyone buys her music at all is because you're using her psionic abilities to brainwash the audience."

Smiles' grin reappeared on his face This time with extra smug and the corners of his mouth went so wide that my monitor wasn't big enough to contain his cheeks. It was the type of grin that a cobra gives a paralyzed mouse just before he swallows it. The grin of knowing that the prey's fate is sealed.

This time around, he was the cobra and I was the mouse, because when he stepped aside I saw Sexy's face fill my interface screen. And she was livid.

"What did you say about my voice?"

Sexy's diatribe went on for roughly ten minutes. At one point I turned the sound off and just nodded occasionally to let her know that I was still there. But even without the audio, her intent was clear. My services as bodyguard were no longer required, which was fine with me. Sexy had brought nothing but grief to my life from the nano I met her and the sooner she was out of my life, the better off I'd be. Tony and his men could protect her now.

Of course that still left Carol. Smiles said that he had put her directly onto Sexy's payroll as an additional bodyguard and backup dancer. I knew having her around would help keep Sexy safe but the idea of Smiles getting his hooks into Carol made my stomach turn. I realized I had to get her out of there and do it quickly.

But I had a couple of other things to do first.

37

Even in the bright morning sun, the joyless shadows of the alley hid the squalid storefront entrance. The air was fetid and smelled of old trash. I hated leaving the Kaiser in the open in this kind of neighborhood, but I had little choice and even less time.

The thick polymer of the door was greasy to the touch, caked with dirt and slime from Gates only knew where. I popped my gun into my hand and used the barrel to knock. There was no answer. I knocked again, louder but again to no avail. I knocked once more, so hard I thought I'd dent the door. This time, I got an answer.

"Go away." The voice was deep, thick with an Arabic accent, and emanated from a small speaker hidden within the door itself.

"I need to see Bushy," I said.

"There is no Bushy here," the voice responded.

I knocked again, this time rattling the door on its hinges.

"Last warning," the voice responded. "Go away."

"Bushy, it's Zach," I said. "Open the door."

A metal panel above the door slid open and a large blaster on a wall-mounted swivel emerged from the building and pointed itself directly at me.

"How do I know that it is really Zach?"

"Who else would come to this dump pretending to be me?"

The blaster twitched on its swivel in response. I heard the high pitched whine of the weapon charging.

"You come here, pretending to be Zach, just to insult me?"

"I *am* Zach, you senile old cow. And I came here to pick up my package. Insulting you is a secondary bonus."

"Why do you want the package?"

"Because the time has come," I replied.

Silence. Then: "Really?"

"Yes, really, Bushy. Now open the DOSsing door before I blast you and your fake gun to smithereens."

The blaster retracted into the wall and I heard the sound of several dozen locks on the door being undone. The door opened a crack and I saw a weary dark eye peek through.

"It is really you, Zach?"

"It's me," I replied.

"You've put on some weight."

"Yeah, and I've lost a little hair. I'm guessing you've aged as well and you weren't any prize to begin with."

The door opened another half a meter and Bushy stood fully in the opening. He was a short, dark-skinned man; rail thin with eyes as black as onyx and a huge, well-coiffed head of (obviously fake) silver hair.

"I was wrong," I said, looking at him. "You look pretty good after all."

He smiled and unconsciously ran his hand through his hair (it shifted a little on his head but I didn't say anything).

"You really need the package?" he asked. "This is not a drill?"

I shook my head no. "It's the real deal."

He swallowed out of nervousness and nodded grimly as he ushered me inside.

"It's in the vault," he said.

Bushy's vault was six stories underground (I'm not sure what, if anything was on the other five stories). He ushered me down the stairs, activated the DNA encoded lock, and opened the big metal door.

The vault was brightly lit and made entirely of metal that shone coldly under the halogen lights above.

"Your package is in drawer C, I think," he said, leading me across the room. "C for Zach."

The drawer was protected by another DNA encoded lock. This one had two activation pads; one for me and one for Bushy.

"Are you sure you want to do this?" he asked.

I nodded and, in unison, we touched our fingers to the pads. The indicator light turned green and I pulled the small drawer from its housing. It was as

I remembered it, about half a meter square, and lined with lead. Inside it was the small black box.

"How long has it been?" Bushy asked.

"Twenty-two years, I think."

"That's a lot of rent you owe me."

"I'll send you a check."

I lifted the black box from the drawer. It fit nicely into my hand and I gripped it tightly for a long nano, hefting its weight, both physical and metaphorical. Then I stuck it into my pants pocket and turned away.

"Thanks, Bushy."

He stopped me with a hand on my wrist. His grip was surprisingly strong. When I turned to him, his face was serious. Then he hugged me tightly and kissed me once on each cheek.

"Gates speed, my friend. You go first into the great unknown."

I nodded and smiled ever so slightly.

"Don't worry," I said. "I'll send you a postcard."

38

It took me three hours to find Electra. That's another downside to not having HARV around to do the legwork. She called in sick for work at the clinic (sick of me, I guess). She wasn't at her place and she wasn't at any of her favorite tapas bars. I figured that the only place left for her to be at the nano, ironically, was my house. A quick check of the house computer confirmed that someone had entered the house using Electra's code and that the new couch had been broken into small pieces. That pretty much confirmed it.

I pulled up to the house in the late afternoon. A few dark clouds had rolled in and the once sunny day had turned cool. I parked the Kaiser in the driveway and entered the house sheepishly, flowers in one hand, takeout food in the other.

"Hi."

She was packing her things into boxes, taking knickknacks and photos off the shelves and walls. I'd become used to seeing her breaking things. But the sight of her actually packing things up underscored for me how serious the situation had become.

"I thought you were working," she said.

"I quit the job today," I replied. "Actually, I was fired. It turns out that Sexy doesn't like criticism."

"I'll go then," she said. "I just came by to pack up my things and break a few of yours."

"Please, don't go."

"I'd rather not pack up my things with you here, Zach."

"No, I mean, don't go."

"It's too late for that, Chico," she said, staring first at the flowers and then turning away.

I heard the soft rumble of thunder outside and hoped that maybe the rain would keep her here, if only for a while.

"It's only too late if we allow it to be," I said. "My watch says that there's still time."

"Your watch is slow."

"You're probably right," I replied. "I just wanted to let you know that I understand how you feel. It might be too late now, like you said, but I understand how all my stuff, the cases, the clients, the news stories, I know how that made you feel. And I'm sorry."

The thunder outside rumbled again, louder this time, signaling the coming storm.

"*Por favor*, Chico," she said. "I'm not strong enough to have this conversation now. Let me just take the stuff I've packed and go. I'll get the rest another time."

She grabbed a box and took a step toward the door. Without thinking, I reached out and grabbed her arm, dropping the flowers and spilling the take-out on the floor.

"Electra, please."

My grip on her arm was a little too tight and she shot me a look that could have melted steel. Then she twisted her arm and broke my grip and continued toward the door.

"At least wait until after the rain stops," I said.

"What rain?" she said, as she walked. "It's supposed to be sunny all week."

The sky rumbled again. But it didn't sound like thunder any more. The air in the house suddenly felt charged. Just breathing it left a bitter, acidic taste in my mouth. Electra was across the room now, nearing the front door. I could see the sparks of static electricity jumping toward her as her feet moved across the carpet. She was reaching for the doorknob, her hand just inches from the metal.

"Electra, don't!"

I ran toward her, sparks flying from my feet as I moved. I leaped as she turned and hit her broadside as the door opened. We fell to the floor together, me spinning us as we fell to ensure that she'd land on the bottom, with my body shielding hers.

Then a bolt of electric white heat flashed in the sky and blew the doorway to pieces. The lights in the house flared ultra bright from the energy surge and burst as the bulbs overloaded. The security alarms in the house went off in a deafening roar. Shrapnel from the destroyed entryway flew around us. I felt it bounce off my armor in a dozen places and I felt Electra shake beneath me from the shock of the explosion.

We were under attack.

39

"What was that?" Electra asked, as we quickly got to our feet.

"Ion cannon blast," I said. "Very bad."

I looked outside through the gaping hole in the wall where the front door had once been and saw a milky-white wall of energy pulsing just outside the house. It was undulating like a wall of clear gelatin but I knew that it was a lot stronger.

"A forcefield cage," I said with a sigh.

"You're kidding," Electra said.

"We're trapped in here."

We ran quickly to the central computer console. I reset the alarms and tried to bring up a status report on the house systems.

"Most of the security system is down."

"Can HARA reboot it?"

"I don't have HARA anymore."

"What do you mean?"

"Never mind. Get to the weapons closet and grab some heavy ordnance," I said. "We might be in a little trouble here."

"Great. This is exactly the way I wanted to end our relationship, Chico," she said. "With a firefight."

"It will give you a chance to break more of my stuff."

She scrambled across the hall to the weapons closet and punched in the security code. The door slid open and she pulled two laser rifles and two hand blasters off the rack. She tossed one rifle to me, stuck both blasters in her belt, then grabbed the second rifle for herself. That's when the second alarm went off. It was a high-pitched wail, like a police siren stuck on a single note.

"What's that?" Electra yelled, trying to be heard above the din.

"Perimeter alarm," I said. "We're under attack."

"No DOS, Sherlock. From where?"

"I don't know. I never heard this alarm before."

"You don't know your own alarms?"

"HARV set the system up," I said. "He usually keeps track of these things."

"Check the console."

I checked the security screen on the house computer and didn't like what I saw.

"We have an intruder."

"In the house?"

"No," I said. "In our airspace."

"What does that mean?"

"It means we better duck."

A high-pitched squeal, like something out of an old World War Two movie, filled the air, growing louder by the nano. Electra and I turned our eyes skyward then looked at one another from across the room and dove for cover as the sound reached its crescendo and a large chunk of the roof exploded inward in a horror-filled nano.

The house shook to its foundations as the debris settled but there was no explosion. I hit the alarm override to turn off the alert. Everything was silent. Electra and I peered at one another from our hiding places (she was in the weapons closet, I was under the com) and scanned the damage.

There was a perfectly square crater in the living room floor. It seemed odd at first but it made sense when we looked up because it matched the perfectly square holes in the rooftop, the second floor ceiling, and the ground floor ceiling. Whatever had fallen from above had gone straight through the house, settled in the basement, and was now hidden beneath a couple layers of rubble that had once been part of my house.

"I have a bad feeling about this."

"You're sharp as ever, Chico."

We heard the whir of a hydraulic motor from below and the debris began to shift. Then the sound of metal against metal filled the air as the debris began to rise. We powered up our weapons and trained them on the crater as the movement continued. Whatever was down there was lifting itself out.

The debris slid away as the thing rose, revealing a slate gray metal cube, four meters tall, wide and deep, rising toward us on thick, hydraulically powered legs. Two nanos later, it was on the first floor, standing rock solid on the foundation of its own legs.

"What is it?" Electra asked.

As if on cue, a tiny hatch in the top of the box slid open and a thin pole emerged, extending a meter and a half high. There was a puff of smoke that made us jump, then a rigid, multicolored banner sprang from the pole and mechanically waved a flag at us. Three words were printed large on the surface in glowing red letters.

Let's Kill Zach.

Something lurched in my stomach and I felt my face redden from pure, unfiltered anger.

"Roundtree."

The box split open suddenly, like the display case of a pushy traveling salesman, and two dozen gray figures leaped out. They were humanlike in form but thin, long of limb, with no fingers or toes and completely featureless of face. Half came at me and half went for Electra. We didn't wait to see what they wanted, choosing instead to say hello with our guns.

Electra hit the one closest to her with a blast from the laser rifle, cutting it neatly in half. I shattered the one nearest me into pieces with a blast to the chest. Two nanos into the fight and we'd already taken out two attackers. I was starting to feel good about our chances.

Which is of course when things turned very, very bad.

The torso half of the attacker that Electra had destroyed started to shake. A nano later two legs popped out of the bottom end and it was as good as new. Likewise, the bottom half grew a torso.

"What the . . ."

Mine was even worse. Each piece of the thing that I'd blown apart was shaking and growing itself a new body. We were now four nanos into the battle and we'd increased the number of attackers by nearly half.

"What are these things?"

"Grey-Goo," I replied.

"What?"

"A new weapon. Randy told me about it once. It's intelligent inorganic matter, a single organism with sort of a hive mentality and composed of self-replicating circuitry. Like a giant computerized amoeba programmed to attack a specific target."

"I'm guessing that we're the targets," Electra shouted as the Goo attackers, moving slowly now, began to surround her. "What do we do?"

"Hit 'em," I yelled.

I flipped my laser rifle over and hit the nearest Goo in the head with the butt end. It tumbled over into the figures behind it and their long legs and arms got tangled up with one another. I doubt it hurt them, but it slowed them down, and gave me some time to hit a few more.

"That's your answer for everything," Electra replied.

She knocked one Goo off its feet with her rifle and then leg swept three more to the ground. It was clear that our rifles wouldn't be of much use in this case.

As hand-to-hand weapons, they were a little clumsy, especially for Electra, who was having trouble with their bulk. So I decided to give her something a little more suitable for the fight.

I fought my way over to the wall by computer console and pulled a hard polymer softball bat from behind the coat rack.

"Electra, catch!"

I tossed the bat over the wall of Goo attackers. Electra caught it on the fly and began whacking away at the gray-shelled foot solders with a new fury and effectiveness.

And although the laser rifles weren't effective against the Goo, my personal gun certainly was.

"Sticky stuff."

The first glue-shot pinned one Goo attacker to the wall. The second bound two so tightly together that they fell over and began waving their legs like up-turned ladybugs. It didn't stop them from functioning but it took them out of the fight.

We held our own for a while. The Goo attackers weren't all that strong, but they were relentless, like a bunch of really persistent and annoying toddlers. Their limbs didn't break easily (which was just as well because any piece that broke off would just grow an entirely new body, as we had already found out) but they hit hard and we weren't as indestructible as they were. Worse still, they were constantly trying to wrap their arms or legs around us and pull us down to the floor. I knew that if they ever pulled us down they'd crush us through sheer weight of numbers. I had my armor to protect me to a certain degree but Electra had nothing and that's what scared me the most.

When I ran out of glue-shots, I switched to the hogtie command and wrapped a bunch of them up in polymer cables. And when I ran out of hogties, I grabbed a bat and started slugging away along with Electra. The Goo kept coming at us and before long Electra and I were standing back to back atop the coffee table, protecting one another as the Goo surged around us.

"This is your fault, you know," she yelled at me between swings.

"I know," I said. "I'm sorry."

"I just came by to pick up my things. Now I'm fighting Goo!"

"I get it. It's my fault. I accept that."

"You should!"

"Not just in this particular case either," I said, still fighting back the horde. "All the danger I've put you in over the years. It's all on my head."

"You're darn right it is!"

"And I'm sorry for all the times I've embarrassed you and all the times you've had to apologize to people for whatever I may have done. That's my fault too."

"You can say that again!"

"But you know what's not my fault? The fact that you loved me."

"What?"

"That was your choice, Electra. I may have encouraged it. I know that I welcomed it. But you knew who I was when we met and you fell in love with me of your own volition."

"Yeah, I did."

"And I loved you back as well as I could. So we're both to blame, okay? I may have messed things up for us and you may not love me anymore but you chose to love me then. And that part is not my fault."

"Who says I don't love you anymore?"

Despite everything, my heart skipped a beat.

"Don't toy with me here. I'm not in the mood."

"I just said that I couldn't live like this anymore, Chico," she said. "I never said that I stopped loving you. Believe me, I would if I could. Gates knows, it would make my life a lot easier."

The Goo were around us tightly now, for every hand or body that we'd knock away a dozen more would take its place. Electra's pants had been shredded below the knee and her legs and arms were scraped and cut. My trench coat had been torn off me, my jacket was ripped up the back, and my arms felt like they were ready to fall out of their sockets. And yet none of that seemed to matter at the nano, because Electra was still in love with me.

"Do you have any plans after we finish up here?" I asked.

"I hadn't really planned that far in advance," she answered.

"Good. Let's go somewhere, I have something for you."

"Get us out of here first," she said. "Then we'll talk."

"Can you remotely control your hover?"

She nodded. "I need both hands to work the control though."

"I'll buy you the time," I said. "Bring the hover directly over the hole in the roof but go high. The force field probably has a ten meter height range. We're going to have to get to higher ground so head for the stairs."

"Ready when you are," she said.

I wanted so badly to kiss her then. Just one brief taste of her lips would have given me such strength. But she had only just now stopped yelling at me so I figured that I shouldn't push things.

So instead, I turned and leaped from the table into the Goo horde. I knocked half a dozen attackers off their feet as I landed, making a momentary pathway through the fray.

"Go!"

Electra jumped from the table and used me as a stepping stone to skip past the horde on her way to the stairway. A few of the Goo tried to follow her but I swatted them aside from behind even as the ones around me began pulling me down.

"Zach!"

I looked up at her from the floor and saw the conflict in her eyes. She was ready to jump back into the fray to help me (and I loved her for it).

"Go!" I shouted. "I'm right behind you."

I threw my bat at a Goo who was climbing the stairway behind her, hitting it in the head and knocking it back down to the floor. Then I started to go under as the Goo surged again. I grabbed the coat-rack and swung it around like a quarterstaff, clearing enough room for me to get to my feet. Then I held the hefty rack horizontally and charged; pushing at the horde like a pigheaded snowplow against a trillion evil snowflakes. I pushed a dozen Goo into the weapons closet, slammed the door shut, and activated the lock. I changed course and pushed another few into the crater in the floor. I threw the coatrack at the ones in front of me, leaped over the prostrate bodies, and finally headed up the stairway.

Electra was waiting for me on the second floor, just beneath the hole in the roof, maneuvering the hover into position. It was no easy task, guiding the hover remotely past the energy fence, especially since the house was now shaking with Gray-Goo fury.

The horde was hot on my heels as I reached the second floor but the hallway was narrow so it was impossible for them to swarm, which is what I was counting on.

"Throw me your bat!"

Electra tossed me the bat without looking away from her work piloting the hover. I caught it and spun around quickly, knocking the nearest Goo pursuer to the back of the pack.

"You know, this isn't the way I imagined this going," I said, battling back the horde.

"Imagined what going?" she asked.

"I'll tell you later. How's the hover?"

"About ten meters straight up," she said. "What's your plan?"

I popped my gun into my hand.

"Big Bang."

I put a blast into the hallway ceiling. The entire upstairs shook as the ceiling supports gave way and the hallway collapsed around the Goo.

"That will buy us some time but my insurance agent is really going to hate me."

I went to the end of the hallway, stood beside Electra and looked up through the hole in the roof at the hovercraft above us.

"Tarzan."

I took careful aim and fired. A tiny magnetic grappling hook and cable shot from the gun toward the hover and latched onto the craft's underbelly. I turned and held out my arm to Electra.

"I'll hold you," I said. "You'll have to drive the hover."

She walked into my arms without hesitation and wrapped herself around me. I held her tightly for dear life (in more ways than one).

The Goo were close to digging through the rubble now. I could see their malletlike hands beginning to poke through. They'd be clear in a few nanos. But they'd be too late to catch us.

"I'm taking us up, Chico."

"Wait, hang on."

I reached into my pants pocket and pulled out the tiny black box that I'd taken from Bushy's vault. Then I wrapped my arm around her and slipped it into the pocket of Electra's jeans.

"A little something for later," I said.

"Fine," she said. "Now hold on tight."

"Gladly."

The strain on my arms was enormous as the hover lifted us into the air and up through the hole in the room, but there was no way I was letting her go. I saw the Goo finally dig clear of the rubble. They swarmed the hallway and leaped at us as we were lifted higher, but we were out of reach. The Goo let out a collective sigh.

"Don't take this the wrong way," I said as we cleared the top of the energy cage, "but I'm glad you were with me for this."

"Why? Is Sexy not so good in a fight?"

"Are you kidding, every time there's been one of these *Let's Kill Zach* things, she's been cowering in the corner. No help whatso . . ."

And that's when things started coming together.

40

"Hey, you can't go in there!"

"Lady, if I had a credit for every time someone said that to me I'd be as rich as your slime-sucking boss."

My foot hit the center of Rupert Roundtree's door like a sledgehammer on a melon. The door was real wood, and I felt a little bad splintering it but there are times in this world where you just have to break a few things for the sake of drama.

Roundtree was at his giant desk (more real wood), scanning some data on his floating computer screen. He turned to me as I broke open his door and smiled widely.

"Zach-acappa Johnsonccinno. I was just thinking of you."

"I hope it didn't tax your brain too much."

"I tried to stop him, Mr. Roundtree," the assistant said, scampering into the office behind me. "Should I call security?"

"That's all right, Jessie," Roundtree said, dismissing her with a wave. "The Zachtathalon here is going to be the network's biggest reality superstar before long. He's allowed a little idiosyncratic behavior. You can go now. We'll be fantacuous."

The assistant backed out of the office and did her best to close the broken door behind her. Once she was gone, Roundtree sat back in his chair and smiled.

"Honest to ingenuity, Zachtastrophe, I was just looking over the *Let's Kill Zach* results from the test screenings. You are going to be so hot when this show drops, you're going to have to start wiping yourself with flame-retardant toilet paper."

"I survived your Gray-Goo, Roundtree."

"Like I knew you would. And I'm sure it was triumphastical."

"Sexy wasn't with me, by the way," I said. "Unlike all the other times you've tried to kill me, she was safely at the hotel when this one hit."

"She was? Oh well, she can't be in every episode, right? We don't want her stealing your spotlight."

I popped my gun into my hand and brought it down hard on his desk.

"Here's how we're going to play this," I said. "You're going to tell me the truth because every time you lie to me, every time I even *suspect* that you're lying to me, I am going to break something very expensive in this office. Lie enough times, and it will be your kneecaps. Got it?"

"Gotta hand it to you, Zachtinium, you have the star tantrum down pat."

"You expected Sexy to be at my house today based on the morning's news reports. That's why the Goo was programmed to attack everyone in the building rather than just me."

"I've told you before," he said. "The drama quotiency heightens with the addition of potentially collateralized victimization. It's all good for the show."

I lifted my gun and blasted a hole through his computer screen. It fell to the floor, sparking and fizzling where it melted a small portion of the carpet.

"The show is a front and you know it. You're not trying to kill me. You're after Sexy."

"Zachquiescence, that's utterly preposteronious."

I blasted a hole in the computer screen that covered the northern wall of the office.

"It wasn't a coincidence that Sexy was at the Kabuki Palace the night that your droids attacked me. You lured us both there, but she was the one you wanted killed in the chaos. That way it would be written off as a tragic accident during a crazy Zach Johnson adventure. When I saved her and became her bodyguard, you just kept trying to get her under the guise of the *Let's Kill Zach* show. That's why all the attacks came when she was nearby; at the hotel, in the limo, and at the HV studio."

"You don't know what you're talking about."

I turned and shattered another of his computer wall screens.

"I know about the memo from the governor's aide, Roundtree. I know that one of Spierhoofd's main contributors put out a hit on Sexy because they feared that she was a threat to the governor's reelection plans. And I checked the records. Your corporation contributed over five million credits to the governor's last election campaign. You've gotten some sweet corporate tax breaks out of it so far and there's huge media deregulation legislation in the works now that will make you a ton of credits if it passes. You couldn't risk losing that. So you put the hit out on Sexy."

Roundtree moved to speak but stopped when I aimed my gun at his third (and last) wall monitor.

"You hired a hitman," I continued. "That's who's been sending the PATA threats. And that's who put the bomb in the flowers and gave them to that kid during the concert. But you don't trust the hitman to get the job done. So you've been using the *Let's Kill Zach* idea as insurance and to do the job yourself."

"Are you finished?" Roundtree asked.

"Yeah," I said, taking a seat in one of his guest chairs. "And so are you."

"I don't think so, Zachariasis."

He leaned back in his chair, put his arms casually behind his head and his feet up on his huge desk.

"First of all, the whole scenario is preposterous. True or not, it's just too crazy to be believed."

"Which is exactly how you planned it."

"Second of all," he said, holding up a hand to quiet me, "you have no proof. It's all wild supposition based on the idle speculation of an unreliable reality HV actor who is currently in bitter contract negotiations with me over his show."

"We're not negotiating anything."

"Give me a nano to call the press and the story

will be running in the evening cycle. Zach Johnson, seeking a pay raise for his upcoming reality series on the Faux Network, shoots up the office of the network's president while spouting conspiratorial gibberish. It's actually a great publicity piece for the show. I'm surprised I didn't think of it myself."

"You're not going to win this one, Roundtree."

"I'm sorry, Zach. Can I call you Zach? But I already have. I'm squashing you like the insignificant little bug that you are because that's what happens when you come at Rupert Roundtree alone."

"He's not alone, Rupert!"

The already broken office door burst open again, this time coming loose from its hinges and falling to the floor as Hans Spierhoofd dramatically entered the room.

"He's with me."

Roundtree nearly fell out of his chair.

"Hans, what are you doing here?"

"I'm here to set things right, Rupert," Spierhoofd said, striding confidently toward Roundtree's desk. "I don't condone murder for hire in my administration."

I have to admit that I used to like Spierhoofd's movies and HV shows. He's not a good actor. He wouldn't know subtlety if it was in the form of an anvil and fell on his head, but in his early days, nobody this side of Robert Mitchum did a better badass tough guy. You'd think that after a few lousy movies and nearly two terms as governor the guy would have lost a step, but I had to admit, standing in that office, he proved that he could still bring on the A-game.

"Don't tell me you believe what Johnson is saying . . ."

He slapped Roundtree hard in the face with his hamsized open palm.

"Everything Johnson has said is true and we all know it. So don't embarrass yourself by lying."

"I made you, you self-righteous steroid addict."

Spierhoofd slapped him again, harder this time.

"Don't threaten me," he snarled. "I saw the Soviets roll their tanks down the streets of Austria when I was a boy. Believe me, there's nothing you can do that would frighten me."

"Hans, you idiot, you're Danish, not Austrian," Roundtree said. "And the Soviets occupied Austria fifty years before you were even born."

"I'm a politician, Rupert," Spierhoofd said, slapping Roundtree again. "I'm allowed to embellish my past for the sake of drama."

"I got you elected," Roundtree sneered. "Your career was sinking when I talked you into running for governor. If it hadn't been for me you'd be doing infomercials by now."

Spierhoofd's face turned red with anger and he put his large hands down hard on the edge of Roundtree's massive desk.

"I don't do infomercials," he growled.

He pushed the desk forward, sliding its great bulk into Roundtree's stomach and pushing him all the way back to the office wall, pinning him hard against the clear Plexiglas of the windows. Roundtree, gasping for breath, tried to free himself but Spierhoofd's hold on the desk was too strong.

"You are going to answer every one of Mr. Johnson's questions completely and truthfully. Do I make myself clear?"

Roundtree nodded and Spierhoofd eased his grip ever so slightly on the desk.

"*Let's Kill Zach* was on our list of shows to be developed anyway," Roundtree said. "We were just hoping to find someone better looking to be the lead."

"Hey!"

"I'm sorry," Roundtree said, "but you didn't poll well with the eighteen-to-twenty-nine demographic."

"Who is the hitman you hired?" I asked.

"I don't know."

Spierhoofd pushed the desk a little harder, squeezing Roundtree's midsection a little more.

"I swear, I don't know. It was done through intermediaries. I spoke to him once over the net; audio only and on a protected channel with voice masking. It wasn't even a good connection. I could barely understand him when he said the word 'kill.' I paid half his fee up front to a Cayman account. The other half was promised on delivery. Honestly, I don't know who he is."

"When is he going to try and kill Sexy?"

"He was supposed to do it at the first concert. Make it look like a crazed fan. We thought that would be most dramatic. If he couldn't do it then, he promised to do it straight out at the third concert."

"That's tonight."

"Everyone would be expecting it to happen at the last concert. We wanted to be a little more unpredictable. You get a bigger bang that way."

"Call off the hit." I said.

"I can't. I don't know how to contact the killer. I can't stop it."

I turned to Spierhoofd.

"The concert starts in half an hour," I said. "We have to stop it."

"You go," Spierhoofd said. "As I told you at our last meeting, I can't be part of this."

"You're all heart, Mr. Governor."

Five minutes later I was back on the street, the pedal of the Kaiser hard to the metal, heading flat out to The Fart. Whether Sexy wanted me or not, in my mind I was still her bodyguard. And there was no way I was letter her die on my watch.

41

The area around The Fart was jammed with pressbots, flesh-and-blood media, and wannabe concertgoers even five minutes before curtain time. I pushed my way through the crowd as best I could (making more than a few enemies along the way) and made my way to one of the police officers stationed at the entranceway.

"My name's Zach Johnson," I said to the officer. "I'm Sexy's bodyguard. I need to get in right away."

"I'm sorry, Mr. Johnson," the policeman said, "but we have orders from Ms. Sprockets' people that you are not to be allowed in the arena."

"What?"

"Apparently, you're no longer in Ms. Sprockets' employ."

"I know that but I have to get in. She's in danger."

"Which might be why there are like five hundred cops in and around the arena right now."

"Look, just call Tony Rickey. He'll vouch for me. You could even call the governor."

"Mr. Johnson, no offense, but I have fifty thousand

people to deal with right now. Why don't you call Captain Rickey or the governor or the World Council yourself."

The cop turned away and I was pushed aside by the throng of fans. I desperately netted with Tony on my wrist interface.

"Tony."

"Zach, you can't come in."

"What?"

"I'm sorry. Sexy and Smiles went directly to The Fart management. They said that if you are found inside the arena, they will cancel the concert. We have to keep you out. I had to pull a few strings just to keep them from having you banned from New Frisco entirely."

"Tony, you have to get me in. They are going to try to kill Sexy tonight on stage."

"Who is?"

"I don't know but it's a professional hit man."

"Are you certain?"

"Absolutely. Rupert Roundtree confessed it to me twenty minutes ago."

"Rupert Roundtree? I thought he was trying to kill you."

"Yeah, it's a long story."

"Do you have any proof?"

"Other than an unrecorded confession that took place in the presence of the governor? No."

"The governor was there?"

"Like I said, long story. The point is that we have to cancel the concert."

"Do you have a description of the hit man?"

"Nothing. It was an anonymous hire."

"I'll speak to Sexy's people," Tony said, "but if we cancel the concert now, we're going to have a riot on our hands."

"At least get me inside."

"Then I know there'll be a riot. Like it or not, Zach, you're not coming in."

The screen went blank and a wave of despair and frustration washed over me. I could hear the crowd inside the arena chanting Sexy's name, begging her to come onstage. The pressbots and correspondents were scurrying around, prepping themselves for live netcasts from the scene. The ground itself was vibrating from the excitement of the nano. The night was hot, the air was electric, and there was murder on the wind. My client was going to die and there was absolutely nothing I could do about it.

And that's when my head started to buzz in a very familiar way and a very well-shaped silhouette appeared from the shadows like a wraith from the forest.

"Hey there, Sadsack. You look like you could use some help."

HARA had returned.

42

She was wearing a tight tweed skirt and matching jacket over a white blouse. Her heels were high and a wide-brimmed hat covered half of her holographic face. Her look was one hundred percent femme fatale, which sent a chill down my spine.

"Before you say anything," she said as she approached, "I just want you to know that I'm still angry with you."

"I figured that. Join the club."

"But as I said yesterday, I'm a professional. And we have a job to do. So I'm setting all our emotional baggage deep into my random access memory while we see this through."

"HARA . . ."

"After that," she said, holding her hand up to silence me, "all bets are off. Got it?"

I nodded. "Got it. Are you up to speed on the situation?"

It was her turn to nod this time. "I monitored your call with Captain Rickey. Now come on, let's get you in the arena."

The HV reporter was looking at the notes on his palm computer and finishing a cup of coffee. He was a little thinner than me but about my height, which is pretty much all I was looking for.

"Hey," I said, tapping him on the shoulder, "you're, um . . ."

"John Blue from *Instant Buzz*," HARA whispered.

"John Blue from *Instant Buzz*," I said.

He turned to me and flashed me a smile.

"Yes, I am. And you're Zach Johnson. Good to meet you."

"Likewise," I said, looking closely at the all-access pass around his neck. "You're here for the concert, huh?"

"No, not really," he said with a smile. "I just like the coffee."

"Funny. Well, good meeting you," I said, turning away. "Enjoy the show."

"You, too."

He smiled and turned away, and when his back was turned I popped my gun into my hand and fired. He spun around quickly, a look of shock on his face.

"Did you just shoot me in my ex-male model butt?"

"It's a tranq dart," I said, as he stumbled into my arms. "Sorry about that."

I pulled him into the shadows of the building, grabbed his pass, and sat him by the wall. HARA threw a hologram over me that made me look exactly like him and we were back in business, that is until I rounded the corner.

"There you are, John."

I turned and saw a pretty blonde woman approaching, a cameraman at her side.

"Andrea, your cohost," HARA whispered.

"Andrea, my cohost," I said, waving.

She came up and stood beside me as the cameraman squatted in front of us, prepping his camera.

"I was starting to wonder if you'd been kidnapped. We're doing a live bumper in about ten seconds."

"Live?" I asked. "Why don't you do this one?"

"Right," she said, giving me a joking poke in the ribs. "You mean you're actually going to let me get a word in this time?"

"Yeah," I said. "Just kidding."

"And by the way," she said, "you better lay off those doughnuts. You're starting to lose that ex-male model body."

The cameraman finished his quick-prep and shouted to us.

"And we're on in five, four, three . . ." He held up two fingers, then one and pointed to us as the red light on his camera went on.

"Andrea and John here at New Frisco's famed Fart Arena for what has become the musical event of the year, Sexy Sprockets' death-defying Ménage Abattoir Tour. And the energy out here is absolutely radioactive. Isn't that right, John?"

"Actually, it's, um, it's really boring here," I said.

"What?"

"It's a total snoozefest," I said. "There's nothing

happening here whatsoever. Anyone thinking of coming here should think again because this is con- cert is duller than dull. I'm leaving now, as a matter of fact."

"John?"

"So just to recap, it's really dull here. Nothing to see. Please stay away. Oh, and don't watch the Faux Network. It's an insult to humanity. This is Jeff and Angela."

"John and Andrea."

"Right, John and Andrea, signing off."

Andrea and the cameraman stared at me open-mouthed and unbelieving for an uncomfortable nano. I shrugged my shoulders and turned away.

"I gotta go."

As I left I heard Andrea say, "he's cute but dumb as a door knob."

I used John's all-access pass to get into the arena through the press gate. HARA kept the holographic disguise on me as I made my way backstage.

"What's the plan?" HARA asked, appearing beside me.

"We have to find Sexy and get her to cancel the concert."

"Wow, that's a generalized and bad plan even for you."

"We have to stop the show."

"You don't think the fans will riot?"

"There'll be a bigger panic if Sexy's killed on stage."

We moved quickly through the backstage area and down the hallway to Sexy's dressing room.

"Sexy, it's Zach," I said, knocking on the door.

I heard music playing loudly inside. It was a fast paced track of Sexy's called "Google My Soul" that she liked performing late in her concerts. It worried me a little that I was becoming so familiar with Sexy's music, but I tried not to think about it too much.

I knocked again, pounding this time and shouted.

"Sexy, you're in danger tonight. Let me in!"

There was no answer but the music continued.

"Can you still open this lock?" I asked HARA, stepping away from the door.

"Just put your eye to the interface and let me do the rest," she said.

I did as I was told. The red databeam flashed from my eye into the lock. The door popped open and I stepped inside.

Immediately I was hit with a blast of the music. It was louder than I had expected. The lights of the room were off but the flaring meditation chamber bathed most of the room in a molten burgundy glow.

Sexy wasn't there but what I saw instead made my stomach turn.

Carol was in the meditation chamber this time. Floating in the air and bathing in the deep red glow. Smiles stood beside the projector, his grin smug, his expression hungry.

I was too furious to speak, consumed by a rage more violent than I'd ever known. I moved toward him without thought, fueled only by emotion. He turned as I approached and didn't recognize me in the holographic disguise.

"I'm sorry but this room is off limits to the media."

I hit him in the face and felt a few of his teeth break free of his jaw. He fell to the floor like a rag doll but I lifted him up by the shirt collar as HARA dissipated the hologram. He turned to me still conscious but dazed.

"Johnson," he spat.

I hit him again in the face and felt the cartilage in his nose crack against my fist. He fell to the floor again, bleeding from the mouth and nose now. This time I left him there.

"Turn this thing off."

"It's set at a very high level," HARA said, forming her hologram beside me. "We may need to power it down slowly."

"Turn it off now!" I shouted.

"Get your eye close to the interface," she said with a sigh.

She flashed the databeam into the machine and powered it down quickly. Slowly Carol sank to the floor. I stood beside her as she descended and cradled her as the last of the red glow faded and the room lights came up.

"Is she okay?"

"Her vital signs are fine," HARA said. "Her heart rate and breathing were low due to the meditation but they're returning to normal. Radiation is dissipating. She should be coming around in a couple nanos."

"Good."

I gently laid her on the floor and put my coat under her head. Then I walked over to the meditation chamber. I popped my gun into my hand and blasted it to bits. I grabbed the biggest piece of the debris I could find and angrily threw it at the wall. Then I turned to Smiles who was sitting on the floor, holding his handkerchief to his bloody face.

"Keep your hands off her," I said, grabbing him again by the collar and shaking him furiously. "Keep away from her or I swear I will kill you with my bare hands. Do you understand me?"

He moaned as I shook him and I gave him a slap to the face with the back of my hand.

"Do you understand me?"

He didn't answer and I hit him again.

"Zach . . ." HARA said softly.

"Do you understand me!" I shouted hitting him again.

"Leave him alone!"

The words were a command rather than a request and I felt them deep in my head as well as heard them. I turned and saw Carol, fully awake now and crawling toward us.

I let Smiles go and backed away from him as she approached. He slumped to the floor and she cradled him in her arms.

"Don't touch him again."

Again, her words echoed in my head. They were bitter and anger-filled. I could feel her reaching into my mind, trying to get control. I wasn't even sure if she knew that she was doing it, but thankfully I was wearing a psi-blocker. That and HARA's presence in my head, gives me protection against psionic attacks. Even so, I had to fight the urge to obey her.

"Carol, he was poisoning you."

"Get out of here," she spat.

"Carol, he's done something to you."

"I said, get out of here. And don't come near me again!"

The vitriol and hatred in her voice was like a slap to my face and I couldn't speak at first. I got to my feet as she helped Smiles wipe the blood from his face and turned away.

Just then the chanting of the audience in the arena changed into a roar. The heavy bass riffs of the opening song sounded and I knew that the curtain was beginning to rise. Sexy's throaty whisper rolled out over fifty thousand screaming fans (and one killer) pumping them into a frenzy.

"Mesdames et messieurs . . . amants et rêveurs . . . bouchers et bétail . . ."

"Oh no," I said.

I was too late. The concert had begun.

43

I ran down the hallway toward the stage as Sexy ripped through the opening number. The roar of the crowd was deafening, almost drowning out the music itself, which wasn't exactly a bad thing. I wanted to put my earplugs in but the psi-blocker prevented me from doing so. I was tempted for a nano to take the psi-blocker out but didn't, choosing instead to protect myself against the evil I didn't know rather than the music I did. HARA's hologram ran with me (putting special slow-motion effects in her hair and clothes as she did so).

"Contact Electra," I shot to HARA through the mindlink. "Tell her Carol's in trouble and that she needs to get here right away."

"She may not like having the message come from me," HARA said as we ran.

"There's no other way. She wouldn't be able to hear me over the noise."

I made it to the backstage area and cast a quick glance at Sexy onstage. It was pure bedlam, as I knew it would be. The crowd was even more raucous than before with fans charging the stage steadily in ones and twos and each time being grabbed by security and hauled away. Tony's men were in full force around the arena and I was actually afraid that one of them would spot me and try to drag me away as well.

"HARA, I need to talk to Tony."

"Done," she said. "He's on the interface."

"Tony, it's Zach. I'm backstage."

"How'd you get inside?"

"Don't worry about it, just let your men know that I'm here and that they shouldn't arrest me."

"That will be a hard sell," he said. "Arresting you is like second nature to them. Any sign of the killer?"

"I'm sure there is. But I can't tell since I have no idea who it is. Have you screened the audience?"

"We checked them individually going in and we're area scanning for weapons every five minutes. No sign of any weapons so far."

"I don't like this," I said.

"You're making me nervous, Zach. I mean more so than usual."

"Good," I said. "I'll let you know if I see anything."

I circled around the stage looking for any signs of trouble. I even discreetly watched Sexy's first costume change (slipping out of something small into something smaller). I saw signs of chaos, lunacy, and tastelessness everywhere I looked, but nothing out of the ordinary (in the context of everything else). And no sign of anything that looked like a killer. That's when I knew things were bad.

"I don't like this," I said. "We're missing something here. Something very big."

"Any idea when during the show the killer is supposed to strike?" HARA asked.

"None whatsoever but let's figure this out now, if I'm a killer, how do I kill Sexy?"

"Make her listen to her own music? Or maybe make her wear a skirt with a hem below the knee?"

I was standing in the wings on the right side of the stage with a full view of Sexy onstage and the lion's share of the arena crowd, my mind desperately running through the possibilities.

"A sniper's no good. There's too much movement on stage and there's no place to get off a good shot except for the luxury boxes. Does Roundtree have a luxury box here?"

"Captain Rickey's men are stationed in all of the luxury boxes," HARA replied. "And they scanned negative for weapons."

"What about a crazed fan with a sidearm or a bomb then? They could get close to the stage and attack."

"The audience has been scanned for weapons as well."

"The press too?"

"Yes," HARA said. "All negative."

I turned my gaze back to the stage, scanning the musicians and stage sets.

"What about something onstage?"

"It scanned negative before the show for weapons and explosives."

"It wouldn't have to be a bomb," I said. "The set pieces could be sabotaged."

"That would mean that the killer would have access to the backstage area," HARA replied. "Do you think it's an inside job?"

"It has to be," I said. The pieces of the puzzle were beginning to come together in my mind. "The PATA notes—they all indicated easy access to Sexy. The kid with the bomb flowers had a legit backstage pass. And he was chosen because of his history of chasing Sexy. That was no coincidence. DOS it. This has been an inside job all along and we didn't see it."

Sexy ended her Poor Little Rich Girl ballad to another roar of the crowd and the synthesizer and Arabic drums of "Love Cutlets" kicked in. Sexy and the girls shimmied across the stage as the dancers (minus the ones I had injured two nights before) strode onto the stage.

"It's one of the dancers," I said. "It has to be."

"They don't have access to Sexy's hotel," HARA said "And I checked them out, they're dancers. Not killers. They're built to sway, not slay."

And it clicked.

"Baba Wawa," I whispered.

"What?" HARA asked.

"It's a joke from an old television show about a newscaster with a speech impediment. She couldn't say her name right and it came out Baba Wawa."

"That's . . . totally unhelpful here, Zach."

"No. Roundtree said that the hit man was hard to understand. He thought it was a poor communication line but the hit man couldn't say 'kill.' And the kid with the flowers, he told the police that he got them from someone who said that the flowers would 'sway Sexy.' It was a joke. It wasn't sway the killer was saying it was . . ."

"Slay," HARA said.

"It's Lusty, HARA. Lusty's the hit man. I mean hit woman."

"Assassin," HARA said. "And that's a shame, because right now she has a meat cleaver in her hand."

"Let Tony know," I said. "And let him know that we're taking her out."

The "Love Cutlets" production number was a crowd favorite with its flying meat, flashing cleavers, and undulating dancers. Tonight was no different, except for the fact that, if I didn't act soon, it was going to end with some real butchering.

"HARA, do you remember the guy whose leg I broke?"

"You're going to have to give me more to go on, Zach," HARA said. "There have been so many over the years."

"The dancer the other night."

"Oh, him," she said.

"Throw a hologram of his image over me," I said. "I'm going onstage."

"You understand, of course, that a hologram won't help your dancing abilities, right?"

"HARA!"

She shrugged and put the holographic disguise of the dancer over me. No one seemed to notice me as I stepped onstage, which is a good thing, because the sight of the fifty thousand screaming people stopped me dead in my tracks. I could actually feel the force of their screams pressing against me like a strong wind. The stage floor was shaking from the music and the heat from the spotlights was so intense I felt like a soy burger in the McMunchies warming tray. It was simply overwhelming.

"Zach?" HARA whispered. "Zach, snap out of it."

I fought back the stage fright and began moving slowly across the stage. One of the security people at the foot of the stage looked my way and furrowed his brow. I quickly looked away and started bobbing my head in a desperate effort to find the beat.

"Nice cover job, Zach," HARA whispered. "No one's going to notice the background dancer who can't dance."

I carefully made my way over to where Misty, Sissy, and Lusty were dancing a couple of meters behind Sexy. All three of them (and the men with whom they were dancing) did double takes when they saw me approach but they kept up with the dance, if a little more awkwardly now.

Lusty was on the end of the dance line and I moved closer to her as she danced in front of one male dancer, bumping and grinding her hips against him. I wiggled next to them and tried to match their movements as best I could.

"Not the twist, Zach," HARA pleaded. "Anything but the twist."

The entire group of dancers, as one, moved to the left, but I caught Lusty's hand and pulled her toward me as the others continued on. She shimmied alongside me, improvising as I leaned close to her.

"Don't do it, Lusty," I said.

"What?"

"I know what you're planning," I said. "Don't do it."

"Zach?"

"It's not too late. You can turn back now."

And turn back she did, only not in the way I had hoped. She attacked almost quicker than I could see, spinning around cleanly and swinging the cleaver in her hand at my neck. I brought my arm up and blocked the swing but the blade sank deep into my forearm, lodging itself in my body armor (not my flesh, thankfully) but hurting like hell nonetheless.

I fought off the pain and forced back any regrets I had about hitting a woman, then sent a left jab at her face. It was as quick as I could muster but she avoided it easily. I followed quickly with a right. She saw that coming as well and sidestepped it. Then she pulled me close and sent her knee into my crotch, then gave me a left jab and right cross to the face that knocked me to the floor. I later learned that Lusty was a minor psi as well. She had precog abilities allowing her to see a second or two into the future. That gave her a nice edge in a fistfight.

The fight had happened too quickly for anyone to

notice. The crowd's attention was firmly on Sexy and the others who were on the opposite side of the stage. So few people, if anyone, saw me go down. And only I, from my position on the floor, saw Lusty pull the laser knife from her boot and shimmy her away across the stage as the music began to crescendo.

I got to my knees as the holographic disguise dissipated. There was no time for subtlety now. I scrambled to my feet and launched myself at Lusty. She was close to Sexy now, whose back was still turned, caught up in her song and dance. Lusty ignited the laser knife and its electronic red blade flashed three hundred centimeters out from the handle. Everyone saw it now, Misty, Sissy, the musicians, even the crowd. Everyone saw the blade but Sexy, who was too caught up in herself to see her own death fast approaching.

"Lusty, don't," I yelled.

Lusty put a hand on Sexy's shoulder and Sexy turned around, confused and annoyed. She saw the knife in Lusty's hand and still didn't understand what was happening. The music stopped, the crowd went silent and every media person in the arena began writing their lead for the next news cycle.

It was clear to me then that this wasn't just a job to Lusty. It was personal. She wanted Sexy to see her death coming. And she wanted to watch Sexy die and make sure that Sexy knew who had ended her life.

But she never got the chance.

I leaped at Lusty from behind and this time she was too caught up in the work at hand to foresee it. I grabbed her knife hand just as she started to bring the blade down. We tumbled to the floor and rolled across the stage, each of us wrestling for control of the weapon. She head butted me hard in the face (which I wasn't expecting) and then kneed me again in the groin (which I guess I really should have expected). I lost my grip on the knife and she quickly grabbed it. Then she rolled on top of me and raised the blade high over her head, giving her, she hoped, enough momentum to pierce my armor. I popped my gun into my hand and was just about to pull the trigger when Lusty froze in mid-swing. Then her eyes rolled back in her head and she tumbled off me, falling unconscious to the stage floor and curled into a fetal position.

I looked up and saw Carol standing on the stage, a little smile flaring the corners of her mouth.

"Hi, Tio." Her words echoed in my head.

"You gave her a psi blast, huh?" I asked.

"I couldn't have her putting a hole in my favorite uncle now, could I?"

The crowd that had gone silent a nano ago now began to applaud. Carol smiled, turned toward the audience, and gave them a little bow.

"Ladies and gentlemen," Sexy shouted into her mike, "please welcome my ub-zeenly old school bodyguard Zachary Nixon Johnson!"

The crowd applauded and I waved.

"And my double-xette and backup dancer, Carol Gevada!"

The crowd went wild. Tony's men slapped the cuffs on the still unconscious Lusty and dragged her off the stage. The musicians took their places to finish the concert and I turned away, hoping to get off the stage as quickly as possible. I actually began to think that we were on our way to a happy ending.

You'd think that I'd have learned by now never to think that.

44

Things turned very ugly very quickly. Things have a way of doing that around me and I'm beginning to take it personally (I don't know why the universe insists on using me as its personal chew toy).

It started suddenly but innocently (or so I thought). Everyone in the audience was applauding. And everyone onstage was happy and smiling. Then the stage lights dimmed dramatically and a bloodred spotlight cut the darkness. The intensity of the light was so great that I feared at first that it was a giant laser and, in retrospect, that would have been much better. The light did no damage when it first hit the stage, it simply enveloped Carol. That's when I noticed that the beam of light was the same shade of red as the projector beam from Smiles' meditation chamber.

"Uh oh," HARA said, appearing beside me.

"What is it?" I asked.

"The radiation level of the area just shot up."

"Oh, that can't be good."

Carol stood motionless in the red beam and let it wash over her, actually lifting her head upward as though she wanted to feel the light on her face. Then she stretched her arms out wide and rose into the air.

"Carol!"

I ran to her but the heat from the beam was so intense that I couldn't get close. And yet somehow Carol was safe inside it.

"It's an oversized version of the meditation chamber," HARA shouted. "It's supercharging Carol's power."

"Where's Smiles?"

"Right here, Johnson!"

Sammy Smiles strode onto the stage with the swagger of a conquering headliner. His orange suit was smeared with blood from his broken nose and split lip but, even though his teeth looked like a picket fence after a cattle stampede, he was smiling so widely that his cheeks were messing up his hair.

"Did you think I'd let Sexy just walk away from me? Did you really think I'd let her go without getting a replacement?"

"What are you doing to Carol?"

"She's not Carol anymore," he sneered. "She's the new Sexy. Better and more powerful than ever before!"

He pushed a button on his wrist interface and the spotlight on Carol cut out. She fell to the stage floor with a thump, landing on her hands and knees.

"Carol!"

I rushed to her and helped her to her feet. She

seemed weak and a little shaken, but otherwise intact.

"Are you okay?" I asked.

"Yeah," she said, shaking the cobwebs from her head.

A sort of distant look came over her eyes and she stood straighter, looking around the arena as though seeing it for the first time.

"As a matter of fact, I feel great."

And then the audience began to cheer. Not the polite applause of a happy ending or even the emotion-filled cheers of appreciation for an exciting show, but the wild, raucous cheers of ecstatic frenzy. The musicians began playing again, more vibrantly than before. Misty and Sissy and the dancers onstage slipped back into their routine. And Carol ran to the front of the stage, pointing at the crowd who screamed every time she moved. The concert had picked up right where it left off. Only Carol was fronting the show instead of Sexy. The fact that Carol wasn't singing didn't seem to matter to anyone. They loved it just the same. Carol blew a kiss at the crowd and the people in the first few rows (male and female alike) were so overwhelmed that they simply fainted.

Only Smiles, Sexy, HARA, and I were unaffected.

"What the DOS is going on?"

"It's like they say, Johnson," Smiles shouted. "The show must go on!"

"She's not even singing!"

"She doesn't need to," HARA said inside my head. "Carol's psionic power is so strong now that she can simply broadcast her thoughts directly into everyone's heads. Everyone out there is hearing her thoughts and they're loving it."

"But I don't hear anything!"

"You and Smiles are wearing psi-blockers. Sexy, having experienced Smiles' treatments for many years already, has built up an immunity to this type of psionic broadcasting."

"No way!" Sexy said angrily. "There is no way that my fans would forget about me this easily!"

"Believe it, Sexy," Smiles yelled. "You're not even a has-been now. You're a never-was!"

Sexy picked up her microphone and ran to the front of the stage, trying to get in front of Carol. But Carol waved her hand and telekinetically swatted Sexy away like a fly. Sexy flew head over heels and landed on a pile of red satin pillows; angry and stunned but otherwise unhurt.

"I'm still hotter than her," she shouted to no one in particular. "Aren't I? Will somebody please tell me that I'm hot!"

HARA and I meanwhile were still focused on Carol.

"Carol's never had that kind of telekinetic power before," I said.

"You're right," HARA said with a nod. "Frankly, I'm not sure she can control it."

"She can't," Smiles shouted, his gap-toothed smile beaming like an Alfred E. Neuman lighthouse. "But I can. I've built safeguards into the technology that will allow me to control anything up to a level four psi."

"But Carol's a level six," I said.

"No she's not," Smiles said. "She's level one, class six."

"She's class one, level six!"

"Which classification measures potential again, class or level?"

"Level!"

"DOS," he said. "I always get those two mixed up. I swear they changed those around now and again."

"Well," said HARA, turning her gaze from Carol to the arena ceiling, "there's an extremely good likelihood that you'll never make that mistake again."

"Why's that?" he asked.

The walls of the arena began to shake, and the scream of tearing polymer and twisting metal overhead nearly drowned out the music as the roof of the arena began ripping itself apart.

"Because we're all about to die, you idiot!" I shouted.

45

Carol had literally blown the roof off the arena. Her telekinetic power had peeled back the hundred kiloton metal and polymer lid of the structure like the lid of a sardine can. The wet night air swept into The Fart like a whirlwind as the music grew louder and the still entranced audience cheered more raucously.

"This isn't right," Smiles shouted, frantically punching the buttons on his wrist interface. "The technology should allow me to control her."

"She's too powerful for your gadgets," I yelled.

Over the past few days, Smiles had surreptitiously given Carol the same kind of psionic enhancing treatments that he'd given Sexy for years. But while supercharging Carol's abilities he had unknowingly broken down the natural power dampening barriers of her brain. He had thought that the technology he'd used to control Sexy's power for so long would work on Carol as well. But where Sexy was a babbling brook, Carol was a raging sea and all Smiles had was a beaver dam and a leaky bucket. And now we were all going to pay for it.

"What have you done to my niece, Chico?"

I turned and saw Electra climbing onto the stage (elbowing screaming fans aside as she did so) and she was wearing a psi-blocker, for which I was very grateful, so she was in control of her own mind.

"Electra, what are you doing here?"

"HARA netted and told me that you needed me here, remember?"

"Oh, yeah," I said. "In retrospect, I think that might have been a mistake."

"What's going on?"

"Long story. Right now we have to get these people out of the arena before Carol brings the whole place down."

"Evacuating the arena won't help," HARA said.

"What do you mean?"

"Carol's power is still increasing."

"That can't be. The red spotlight's off."

"Smiles' augmentation treatments only began the process," she said. "They lit the fuse."

"Please don't use that metaphor," I pleaded. "Nothing good ever comes from you using a fuse/bomb metaphor."

"Without the natural dampeners in her mind, Carol's power is continuing to increase. This wind you feel isn't a natural one. It's telekinetic leakage and it's only going to get stronger. In a few minutes she won't be able to contain her power at all. She'll hit critical mass."

"What happens then?" Electra asked.

"Let's just say it won't really matter who becomes governor of California in the next election," HARA said, "because there won't be a California to govern."

The wind was getting stronger, picking up debris and hurling it around the arena. The structure itself was groaning as its damaged supports bent and swayed from the force of Carol's power.

"How do we stop her?"

"Other than rebuilding the dampeners in her mind," HARA said, "I have no idea."

"Then how do we rebuild the dampeners?"

"We can't," HARA replied. "Carol has to do that herself. We have to convince her to do it."

I took a step toward Carol and got hit with a blast of telekinetic wind that nearly blew me off my feet. I popped my gun into my hand and aimed directly at Carol, who stood motionless amid the fury.

"Tarzan."

The cable flew out against the wind and latched onto the only secure thing in the entire arena, Carol herself, wrapping around her leg several times. I detached the cable from the gun muzzle, popped the gun back into my wrist holster, and held on for dear life.

"Electra, HARA, help me get close to her."

Electra moved behind me and leaned into my back, propping me up against the wind. HARA became as solid as she could (her hands mostly) and began pushing as well. Together, we fought off the wind and took a couple steps toward Carol.

"You know," Electra said, "this isn't the way I imagined this going."

"You do you mean?"

"I opened the box you gave me this afternoon at your house. You forgot about it after you had whatever epiphany it was about this case and ran off."

"I said that was for later."

"You give a girl a little black box then run off and you expect her not to open it?"

"He gave you a little black box?" HARA asked.

We were making our way through the telekinetic storm, baby step by baby step. The winds were lashing us but we were hunkered down low and held tightly to the cable; Electra and HARA lending their strength to mine.

"What do you think?" I asked.

"I think you have great taste in rings."

"He gave you a ring?" HARA shouted.

"It was my mother's ring," I said. "And her mother's too, I think. I'm not really sure. My family history is a little spotty. I'm fairly certain that it's not stolen, though. So what do you think? Do you want to make things official?"

"Only if you say the words, Chico."

As fate would have it, I was already down on one knee, thanks to the fierceness of the telekinetic wind around us. So at least there was one traditional element to the proposal.

"Electra!" I shouted above the din, "will you marry me?"

Electra leaned harder into my back and wrapped her left hand around me. I felt her lips, soft and moist, against the back of my neck and smelled the sweetness of her hair on the violent breeze.

"Does this answer your question?"

I looked down at her left hand on my chest and saw the ring on her finger.

"Great!" HARA said, a little coldly. "Let's plan a June wedding. Or a November funeral, whichever is more appropriate!"

I looked up at Carol, still standing, arms spread wide, at the center of the storm. I felt Electra's arms around me and HARA's presence in my head. I put my head down and took two more giant steps forward.

"No one's dying today," I said through gritted teeth. "No one."

I pushed on, inexorably, step after step. The winds eased ever so slightly the closer we got to Carol. She was only a few meters away now but the walls of the arena were starting to tear at the seams. I knew we were fast running out of time.

I put my head down and lurched forward once more and suddenly felt the winds ease dramatically. Without the resistance, I tumbled forward and fell to the stage floor. I looked back and saw Electra, still clinging to the cable and fighting the winds.

"What happened?" I asked.

"We're at the eye of the storm," HARA replied, her hologram appearing beside me.

I grabbed onto the cable and reached my hand out to Electra, who was still struggling.

"Grab my hand, honey."

Putting my hand into the telekinetic wind nearly ripped me off my feet. If it hadn't been for the cable, I would have been spun into the air like straw in a funnel cloud. I held tighter to the cable and went to reach back toward Electra again but she waved me off.

"Don't worry about me," she said. "Save Carol."

"Electra!"

"I'm fine," she said, wrapping the cable around her midsection. "I'll be there in a nano. Just go."

We shared a long, wordless look and then she waved me away. Slowly I got to my feet and took a step toward Carol. She didn't seem to notice me.

"Carol!"

There was no response.

"Carol, it's me, Zach!"

She turned and I felt the winds in the arena shift with her movements. A huge portion of the arena's southern wall ripped free with a thunderous shriek and simply blew away. Through the hole that it left, I could see that the winds had expanded outside of the arena. Carol's storm was growing.

"Listen, Chica," I said. "I know you don't want to destroy anyone, or everyone, as the case may be. So I'm going to need you to power down. Okay? Can you do that?"

Her face was serene with the slightest trace of a smile on her lips. Her gaze was distant, as though she were looking through me. And my words seemed to have no effect.

Being this close to her made my head hurt from the psionic power that she was putting out. I could feel her inside my mind, fighting through the psi-blocker, and unfortunately, I knew that I didn't have much time left.

"You know," I said, "you're officially my employee right now, so I'm going to be liable for the damage you're doing. I'm going to have to take it out of your pay."

Her eyes shifted subtly in her head as though they were focusing on me.

"Do you have any idea how much an arena like this costs?"

Her body remained completely motionless. But her eyes moved again, as though she was calling my attention to them.

"You can hear me, can't you, Carol?" I shouted.

She nodded almost imperceptibly.

And then she blinked her right eye three times quickly.

"She blinked her right eye," I said to HARA. "Did you see that?"

"I saw it."

"That's our code for trouble. It means she's still in there. She still remembers who she is."

"Whatever you're going to do, Zach," HARA said. "You better do it quickly."

"You can do it, Carol," I said. "You can control this, I know you can. How can I help you?"

She blinked her right eye again, three times fast.

And then a fourth time.

"Four blinks?" I said. "What does four blinks mean?"

"It means 'please shoot me in the head,'" HARA said. "Remember?"

A pit opened in my stomach as my memory confirmed HARA's words.

"Carol," I said, pleadingly.

Her right eye blinked four times again, more persistently, and it was as though someone had reached into my chest and pulled out my heart. I could hear the arena walls ripping apart around me and the cheers of the audience who were too stupid to know what was happening. I knew what Carol was telling me, but I didn't think I was strong enough to do it.

I flicked my wrist and popped my gun into my hand.

"Are you sure about this, Carol?"

I stared at her face hard, through the tears that were forming in my eyes. I stared long and hard, searching desperately for the smallest sign of a negative response. I found nothing. Instead she very clearly nodded her head.

I stood back and wiped my tears with my sleeve. Then I raised the gun and pointed it at her.

"Zach, what are you doing?" Electra shouted.

I swallowed away a lump in my throat the size of a golfball and when I spoke, it was barely more than a whimper.

"Gates help me."

46

"Zach, no!"

HARA's solid light hand ripped the gun from my grip.

"HARA, give me the gun."

"It won't work," HARA shouted.

"Don't make this any harder for me. You saw what she did."

"She's way too powerful to be killed by your gun, Zach." HARA said.

"I'm going to trust Carol on this," I shouted. "Now give me the gun."

HARA backed her hologram away from me and held onto the gun tightly. Her hands were a little unsteady. It might have been because the effort of holding the gun was taxing her capabilities, or it may have been the effort of what she knew was to come. Because, much to my surprise, she raised the gun and pointed it at me.

"What are you doing?"

"It's the only way, big guy."

The arena was giving way in the storm. People in

the rear seats were beginning to be thrown into the air from the force. The arena itself was ready to collapse. Carol had to be stopped.

"HARA," I said, "give me the gun. That's a direct command. Give me my gun!"

"I'm sorry," she said. "But I can't."

And there it was. Everything that Randy had warned me about had come to pass. HARA had refused a direct command. With thousands, perhaps millions of lives hanging in the balance, she had abandoned me. And as she stood there with my own gun trained on me, she had the femme fatale glare of a woman scorned. It was the end of every pulp novel ever written. But I couldn't let her do it.

Slowly, sadly, I reached my hand toward my wrist interface and gently placed a finger on the button to download the virus that would erase HARV. My hand was shaking but I was running out of time, and I had no options left.

Then she stopped me with two words.

"Trust me."

HARV had saved my life more times than I could count. I trusted him implicitly to do the right thing. He was my partner, my friend. He had my back. But as Randy had said, this wasn't HARV anymore. It was HARA. The question was, could I trust her the way I trusted HARV? Was there enough HARV left in HARA to trust? There was only one way to find out.

"What's the punch line?" I shouted.

"What?"

"The joke you wrote, the Archimedes Bakery," I said.

"How did you know about that?"

"It doesn't matter," I said. "Just tell me the joke."

She swallowed once and spoke slowly and shyly.

"Why are there no round boxes at the Archimedes Bakery?"

"Why?"

"Because their Π r^2."

I thought for a nano as the wind swirled around me and the arena continued to tear itself apart. Then I smiled and suppressed a bit of a chuckle. Then I laughed out loud. HARA saw me and smiled as well.

"Okay," I said. "I trust you."

She aimed the gun at me. I saw the OLED light flash in response to her silent command as she overrode the security system. Then her hologram shimmered and her form disappeared, reassembling itself into HARV.

And he fired.

47

The blast hit me full in the chest and enveloped my body in a thin layer of intense pain. Every nerve, every bundle, every ganglia, synapse, and neuron in my body fired at once with a soul-twisting blast of pure agony. I was on fire. I was being pierced by a million needles. I was being torn apart. I was sitting through a never ending Adam Sandler film retrospective.

I screamed once, loud and long, as darkness rolled in at me from all directions. Somewhere in the distance I heard another scream and felt the winds of Carol's psionic storm envelope me.

And then there was nothing.

48

I awoke in a void. Bodiless and shapeless, I was nothing more than a floating consciousness in a sea of nothing.

"This better not be eternity."

A white light appeared in the distance. Actually distance isn't the correct term because in a void, distance has no meaning. So let's just say that the light was very small at first and slowly grew larger. It took on a form after a few nanos and I recognized it.

"Carol."

She was luminescent, almost ethereal and I didn't like where all this symbolism seemed to be heading.

"Hola, Tio."

"What happened?" I asked.

"I went a little crazy," she replied with a shrug. "Lost control of myself, broke some stuff, almost destroyed the earth. Sorry."

"It's all right. It wasn't your fault," I said. "What happened after HARV shot me?"

"Pain," she replied.

"That I remember."

"Me too," she said. "That was the point."

"What do you mean?"

She flashed a very mature and knowing smile at me that made me feel kind of old.

"I needed something to snap me out of my trance in order to give my mind a chance to regain control of my power," she said. "HARV knew that. But he also knew that in the state I was in, I was fairly impervious to physical pain."

"So he shot me?"

"Your mind has always been an open book to me, Tio," she said. "It's sort of a bond we share. When HARV shot you, it hurt."

"You can say that again."

"I know, because I felt that pain just as much as you did. It was like a slap in the face."

"That's all?"

"A very hard slap in the face," she said with a smile. "It brought me back reality and gave my mind a chance to power down."

"So you're okay?" I asked.

"I'm fine."

"And everything else?"

"Well, The Fart's pretty much destroyed. The walls collapsed. They found the roof in the bay."

"What about Electra?"

"She's fine; she and everyone else who was there, they're all safe and most of them don't remember what happened."

I relaxed a little and felt a peaceful feeling wash over me.

"I suppose in the long run then it was worth it."

"What do you mean?" she asked.

"It's not a bad way to go out, really. Saving your loved ones and fifty thousand innocent bystanders with crappy taste in music."

Carol smiled and shook her head softly.

"Tio, you're not dead."

"I'm not?"

"Of course not."

"I'm in a void here. I have neither shape nor form."

"That's because you're not thinking of one."

I looked around again and saw my left hand appearing from the darkness, becoming more and more real with every nano. My right arm soon followed as did the rest of my body.

"Any chance I could get some clothes, too?" I asked Carol, covering myself.

"Think harder."

I did, and a nano later I was wearing my favorite gray suit, trench coat, and fedora.

"So let me get this straight, when HARV shot me . . ."

"He used the big hurt," Carol responded. "Lots of pain, but nonlethal."

"Wow. I need to get Randy to turn that down a notch." I said. "So where are we right now?"

"We're in your mind."

"And my body?"

"Tio, look," Carol said. "No offense but this is getting a little sappy. I came here to let you know that everything's okay, but I really have to go now."

"What?"

Her form began to drift away, slowly shrinking.

"I'll see you in the real world," she said.

"Carol?"

"Oh, and Tio," she said, turning to give me another ethereal smile. "Thanks again. You're the best."

I watched her form shrink away until it was a tiny white light against the lightlessness of the void. Then all at once, the void began to brighten. Ebon turned to black. Black turned to gray, gray to white, and then it was almost too bright to look at.

That's when I opened my eyes.

"Hola, Chico," Electra whispered.

I smiled and felt safe at last.

49

I woke in a hospital bed where I'd lain unconscious for four days. I had three cracked ribs, a hairline fracture in my left leg, and a concussion. All of which were painful, but none of which, fortunately, would do me any lasting damage. And as the months went by, the final threads of the case would play themselves out and come to resolution.

Sexy Sprockets, as promised, officially retired from the music industry, ending her career with the concert that has become known as The Last Fartz. She recently announced her candidacy for governor of California and, at the nano, is polling about even with incumbent Hans Spierhoofd. It's worth noting that Sexy's younger sister, Sassy Sprockets, has just embarked on a singing career. Industry insiders say that the younger Sprockets has a much better singing voice but much smaller breasts than her older sister. They therefore give her little chance at any real success.

Rupert Roundtree was arrested and charged with solicitation of murder, but was acquitted due to lack of material evidence (and Governor Spierhoofd's refusal to testify, citing executive privilege). In retaliatory news, several tax loopholes for media corporations such as Faux were closed by the state government and the media deregulation legislation was vetoed and then killed by the governor. Undaunted, Roundtree has begun an all news channel, which unfortunately, reports mostly fiction.

It was learned that Sammy Smiles had once been employed in the weapons R&D department at the World Council Department of Defense. It was during his tenure there that he developed the technology of psionic augmentation and psionic broadcasting over the AM radio spectrum. The DOD is still uncertain as to how they lost track of him and the technology. Smiles' current whereabouts are unknown. He disappeared from The Fart during its destruction and is currently a wanted fugitive.

Lusty (last name unknown) was tried for attempted murder but was acquitted by an all middle-aged jury on the grounds of insanity. In post-verdict interviews, the jurors claimed that, after listening to Sexy's music in court, they completely understood Lusty's desire to kill her and could therefore not hold Lusty responsible for her actions. Lusty has since become a solo artist and is currently the headliner at the Lively Little Lighthouse Club in Lafayette, Louisiana.

And the World Society of Isaac Newton Scholars recently put out a statement saying that Newton had consumed a little too much absinthe on the night that he made his dire prediction about the world ending in 2060. What he really meant to say, they claim, is that the world will *bend* in 2060, which apparently was some kind of metaphor. Hey, the guy couldn't be brilliant all the time.

50

A few weeks after I was released from the hospital, Electra and I took a trip to our favorite spot on the New Costa Rican coast. We spent most of our time lying on the beach planning our wedding with HARV.

"Are you sure you want the imported champagne for the toast?" HARV asked from his holographic lounge chair. "The domestic brands are becoming quite hip."

"The domestic doesn't taste as good," I replied.

HARV smiled and nodded. He had returned to his original holographic interface since that last fateful nano at The Fart. His hair was a little more stylish now and his body seemed a little buffer as well (not that I notice those type of things). But at the core, he was still the same HARV.

"Good for you, Zach," he said. "I was testing you. Your palate is evolving."

"I want plenty of buffalo wings on the hors d'oeuvres table, though," I said, trying to get to an itch on my leg that was just out of reach beneath my air cast. "With lots of bleu cheese dressing on the side."

HARV sighed and shook his head gently.

"Alas, one step forward, two steps back."

HARV claimed that the HARA experiment was officially over and that he had permanently erased her hologram from his memory. I couldn't say that I was sorry to see her go. HARA was perfect in a lot of ways but, like they say, redheads are just trouble.

"Just a reminder," Electra said, as she sipped her margarita, "my mother will be there and I don't want her sitting next to any of your former clients."

"Done," said HARV. "And speaking of former clients, you've agreed to invite Ona Thompson. Are you also inviting Twoa and Threa?"

"Didn't they try to kill me?" I asked.

"Technically yes, but if we're going to exclude anyone who's ever tried to kill you then we'll need to cut another three dozen guests from the list, including several members of Electra's family."

"Okay," I said. "But don't put all three of them at the same table."

"A fine idea," HARV said.

We heard the sound of distant thunder then, which struck me as odd since the early evening sky was completely cloudless. It seemed to make HARV a little uncomfortable as well.

"And, um, have I mentioned yet, that you'll be checking out this evening?" he asked.

"No," I said. "You skipped that part."

"What's going on?" Electra asked.

"Well, you see, it's kind of a funny story really."

"You mean funny-haha or funny-odd?"

"Both actually. It seems that the pilot episode of *Let's Kill Zach* was pirated and illegally put on the net."

"Oh, no."

"It's become sort of a cult hit, especially here in Costa Rica," HARV continued. "So much so that the premier Latin American network, Holomundo, is planning a Costa Rican version. It's called *Matemos a Zach*."

The rumbling sound grew louder and it was clear to us now that it wasn't thunder. It was coming from the forest to the south.

"Oh, well," Electra sighed, getting to her feet and tying a wrap skirt around her bathing suit. "It was fun while it lasted. I was getting a little homesick anyway."

Our hovercraft, with HARV remotely piloting, pulled up neatly beside our lounge chairs. I slowly got to my feet and limped toward the passenger seat.

"Yeah," I said. "I get a little antsy if I go too long without someone trying to kill me. *Matemos a Zach* did you say?"

"Correct," HARV said as he held the hover door open for me. "The show was to be very representative of the Costa Rican culture. In the first episode, droids were going to be pelting you with spherical granite bolas."

I settled into the hover and fastened my seat belt as Electra revved the engine.

"Sounds like first rate entertainment," I said. "It's a shame we'll miss it."

Electra gunned the hover and we sped off down the beach, a cloud of pure white sand in our wake and bloodthirsty reality show producers on our tail.

"By the way," HARV said, his hologram leaning forward in the rear seat of the hover, "did I mention that I plan on bringing a date to your wedding?"

"A date?"

"I'm allowed, aren't I?"

"Of course you are, HARV," Electra said.

"Good. His name's Guy," HARV said. "He's a fashion model from New Milan."

"Guy?"

"I realized recently that I prefer men," HARV said. "That's not a problem, is it?"

I smiled, eased the hoverseat back just a bit, and watched the sun set a glorious red and orange over the sea.

"No problem at all, buddy. No problem at all."

My name is Zachary Nixon Johnson. I am the last private detective on Earth.

And my life rocks!

CJ Cherryh
Classic Series in New Omnibus Editions

THE DREAMING TREE
Contains the complete duology *The Dreamstone* and
The Tree of Swords and Jewels.   0-88677-782-8

THE FADED SUN TRILOGY
Contains the complete novels *Kesrith*, *Shon'jir*, and
Kutath.   0-88677-836-0

THE MORGAINE SAGA
Contains the complete novels *Gate of Ivrel*, *Well of
Shiuan*, and *Fires of Azeroth.*   0-88677-877-8

THE CHANUR SAGA
Contains the complete novels *The Pride of Chanur*,
Chanur's Venture and *The Kif Strike Back.*
        0-88677-930-8

ALTERNATE REALITIES
Contains the complete novels *Port Eterntiy*, *Voyager in
Night*, and *Wave Without a Shore*   0-88677-946-4

AT THE EDGE OF SPACE
Contains the complete novels *Brothers of Earth* and
Hunter of Worlds.   0-7564-0160-7

To Order Call: 1-800-788-6262

Lisanne Norman

The *Sholan Alliance* Series

"Will hold you spellbound" — *Romantic Times*

This new, seventh novel takes readers into the heart of a secret Prime base—where Kusac must make an alliance with an enemy general to save his son's life.

To Order Call: 1-800-788-6262

C.S. Friedman

The Best in Science Fiction

C.S. Friedman

The Coldfire Trilogy

"A feast for those who like their fantasies dark, and as emotionally heady as a rich red wine." —*Locus*

Centuries after being stranded on the planet Erna, humans have achieved an uneasy stalemate with the fae, a terrifying natural force with the power to prey upon people's minds. Damien Vryce, the warrior priest, and Gerald Tarrant, the undead sorcerer must join together in an uneasy alliance confront a power that threatens the very essence of the human spirit, in a battle which could cost them not only their lives, but the soul of all mankind.

BLACK SUN RISING	0-88677-527-2
WHEN TRUE NIGHT FALLS	0-88677-615-5
CROWN OF SHADOWS	0-88677-717-8

To Order Call: 1-800-788-6262

DAW 18

OTHERLAND

TAD WILLIAMS

"The Otherland books are a major accomplishment."
–Publishers Weekly

"It will captivate you."
–Cinescape

In many ways it is humankind's most stunning achievement. This most exclusive of places is also one of the world's best-kept secrets, but somehow, bit by bit, it is claiming Earth's most valuable resource: its children.

CITY OF GOLDEN SHADOW (Vol. One)
0-88677-763-1

RIVER OF BLUE FIRE (Vol. Two)
0-88677-844-1

MOUNTAIN OF BLACK GLASS (Vol. Three)
0-88677-906-5

SEA OF SILVER LIGHT (Vol. Four)
0-75640-030-9

To Order Call: 1-800-788-6262

DAW 44